Contents

My Best Friend is a Demon
By Stephen W. Scott

"You can't defeat your demons if you
keep enjoying their company."
Unknown

All of the people, places, organizations,
and events portrayed in these stories are
either works of fiction or are used
fictitiously. All rights reserved.

ISBN - 979-8993621418

This book is dedicated to the "Married with Children" Podcast Team (original and finishing team) who has been so supportive in my endeavor:

Alex Edwards, Jamie Sammons, Jerry Herring, Dan Chase, Luigi Pedalino, Chris Gunter, Tyler Tingo, Annabel Whitford, and Matt Thompson.

Special thanks to Heather Nuttall Westover for her coaching and editing and Derek Stewart for the cover design.

Chapter 1

Gunner's eyes widened as the hatchet flew at him. Horrified, his heart, nerves, limbs, and muscles all twitched violently. The small axe wobbled, turning on end. The back of the handle hit the shed wall about three or four feet to the left of him. It careened to the ground.

Gunner pulled at the bungee cords that kept him secure to the outside of Uncle Jason and Aunt Jenny's shed. Both cords wrapped around his wrist, with hooks attached to rounded hasps. His stomach and chest pulsed with his rapid breath. "Elise," he said between gasps, "I don't want to play 'circus' anymore."

"Don't worry, Gunner," she said, rearing another hatchet back with her hand. "I'm not aiming at you - but around you."

Elise thought of herself as Wednesday Addams, having black hair, emotionless eyes, a dead facial expression, and always wearing black. Aunt Jenny, Uncle Jason, and Jeffrey commented about it. She had a mean streak, but he wanted her to like him so bad since he had no sister. A year older than Gunner, he recalled her comments that could be dark humorous sarcasm, or disdain bordering on hate.

"Don't drown in the bathtub."

"Your eyes would look really good - if they were in someone else."

"Gunner, would you like to donate a quart of blood?

It's for a good cause."

Once, she handed him some sort of metal object. *"Hold this - but don't let go or you'll get a horrible, painful electrical shock."*

Her twin brother, Jeffrey, was his best friend. They always hung out together watching horror movies, racing their minibikes, and having a good time. It was great because Jeffrey always stood up for him when kids at school picked on him. Sleeping over at his cousin's house was his favorite thing to do on the weekends. Where was Jeffrey? Oh, yeah, riding his minibike to the store to get some snacks.

Petrified, almost crying, he watched the hatchet turn on itself. Although frozen, his legs and arms shook. Why did he agree to this? He thought his cousin, Elise, for a change, was being nice to him. She acted as if she wanted to be his friend, but this didn't look like something a friend would do to him.

Elise's next hatchet's blade thrust itself into the wall about two feet to the right of his head – snapping him back to the present moment. Bawling, he stammered out his words. "Elise, please. I don't wanna play this game anymore," he bellowed.

She ignored him, nodded, and muttered, "Good. It worked." Looking at Gunner, she raised her volume. "We're going to be Circus Stars, Gunner. I'll try to get the next one a little bit closer to you."

"Uncle Jason … Aunt Jenny – help!" Gunner's voice almost hurt. Like a pipe in sub-zero temperatures, his body froze tight as another hatchet flew at him, descending slowly. His eyes snapped shut, trying to stave off the fear that burrowed into his chest and stomach. Hearing a chunk noise, he realized this hatchet embedded its blade into the wall just a foot or so below his crotch. "Aunt, Jenny! Uncle Jason! Help!"

"Elise!" screamed Aunt Jenny, "what the hell are you doing to Gunner?" She seized her wrist to dislodge the hatchet.

"Mom! I wasn't aiming at Gunner – I was aiming AROUND him."

"Stop your Wednesday Addams shit NOW and go to your room." Aunt Jenny looked at him. "Gunner, sweetie, are you okay?" He could not remember her walking up to him. She released him from the bungee cords and hugged him. "I'm so sorry, sweetie," she said, kissing him on the forehead. "Go find Jeffrey, stay with him while I deal with Elise."

The memory faded as Gunner almost awakened. However, with his next breath, he smelled something weird again - like a cloth drenched in some sort of oil. At first, his lungs rejected it, trying to cough it out, but instead it dug into his blood and up to his head. Sleep returned, forcing him to find another memory.

It was about two years later when he was ten and Elise was eleven. Jeffrey had to help his dad with fixing the motor on Uncle Jason's semi. Gunner hated the loud noise, so he remained inside.

"Gunner," said Elise, "do you want to play a game with me?"

He shook his head. "No! You always scare me."

"Gunner, I promise you'll be fine."

"No!"

"Come on, Jeffrey is going to play this with me, too. He said he wanted you to be part of it. He said he'll be there in a few minutes."

His eyes brightened. "Really."

"Really. I promise. Besides, you'll like this game."

She took his hand and led him out to the shed again. Amazingly, Uncle Jason's semi, unhitched, was rolling past the shed towards the fuel pump. Elise waved at her dad and at Jeffrey. They waved back. Gunner had to wave because he loved Jeffrey and Uncle Jason so much. He only wanted Elise to like him just as well.

As the loud semi pulled out of sight, Elise seized his left wrist and wrapped the bungee cord around it. Panicked, he tried to stop her, but she was fast in putting another bungee cord around his other wrist and hooking it to a rounded clasp on the other side.

Terrified, he yelled for Uncle Jason, but the noise of the semi was still powerful. He pulled to the right, still too far away to reach the bungee cord hooks. He tried moving left but at maximum length, he couldn't break his cord or reach the hooks. Unable to escape, he cried, asking Elise to stop and let him go.

She moved closer. "Gunner, calm down. I promise I won't throw hatchets at you."

Between the sobs and his rapid heaves, he shook his head. "No. No. I don't want to. I don't want to."

"Gunner, this is a completely different game. Just calm down and everything'll be fine."

His breaths calmed some, but a small ounce of fear lodged in his throat.

"Just be still," she said. "This game is called William Tell," she said while putting an apple on his head.

Still uncertain, he turned his head. "What's William Tell?"

The apple started to fall, but Elise caught the apple and placed it back on his head. After pivoting it enough to make it stay, she looked directly into his eyes. "Just be perfectly still."

Gunner had an instinct rumbling in his stomach. It churned lightly but tightened into something hard like a rock. An intuition convinced him she had devised some sort of sinister plan. Instantly regretting his trust, his arms wanted to shake, but the bungee cords kept him trapped. "Elise," he faltered, "what's William Tell?"

She walked about 20 paces away from him, then reached behind the hay bale. Quickly, she loaded an arrow to the bow and pulled back on the string. "I'm going to shoot the apple off your head."

A terrifying spasm shot through his whole body as a heavy terror smothered him. It seemed like swirling winds forced his eyelids wide open as his skin shriveled and froze. His chest vibrated like a washing machine out of balance. The apple fell off his head.

"Gunner!" snapped Elise. "I told you to be perfectly still." She rushed back to him and placed the apple atop his head again. She had to pivot the apple a few times to balance it. "Gunner," she looked angry, "quit being a baby and stop crying, okay? Be perfectly still. Trust me. I've been practicing a lot."

She jerked her head to the side and shook it. "Maybe I should wait until the sun sets behind the shed."

He jerked his body violently to break free, but his cords prevented any real leverage to snap them or release their hooks. Fortunately, the apple fell off his head.

Elise growled and marched angrily towards him. "Gunner, I'm losing my patience." She looked around, even exploring the tool bin. Finding some duct tape, she nodded and stripped off a long piece, attached the free end to Gunner's chin, then wrapped it up his head, around the apple, and down to his chin. After a second wrap, she nodded. "Now it'll stay on your head."

Panicked, Gunner's breaths huffed in and out, sounding like a whimper mixed with crying. Wriggling his head, he hoped to dislodge the apple to frustrate her plan. Not working, he gyrated his hips and pulled his arms, but she had wrapped her tape tightly to keep the apple on his head.

Was that pee flowing down his leg? Maybe she could do it, but he didn't trust either her motives … or her aim. Ideas of the arrow slicing through his head, perhaps even impaling his eye, and getting his head attached to the shed made his heart race. It stumbled, picked itself up to run, tripped again and tried to keep going. She pulled the bowstring back, held it, and took a deep breath.

"Elise! What the fuck are you doing with your cousin!" Uncle Jason clutched the bow and pushed it to the left and caught the bow string before the arrow could be launched.

"Dad!" she said, finally showing some anger. "We're playing William Tell."

"Are you crazy or just plain stupid?"

"I can do it if you let me. I've been practicing for weeks."

Uncle Jason used the bow to spank her. "Get to your room while I discuss this with your mother. And you're grounded until you're … 40!"

Uncle Jason apologized profusely while freeing Gunner. Quickly, his uncle's massive arms surrounded him and squeezed tightly. "It's okay, Gunner. You're safe now, okay?"

His nerves, heart, and spirit still felt a deep anxiety, bubbling under his skin, and swirling like a tornado in his chest. Crying on Uncle Jason's shoulder, he hugged back as tight as he could, hoping the fear would die.

Feeling the memory slip to the recesses of his mind, Gunner felt consciousness slowly rise again.

The memory returned, rushing through Elise's consequences for the game of "William Tell." She was grounded for six months, and she was made to go to counseling for a year. Sure, she pretended to be Wednesday Addams, but she took it far too seriously. She kept saying it was a joke, but he still had anxiety attacks whenever she was around.

At this point, to spend time with Jeffrey, he had to come to Gunner's house. It was okay, but Gunner missed Aunt Jenny and especially Uncle Jason. He was such a great guy: playing catch, telling spooky stories, wrestling with him. Gunner's dad never did any of that kind of stuff.

After two years, Gunner was allowed to visit his aunt and uncle's house again. Within a year or so, she pulled another sinister "prank" in the shed. After handcuffing him in the shed, she threatened to surgically remove his penis and testicles. "Gunner," she said, "I overheard your parents talking. They think you masturbate too much" Remembering the icy fear in his belly, it fell deeper into his groin, legs and toes. Petrified, he stood handcuffed as she approached him with the scalpel. Crying, pulling on the cuffs, he wanted to break free and run. He screamed for Mom, Jeffrey, Uncle Jason or Aunt Jenny. Nobody came. He cried, begging her to not do it. He kicked at her, hoping to keep her away.

Jeffrey jumped from behind the toolbox, hiding with his camera. He laughed while Elise just stared at him. Although relieved it was a prank, Gunner was still petrified - and shocked that Jeffrey was part of it!

Finally, Gunner woke up. His blurred vision focused

and … Elise stood over him wearing a surgical mask and holding a scalpel. Realizing he was naked, unable to move, and gagged, a vicious terror carved through his mind, spiraling and tingling down his body – leaving behind a lingering and desperate dread. He felt several tight straps around his body. Helpless, unable to find any solution or agency, his breaths shot in and out of his nostrils, sweat pushed through his pours like geysers, and tears tried to drown his eyes. Unable to find any solution or way out of this, his panicked mind silently screamed for Jeffrey or Aunt Jenny.

Elise is a homicidal maniac!

Chapter 2

Elise

Gunner's eyes batted a few times. Once open, they scanned, froze – and then widened when he saw me. However, he could not move or talk. First, I had shoved a bandanna into his mouth and trapped it by wrapping another bandanna around his mouth and head. He grunted, but it was only in his throat.

Also, Gunner couldn't move as I had immobilized him on a large board. One leather strap was nailed on one side of the board, then was tightly wrapped around his forehead and nailed on the other side. I did the same with four other straps, the first one wrapped around his right bicep, then around his chest, then I wrapped it around his left bicep, then nailed tautly to the left of his body. Another strap wrapped around both wrists, and his waist, and the last one had been wrapped around both ankles, also nailed on both sides of him. It was not easy because I had to use the chloroform on him three times just to haul him to the shed, then two more times to immobilize him with the straps.

Although he was naked, Gunner was far more petrified than embarrassed. Unable to talk, he grunted frantically as his teary eyes pleaded for help. I wish he'd understand that surgically removing his penis and testicles was for his own good. Victor convinced me of this.

"Now cut them off."

Victor's whispers felt cold to my ears and somehow

echoed, although there was really nothing to cause the reverberation.

"Don't rush me. I want to instill as much fear in him as I can."

I adjusted my surgical mask and set out my tools. I ordered them online. Holding a syringe, I nodded. "Okay, Gunner – now for the surgery. Are you ready for your anesthetic? Usually, it's for horses, but I figured out the proper dosage for your weight."

He grunted horrifically while trying to shake his head.

"Oh – you don't want an anesthetic?" I put the needle down and got my scalpel. "Okay – but it's really going to hurt … badly."

All the color left his face as his blood went to … well, you know. His eyes, horrified and panicked, gave me deep and fulfilling satisfaction. My mouth widened, becoming a vile, menacing smile. Relishing the abject terror that teemed in his eyes, the power inside me sent a cold tingle to my skin. Sure – I had joked about it, but nobody knew how serious I was in my mission to turn Gunner into a freak.

Gunner's eyes welled with tears as his body tensed, trying to break free. I checked the nails and straps to see if they remained secure and tight. Although he couldn't move, sweat poured profusely, drenching his whole skin. "Gunner," I said, "maybe I should give you the anesthetic to keep you from twitching. I don't want to mess up this surgery."

His stifled scream bellowed through his throat, and he somehow sobbed through the bandanas. Frantic huffs ran through his nostrils. "Gunner, if that's your attitude, then forget the anesthetic." I touched his shoulder gently. "This is for your own good. I promise that you won't die. You just won't have your dick and balls to play with." He gagged, which concerned me. "Can you breathe? I mean I don't want you to die. I want you to live a long life … without your penis and testicles, that is. If you want, I'll put them in a jar of formaldehyde so you can see them every day."

He gagged again and cried more.

Victor's presence was not with me, but rather infused within me, filling my body and mind with a very hateful, dark presence. Feeling sleepy, his personality became stronger, overwhelming my own. Both warm and cold, his presence spread through my chest and slithered into my arms and legs and his voice got louder. It felt awesome to let him take control and embed himself withing me.

"Sis! What the fuck are you doing?"

Oh no – Jeffrey! His eyes widened in terror, and he stormed at me – trying to seize the scalpel from my hand. I couldn't tell if it was me or Victor who swung the blade at him – barely nicking his upper arm, causing him to scream as blood splattered across my face.

Before I could swing it again, he grabbed my wrist. "Sis!" he screamed. "What are you doing? Mom! Mom!"

"He's ruining everything. Kill him. Cut off Gunner's dick!"

Jeffrey grabbed my other wrist and squeezed, begging me to drop the scalpel. We both stumbled, forcing me to drive the surgical tool into the wooden table between Gunner's legs, just an inch below his scrotum. My brother was stronger than I expected, but Victor helped me, surging in my limbs, particularly in my muscles and bones. Pulling the scalpel out of the wooden table, I tried to stab Gunner's dick. Jeffrey seized my wrist again and somehow pushed me to the side, throwing me out of balance.

My Best Friend is a Demon

The scalpel severed the leather strap near Gunner's right wrist. Shit! I'm so close to my dream of castrating him – but now he has a chance of getting away.

Jeffrey tried to squeeze my wrist harder and slam my hand into the wooden table, but I didn't let go. I refused as my fingers clutched the blade with uncanny strength. Frustrated, I let go of the scalpel and drove my fingernails into the back of Jeffrey's hand. It fell on the table next to Gunner's free hand. He seized it and he kept me away with an impotent stab. Ouch! Fuck! He nicked my finger.

Jeffrey pinned my arms against the shed wall. "Gunner!" he yelled, "Can you get free?"

Gunner gave up on slicing his chest strap and severed the one around his right thigh. He got that leg partially free, but the ankle and chest strap still had him fettered.

Victor's fury spread to my mind and spirit. Unable to tell where he began and where I ended, confusion overwhelmed me – sending me into turmoil. Usually, the high of Victor spreading inside was great – but now I felt tremulous.

My knee shot up, landing on Jeffrey's balls. He gritted his teeth, grunted, but somehow squeezed my wrists tighter. I yanked hard, pulling one hand free, seizing Jeffrey by his neck and lifting him off the ground.

"Sis!" his screams, stifled, were trapped in his throat. "Stop! Please!"

I growled again, saying things I didn't understand. Victor scared me, but I wanted him to like me so badly, I did not fight him. *Victor,* I thought, *please stop it. He's my brother.* My friend had nothing to say, but his furious rage forced me to lift Jeffrey higher.

"Gunner! Gunner," Jeffrey struggled for a breath and his voice, "help me. Please!" His arms flailed violently, finally clutching onto something. I lifted him higher, feeling a sinister laugh erupt in my chest.

Jeffrey doubled his right fist and hit the tool board. What was he doing? Victor growled heavily, making me squeeze tighter. The color in my brother's face faded some, but he hit the board two or three more times. Glancing at the wall Jeffrey pounded, I caught sight of three hatchets barely hanging on a peg. He hit the wall once more, giving enough force to knock them loose. Two of them hit Gunner's panel and fell to the side. The third flipped and the blade severed the strap around his arm and chest.

Turning my head, Gunner pulled his upper torso free, then used the scalpel to cut the straps over his forehead and then his ankles. He jumped off the table and ran towards the door. Damnit! He's getting away! Victor's howl exploded in my voice, straining and hurting my vocal cords.

"Gunner! Help! Please."

Yes – Jeffrey's voice weakened as if about to pass out. Soon, I could chase down Gunner. It'll be easy since he's naked and it's so cold. Looking at Jeffrey, I noticed his eyelids batting, his arms falling, and his whole body weakening.

A hand and a piece of cloth covered my mouth and nose.

"Die, you fucking bitch!"

Was that Gunner? Panicked, I tried to get a breath of air but inhaled a thick odor that stifled my breath even more. My strength faded, as well as my mind. Another attempt at breathing made it worse as the numbing smell crept deeper into my nose and lungs. That little shit was using my own chloroform on me! A third huff had noxious fumes invading my mind, dragging me to sleep.

Chapter 3

Elise

I woke up but couldn't move. My head tilted back as if I slept on a chair. After blinking my eyelids several times, my blurred vision cleared, and a dull, aching pain ran through my head. I grunted, seeing the light that hung from a power cord swing back and forth, left and right. Lifting my head, I tried to stand, but tight straps kept me firmly in the chair.

Muffled sobbing drifted my way from just beyond the dim light. Seeing Mom, I remained calm and spoke with clarity and confidence. "Mother, untie me from the chair. I'm okay now. I had …" I thought about the right word to use, "an episode."

"No, sweetie …" Mom sounded spooked, unsure, and suspicious. "Jeffrey and Gunner told me about …"

"It was a joke. That's all."

"It wasn't a joke, Sis, I saw you."

I did not see Jeffrey who waited just beyond the light.

"Elise – you have someone in you like I did. Who is it?"

Trapped, I confessed, but not giving too much information. "He's my friend. He's my best friend. That's all I'll say."

Gunner appeared in the doorway. "She's right in there," he said while guiding Father Matthew and Sister Regina.

Father Matthew hesitated, removing his coat and putting on his stole. "Elise ..." his calm voice did not soothe the uneasy feeling inside me. His voice, full of uncertainty, softened.

"Elise?" asked Father Matthew, "are you there?"

Victor whispered in my ear. *Don't listen to him.*

I don't have much of a choice, Victor.

"Or are you someone other than Elise?" asked Father Matthew. He and Sister Regina crossed themselves and took a step forward. Victor surged within me, carrying his putrid smell along with his thick hopelessness, horrid fear, and vile hatred.

Father Matthew spoke Latin. Although I could not understand a word of it, Victor kept surging, pulling on the straps, twisting my head, and snapping my neck back and forth. Every limb tried to contort and free itself from the straps.

Father Matthew threw some holy water on me. Victor screamed through me as my skin blistered from scalding water. I convulsed violently, trying to break free from the straps as more pain erupted from inside my core and spread to my flexed arms and legs. More Holy Water touched my skin, making it come alive like powerful wasp stings and blistering my flesh. I screamed with Victor as the pain spewed like lava from a volcano.

"Who are you?" asked Father Matthew. "Are you Vordic?"

Victor fully emerged in my mind – pushing me aside and squashing me down into a deep abyss. The shadow not only blotted out the light but also all the warmth, leaving me in a depressing cold blackness.

Victor had taken control and with it, put me in an image he created for me. It was a cage, ten feet, by ten feet.

He added a bitter cold that bit my skin, and this time, he removed my clothes. It's not like he violently removed them, but he dictated this humiliating visage within me. Although I knew it wasn't real, his overwhelming strength made it my existence. *"Victor,"* I thought, *"you know I hate this. Please let me out."* Every word echoed back, even though no thick walls could be seen. *"I don't like this. Please don't hurt Jeffrey and Mother."*

I immediately covered my breasts and hugged myself in a vain attempt to shield myself from the stifling cold that pierced my skin like freezing needles. Every part of my body shivered.

He snapped me back up, letting me join the conversation. We both spoke at the same time, although his deep bass voice barely trailed my soprano pitch. A subtle sibilance existed somewhere between our voices. Our laughs also mixed, giving the sound an echo that repeated numerous times. "Remember me, Matthew? Florence, Italy in 2003? Matteo and Luca? Two dead boys," said Victor, "ten years old. Your fault. Your lack of faith. Your …"

Father Matthew quieted. His eyes froze as his face whitened - as if he lost his faith and confidence. His fingers shook as sweat seeped from his skin. Some tears followed. I never saw my Priest like that before. Victor's sinister laugh resounded in my head.

"In the name of the Father, Son, and the Holy Spirit!"

Father Matthew's exploding voice frightened me. Angry, he shouted so loud that it pounded my eardrums - making me cringe the same way when I heard the brakes of a train drag across railroad tracks.

"Depart from this vessel," he continued louder, frightening me. It sounded like he was trying to reclaim his faith amidst all the doubt that surrounded him. "Unclean spirit - I condemn you to the abyss!" he said while throwing more Holy Water at me.

Victor retreated deep inside, carrying a frigid cold that wrapped around the inside of my stomach and chest. He surged back up, catching my lungs with a heavy cold net, carrying me into the air. How high was I? Five feet, ten feet? It didn't matter as I struggled to inhale. I begged Victor for help. *"Victor – I can't breathe. Stop!"*

My arms and legs all twitched violently, trying to break the binds that secured me to the chair. My eyes rolled back into my head. A giant heave from my soul tried to expel the cold, stinking blackness, but it refused to budge. Victor's arms wrapped around me, even digging claws into my skin. Lacerations streaked across my arms, legs, and chest. Victor yelled so loud that my ears popped. His stinking breath spread with the force of a tornado, knocking everyone down.

The chair dropped, crumbling under the weight, freeing me from captivity. Winded, sore, I rolled a few times back and forth, wriggling free of the chair pieces. It hurt to breathe - as if I bruised two or three ribs. I grunted, letting out a few breaths. Finding a little bit of strength, I stood to survey my family, Father Matthew, and the sister. They were all knocked out cold. Maybe I should finally cut off Gunner's …

There is no time. Get what you need and leave them. There will be another day. If you fail me once again, I will take full control and keep you in the cage for a much longer time!

I certainly didn't want that.

While humming the tune to "The Addams Family," I searched Mom, Jeffrey, Father Matthew, and Sister Regina for any money. Then, I went into the house and retrieved all the camping equipment I could carry in a backpack. Tools, sleeping bag, some food, lanterns, and several other things.

It's time for Victor and me to be on our own.

Chapter 4

(One month later)

Finishing his shower, Jeffrey went to the kitchen and got his breakfast. Raisin Bran, milk, orange juice, a small cup of fruit, and a cheese stick. His fingers, under duress, wobbled when trying to use the spoon to feed himself. Closing his eyes and holding his breath calmed him down a little so he could finish eating.

Jeffrey's sadness and anxiety left quietly as his eyelids squeezed out several tears. Every morning, he reminded himself of Elise, and that always took him back to the memories of his own possession. He wished those recollections would fade and vanish, but they wormed their way deep into his mind, imprinting themselves on his spirit. Every sound, smell, and image flashed with just enough pain to leave behind a bit of doubt. The memories still burned, leaving a cold sting impossible to forget. He stood, cleaned the dishes and put them in the dishwasher.

Putting a leash on Freddy, Jeffrey took him for a walk. Freddy never lost the excitement of sniffing his world, pooping, peeing, and playing fetch. Jeffrey wished he could find the same happiness his dog displayed. After a dozen or so tosses, Jeffrey sat on the bench Dad had put near the pond. He gazed at the rising sun that lit up the trees and sky, then looked at the magnificent reflection off the still water. Jeffrey's head fell, thinking about his sister. Some thoughts went back to the memory of Dad, and his death. Now, Elise's life was at risk. What would this demon do to her?

Freddy jumped onto the bench and curled up beside him. It brought Jeffrey comfort to feel the soft fur along his dog's back. Strangely, a calm feeling spread through his fingers, hands, arms, shoulders … and his aching heart. "Freddy, where is she? Where's Elise?" Freddy stopped wagging his tail, turned his head and barked, as if either angry – or perhaps afraid. Freddy always seemed to be wary of Elise – and it remained even in her absence. Just the mention of her name triggered anxiety in his dog. Jeffrey walked back to the house with Freddy by his side.

"Mom?" he said, peering around the corner, "I'm heading over to St. Patrick's to see Father Matthew. Then I have a couple jobs to do."

Mom's eyes seemed to lose more color every day, as if they became more exhausted and saddened. Or was she hungover again? He was afraid to ask.

"You're such a wonderful son. I don't know what I'd do without you." Tears welled up in her eyes. "You look like your father … and you have his best qualities."

Jeffrey let her push his hair back, although she really didn't have to do that any longer. Mrs. LaHaye changed his hair style so now it parted higher on the left side, revealing his forehead. His long hair fell to the sides, framing his face. He had a little growth spurt he had anticipated for the last two years, allowing him to almost look at Mom eye-to-eye. His lips twitched upwards in a shaky attempt at a smile, but the worry and sadness kept it from being genuine. "Thanks, Mom." Jeffrey hesitated, scared about asking his next question. "Any leads on a job?"

She stepped towards him and barely stretched a smile. "Don't worry about that. That's my job." Mom kissed him on the forehead. "You be careful on your minibike."

Jeffrey put on his helmet, then kickstarted his minibike. His spirit shook, and it spread to his fingers and hands as the memories of his possession lingered. Should he tell her? he decided against giving her something else to stress over. Quickly shifting to higher gears, the bike jolted to life, creating an unplanned wheelie. After putting the front wheel down, Jeffrey guided the bike to the bumpy driveway, then onto the paved road.

***

The rumbling noise of the minibike quieted. In the shadow of St. Patrick's Cathedral, he glanced at the high structure, particularly noticing the stained-glass windows that provided a bit of illumination. Using a chain, he tethered his small motorbike to the handrailing and put his helmet on the handlebars.

Ignoring the sparse traffic of town, Jeffrey strode up the small hill of steps, and opened the over-sized doors embedded within the fortress-like walls. His footsteps echoed inside the empty cathedral, making Jeffrey feel lonely. He felt it at home, too. Not only with Elise's disappearance, but also Mom regressing into her depression.

The cross, secured to the wall, had a lifelike image of Christ carved of wood. The eyes looked sad – almost lifelike. Jeffrey bowed and crossed himself, hoping to find companionship with Jesus. His savior seemed too far removed - not just in history, but also in humanity. Did Jesus ever fart? Or feel relief after peeing? Did he ever sprain his ankle or decide to skip rocks across a pond? Saying a prayer, he hoped to find some solace and comfort for the tension that haunted him every day.

"Jeffrey – I'm glad you're here."

He smiled at Father Matthew's keen insightfulness. "How'd you know it was me?"

The blind priest seemed to lock himself into place with his cane. He smiled and gently touched Jeffrey's shoulder. "Your footsteps are lighter than a grown man, and I can also smell the mix of oil and grease. The key thing was that I heard the distinct sound of your minibike. Yours has that slight rattle again."

Jeffrey fully smiled. "Yeah. I keep forgetting to tighten the bolt on the exhaust manifold."

Father Matthew's hand clasped his shoulder tightly, then patted him on the back. Jeffrey offered a one-armed hug while his favorite priest messed up his hair. After taking a few deep breaths, they both stepped back to face each other.

"Father ..." Jeffrey hesitated, realizing he probably knew the answer, "have you figured out why I ... remember everything that happened during my possession?"

Father Matthew's disappointed look telegraphed the answer before it fell from his mouth. "We still can't figure it out. Father Bradley has been talking with the top Jesuits at the Vatican, and they're looking into some old archives – hoping to find a clue of some sort."

Jeffrey's heart tore apart, as it devolved to an erratic rhythm of despair. "Why am I the only person in Church history to remember it?" He barely got his words out before his sobs drowned out his voice.

"I wish I could tell you – but there are mysteries in life, belief, and doctrine. We are all working out our salvation and understanding of things." Father Matthew patted Jeffrey's back.

Jeffrey sighed, then let loose a little laugh. "So, I'm a

mystery like the old 'did Adam and Eve have a belly button'?"

It was Father Matthew's turn to laugh. "Well, remember what I said, the Creation Story is …"

Jeffrey finished the statement, although the two said it together, "- not history, it's an allegory to the state of man and God."

"How's your mom doing? I was going to have Sister Regina take me over to your house tonight for a visit."

"Please do, I'm mega worried about her. I know she's worried about Elise, and I think getting turned down for jobs is adding to her depression." A small eruption of anger added sharpness to Jeffrey's words. "It's Mrs. Righetti!" The flames in his soul retreated. "She's spreading rumors that Mom and Dad were Satanists and abused me and Elise." He shook his head. "God, how I hate her."

"I understand."

"Father Matthew, I'm scared," he whispered.

"You feel surrounded by trouble because the future looks bleak – for you, your mom, and your sister."

Jeffrey liked Father Matthew's deep, bass voice that was never used forcefully as a blunt instrument of judgement on him or anyone else. He nodded, realizing his priest knew exactly what he thought.

"What about your sister? Do you think she's still alive?"

Jeffrey leaned back in the pew. "Yeah. I … don't know how to describe it, but I feel … connected to her. And I sense that she's still out in the woods."

"It's been a month."

Jeffrey nodded. "Yeah – but Dad and I were Boy Scouts. He taught Elise and me everything he knew about camping, survival skills, the right berries to eat, along with some traps to catch animals. And a bunch of camping stuff was missing when we all woke up. I'm sure she's alive."

"And she has a friend who's likely helping her."

Jeffrey hesitated. A question burned on his tongue many times over the last month or so, but he could never speak it to cool the hot coals. It was time to douse the flames. "Father Matthew … what happened in Florence, Italy? Who were Matteo and Luca?"

Chapter 5

Elise

I love my new home. It's perfect for what I need to do. It was my favorite place in the forests outside of Newcastle – although it was difficult to locate. Still, I remember finding it with Dad, Mom, and Jeffrey on a camping trip about three years ago. It was off the beaten trail about 20 miles northeast, wedged between two hills that had a stream running at the base. A few caves were nearby, and the forest was super thick.

At the base of the hills was an old cabin, likely built in the mid-1800s. Time and the elements wore it away, leaving a ghost-like structure. It also had a barn next to it that somehow remained much more solid. The old barn had ancient metal tools that had rusted into fragments. The high loft was too weak to support even someone like me who was very lean. However, what made this place appealing was the secret door.

The eight by three feet door was made of thick oak – which was heavy. I could lift it when exerting myself, but I realized it would be easier to use a rope on the old rickety pulley attached to a support beam. One of the things I made sure to have when I left home was some good, strong rope. Even better, I found a chain near the highway I knew I could put to good use.

The door had some stairs that lead to a cellar which was probably ten feet by ten feet, having some tables, and even a couple of wooden slabs resting on masonry blocks.

There was a small fire pit on one side with a large ventilation shaft. Another ventilation shaft rested on the opposite side that helped provide ample airflow. Although he was not sure, Dad thought it was a place used for runaway slaves to hide. Of course, I – or rather Victor – had other plans in mind – and they weren't for a higher purpose.

There was just enough light from the two lanterns I brought with me. It was perfect. It was pitch black when I doused them. There was a large box I used to store supplies: beef jerky, water, animal traps, toiletries and the like. Outside, the stream provided water to drink – and fish to eat.

The sun displayed the beauty of the forest, letting me see so much wildlife: flowers, tall trees with colored leaves, along with animals that wandered around. Fortunately, I had not seen any bears or mountain lions, but seeing deer, birds, rabbits, and other animals pressed me to smile … a little bit.

Ironically, the place was also creepy. The house, mostly in shadows, looked as if hundreds of people had lived there, leaving behind legends of ghosts, demons, and people with sinister motives. What would the walls of the house, barn, and cellar tell me about what they witnessed?

It had been four weeks, but disappointment ran through my mind whenever I thought of Gunner getting away. I was so fucking close to castrating him and forcing him to live without the pleasure of his penis and testicles. I needed to find someone else. I had to be patient. But for how long?

Victor must be sleeping. He had not said anything for a day. My mind went back to when I first met him …

****

"My name is Elise." I said it again, looking directly at the mirror. "My name is Elise." I tried it one more time. "My name is Elise." That was it! I rid myself of the emotions in saying my name.

I said it a few more times, working on keeping any feeling or empathy from my eyes and voice. Dad and Mom said I reminded them of Wednesday Addams – and after seeing the two movies from the 1990s, I had to perfect my tone and look. The old TV show, while corny, was fun to watch and gave the template for the character as well – although I could not bring myself to wear the stupid looking dress. Also, Wednesday did not have glasses. At first, I wanted a sinister frame to house the lenses, however, I realized my glasses were fine the way they were. They had an innocuous look that added some intellect to my emotionless persona.

Feeling something cold brush across my neck made me snap to the left. Was that cool air flowing from the vent? My hands folded over my chest when a cold finger stroked my right ear. While my hair tingled and shook, my breath locked into place. Looking around, I tried to find whoever could have done that.

"Elise."

Who was that? I swiveled my chair and stood, trying to locate the whisper as it seemed to move around.

"Elise."

A steady energy fired through my nerves, creating tremors that seized my fingers, hands, arms, and legs. Strangely, my heart never fell out of sync, nor did my breath run erratically. Within my head, something swirled like a racing house gecko.

My eyes squinted, noticing the subtle red glow in the closet. I always thought something evil lived there. At night, it looked like a black gateway into pitch darkness. The glow changed to a slight yellow, then back to red. Yellow. Red. Yellow. Red. The colors faded into nothing as I stepped closer to the folding doors that stood slightly ajar.

"Elise."

I'll bet it's Jeffrey teasing me. Our constant goal was to scare each other. It's in our genes, I guess. Mom and Dad also liked to sneak up on us and scare us. Dad used to joke that the morning of the Resurrection of Jesus that he snuck up on the women and said "Boo" which is why people say "Jesus Christ!" when someone sneaks up on them. I never really got that joke, but he and Mom thought it was hilarious. You get that when your parents grew up on horror movies of the 1980s and 1990s.

Now my nose cringed as a dank, disgusting smell reached my nostrils. It stank so bad, I turned my head and pinch my eyes shut. My actions did nothing to combat the stench that smelled like … like … something. I did not have anything to compare it to.

Something was there on the closet floor. I rushed to open the folding doors and reached in to attack my brother. The light flooded in – revealing a large teddy bear who had a stupid grin on its face. I kept it to spare Mom and Dad's feelings because I loathe childlike romances and infatuations with the innocence of childhood. Aunt Beth once got me a Barbie doll, but I changed it into a grotesque, wickedly looking doll. Why don't toy companies do that for girls like me? Fuck Barbie! I wanted a Chucky Doll, Talky Tina, the Zulu doll from Trilogy of Terror, a Pennywise Doll, and an Anabelle doll from The Conjuring. I'll add them to my creepy doll collection.

The lights flickered. What is going on? As I turned

around, it seemed as if the walls closed in. My stomach shifted as the room appeared to tilt to the left. Almost losing my balance, I wondered if the room actually swiveled, or if my perception threw off my steadiness.

My jaw dropped, mimicking the creepy dolls I did have. Some were puppets, carved with sinister faces, wicked eyes, and strange grins. Some were painted in ominous colors, making them appear as if they had an insidious entity dwelling within. Perhaps they watched me, waiting for the precise moment to strike. Of course, I was ready with a cross, a Star of David, and even some salt. The others were custom-made dolls with small mouths that did not smile and devoid of friendly eyes. Instead, they were dark, beady and bank – but that was when the eyes were opened. I had to push a button to do that, but to me, they looked creepy with their eyes open or closed. Their cheeks also had no smile at all, devoid of any pleasant emotions. Did they have memories of ancient spirits going back to the beginning of time? Did those spirits have contact with the dark entities that hid in blackness?

I gasped as their mouths dropped open and the plastic eyelids lifted on their own. A fine mist dropped from their mouths and noses, as if they exhaled just like a person. I heard the voice again – except it was louder, but no more than a whisper.

"Elise."

"That is so wickedly cool," I muttered. The anxiety in my chest turned to joy. I always wanted a ghost to share a room with. "Holy Mother Mary May I! Are you a ghost?"

"Yes."

I gasped hearing the cold whisper resonating in my ears … or was it in my head? "Please," I said, "let me be your friend. I've always wanted to be friends with a ghost.

What's your name?"

"*Victor.*"

My hopes faded to disappointment. "Oh, great. I get a boy ghost. I already have an annoying brother and a lame cousin. I wanted a ghost sister." I slapped my forehead. "By any chance, do you have a sister I could be friends with? Please? It's my dream."

"*Elise, I will be your friend.*"

"If I could kick you in the balls – I would."

The lights flickered. All the joy inside me shrank as if a serpent coiled itself tightly around my mind. Another one, a bigger one, did the same in my chest, tightening around my heart. A horrid, frightening dread emanated from my belly. Uneasy, a deep anxiety spread slowly in my mind. Void of any peace, contentment or hope, I almost cried. Is that what Victor was doing to me? I didn't like it. A bitter cold wrapped around me as a vaporous breath fell from my mouth and nose. Immediately, I clutched my body. Arms tight, I tried to find some warmth. It felt like ice particles formed on my skin, nose, cheeks, and ears.

"*We can take care of each other.*"

Its tenuous whisper emanated from my eardrums.

"*We can make plans against your brother, and your cousin.*"

I felt dizzy as the voice circled within my head again.

"*We can scare them. Play tricks on your parents.*"

The inside of my skull froze, emitting a headache that pushed pain out through my ears, sinuses, and jaw. At the same time, the aches and discomfort faded as exhaustion spread through my body. My eyelids became heavier. I tried batting them, but they were overwhelmed by the trance.

The terror returned in full force as I saw him in the

mirror behind me! Although it wore a cloak over its head, the wide slit mouth smiled, spreading over the boundaries of its narrow, sunken cheeks. The eyes, white, rested within a thick blackness. They vibrated, growing into bulbous spreads with red scars. It looked as if its nose had been cut off, leaving only imperfect holes with pieces of flesh and hairs blowing in and out with each breath. They also changed in size, pulsating large then shrinking in sync with the eyes. His mouth opened wide, baring teeth that looked chiseled. I felt a hot, dank breath blowing through my hair and spreading over my neck.

My eyes opened and it stood behind me in my reflection. A hand with long fingers reached down, clasped my shoulder, then held tight. Although I could hear the rhythmic beating of my heart in my ears, I did not feel it pump any blood, leaving me cold. The lights flickered then doused, removing the terror from my heart. Noticing my erratic breath, I took a few deep breaths, held them, and counted. The image was no longer behind me.

Wow! This was so cool!

Chapter 6

"Gunner, open up. It's me."

Recognizing Jeffrey's voice, Gunner slid the small latch he built into his door. After Elise disappeared, he wasted no time fortifying his room for protection. It took him two weeks to put three latches and two deadbolts on his door, bars on the inside of his two windows, and create a slot where mom could deliver his meals. She let him have a little fridge for snacks. His house had an old laundry chute that sent his clothes to the utility room. He hoped to get enrolled in online ed for the upcoming school year.

Gunner started at the top: latch, deadbolt, latch, latch, deadbolt. The door opened and they locked hands with a powerful grip. Gunner cringed at Jeffrey's strength. "Great to see you, dude."

"Great to see you," Jeffrey said while giving him a one-armed hug. "I guess your dad's moved out?"

Gunner sat on the lower bunk bed as the hurtful rejection left by his father festered. A couple of tears wanted to spurt out to provide healing, but Gunner tried to hold them back, yet a few of them seeped through. "God, how I hate him."

Jeffrey sat next to him, offering him a one-armed hug. "It's alright, dude. I'm here."

"I hate him so much." After a heavy sigh, his emotions retreated for a moment, giving him a respite from perpetual sadness. "I really miss your dad. He'd always made me feel better when my dad was an asshole to me."

Feeling his own grief, Jeffrey sighed. "I miss him, too."

Although his eyes faded, a hopeful resolve rekindled. "You gotta get some counseling, dude. You gotta get out of this prison."

Suddenly, Gunner seized, twitching nervously. "I can't. I can't! She'll get me. She'll get me! I know she's going to come after me, hurt me or maybe kill me."

"Calm down, dude."

"I can't. I can't! You don't understand. You don't understand!" He repeated his whisper numerous times, trying to convey the sheer horror and trauma that imbedded deep in his psyche. "She's tried to kill me four times, dude. Four times."

Jeffrey cracked a smile and a hint of a laugh. "You sound like Dr. Loomis in Halloween 2: 'I shot him six times. I shot him SIX times.'"

"You're not funny, dude! You don't understand."

Jeffrey's levity disappeared. "Sorry. But you do need to get out. Come over and we'll watch some movies. Or we can go out on our minibikes."

"I'm not leaving this place until Elise is either locked in a prison or in a mental institution!" Gunner calmed down a little, not wanting to alienate who seemed to be his last friend in Newcastle, or maybe even this whole world. "Why don't you stay over tonight with me? We can watch a couple of movies or something."

Jeffrey sighed. "I can't. Mom's getting worse. She can't find a job. She's drinking more. I don't know what to do to help her."

Gunner's self-imposed loneliness became colder, darker, and bleaker. His room – which included his own bathroom – seemed smaller, as if closing in on him. "Can't you come over some night this week? Please."

Jeffrey nodded. "Sure. If not tomorrow night, the night

after for sure."

Gunner inhaled deeply, trying to find any ounce of courage to free him from his room. It eluded him, just like his … No. He didn't want to think about Dad. It made him feel bad enough.

"Dude – you need some serious counseling. You can do that online now. Please. I wanna help you, but you have to take the first step."

Gunner nodded. "I'll try."

Both boys locked their hands tight, pulled closer to each other and used their free hands to slap each other's shoulder. It was their salute to each other. Finding a little strength, Gunner savored it for the few seconds it lingered, although he wished it would remain with him longer. "Let's at least text later, okay?"

Jeffrey nodded. "Sure."

As soon as Jeffrey left, Gunner secured the door: latch, deadbolt, latch, latch, deadbolt.

***

Aunt Beth's smile lit up the darkened living room, although it did not match her demeanor. Her exhaustion radiated, as if she had not slept for two or three days. It appeared a deep melancholy had descended on her just like it had to Jeffrey's mom. Aunt Beth also had mounting problems: going through a divorce, Gunner isolating himself, and a broken friendship. At least she hadn't let the depression grind her to a halt. She worked furiously on her laptop, finding deals on vacations and business trips for her clients.

She stopped working and looked at Jeffrey. "How's your mother?" she asked. "I really miss her."

"I know," he said quietly. "Not too well. I think her depression is getting worse."

"I wish I could help," she said after letting out a huge sigh. "But she won't let me. You know I've tried, right?" she asked while turning on the lights. She had done so much for Mom, offering to take care of Jeffrey, help Mom get counseling, get off the alcohol, even to work with her at her Travel Agency. Her head tilted to the right, letting her long, dark hair fall in that direction. She had gray eyes that radiated so many emotions: sadness, concern, desperation, and love.

Jeffrey nodded silently, staring at his aunt while standing at the edge of despair and hope, love and fear, anger and sadness. Not knowing which way to step or turn, he hunched his shoulders. "Aunt Beth, I don't know what to do." Unable to face her, his eyes fell to the lightly stained heather gray carpet. "I'm mega scared for Mom, Elise … and Gunner." His head shook. "Why am I the only one that's trying to hold us all together? I mean … I try to be responsible and take care of things … but I don't know if I can live like this much longer."

She wrapped her arms around him tightly. He found it strange that during his possession she found so much terror from him but now she found him vulnerable and afraid.

"I'm so sorry, honey."

He hugged her back, wanting to hold on longer, but they both knew it was time to stand on their own for a short while. Taking a deep breath, Jeffrey found some strength and let a smile break forth for a split second. "Aunt Beth, I have a question I need to ask you. I know you're divorcing Uncle Walt, but … if things don't get better with Mom, can I live with you?"

Chapter 7

Excited, Freddy wagged his tail, barked, and rushed to Jeffrey who dropped to one knee. He rubbed his dog's head, just behind his ears. "Hi, Freddy. Are you happy to see me? Did you miss me that much?" Dropping to the ground, Freddy yelped and rolled onto his back. His tongue lolled out the side of his mouth as Jeffrey rubbed his belly. After a minute, Freddy rolled back to his paws and stood. Emitting a puppy whine, his head dropped as if sad.

"What's the matter?" asked Jeffrey. Of course, he knew Freddy could not talk – but what was amazing about his beagle was that he was very empathetic. Jeffrey found it ironic since his dog was named after Freddy Krueger, but had a caring, supportive soul. "What is it boy?"

Freddy raced to the house, leading Jeffrey through the front door, to the right hallway, past the piano room to the office. Jeffrey's exuberance faded, seeing Mom on the couch, sound asleep. Strangely, it seemed as if Mom's sadness affected her dreams, not even allowing any respite from the melancholy. Worse, he noticed the goblet on the table next to her. It had a tiny bit of wine that gathered at the bottom. Even more indicative were the wine bottles – one being empty and the other was somewhere between a half to two-thirds full.

Jeffrey's chest tightened as if his emotions all rumbled together, wrestling for control. Each one sought dominance in the three or four-way battle. Although he wanted to feel angry, his sadness countered, as well as desperation. Pity and love tried to team together and combat the previous emotions, but they struggled for dominance, taking it for a split second only to lose it to another emotion in the next second.

Jeffrey glanced at the laptop and moved the mouse over the email section. He clicked, opened and read one. After a minute, he went to the next one. Nervously, he went forward again, read the email, then clicked to the next one. After ten emails, his own hope faded. All of them were rejections for job applications, half of which were work at home positions, and the other half from town or nearby towns.

Last night, he found her the same way, and he rifled through all the medical bills from when he was possessed. That was when she had insurance from work and the bills still totaled a little over $34,000. Jeffrey thought of starting a GoFundMe page on Facebook or asking Father Matthew if the Church could help with the bills. Mom, though, was too proud to do that. Or was it stubborn stupidity? The alcohol seemed to make the pride lose ground but gave fuel for her obstinance.

Jeffrey reached into his front right pocket and pulled out the cash he earned for mowing and sacking three bags of mulch today. After facing the cash, he counted it off to $150. It'd only put a dent into the surmounting bills. Worse, he knew the insurance company was still balking at Dad's Life Insurance Policy. Maybe Lillian, Mom's attorney, could help. Sighing, Jeffrey put the cash in Mom's purse.

***

Something tickled his ears. No, it didn't tickle. A chilling malevolence irritated the hair in his ears, making Jeffrey quiver. Was it something in his dreams? Lifting his

37

head, Jeffrey looked around his room, terrified of what he might find. Did Vordic come back? He winced, worried about being thrust into a twisted reality, locked in his mind with the demon again. The first time was terrible enough. He almost cried at the memory, wishing he could forget.

Pressing his eyelids tight, Jeffrey prayed the Lord's Prayer, crossed himself, and clutched the Rosary Beads Sister Regina had given him. Once he finished the prayer Christ taught his followers, Jeffrey started his own silent prayer. *God, please don't let him come back. God, please don't let him come back.* On the verge of tears, the prayer became a whisper in his mouth. "God, please don't let him back. God, please don't let him come back. Please, God, please."

Startled, shaking, his mind launched into a high-alert status. The blunt racket resembled a slam, or perhaps a heavy weight falling to the floor. Its tone suggested an intruder or unfriendly spiritual force. It might be Mom moving through the house. Or perhaps it was just a sudden change in air pressure that slammed an open closet door. What if Elise came back to get some supplies or something? However, none of his theories were confirmed.

Gulping hard, he had to know which theory was true. Pulling the sheets and blankets off his legs, he gently stood. A short, quick bark startled Jeffrey. Holding his chest, he took several slow breaths to slow the eruption swirling inside his torso. Once the energy ebbed to nothing, he glanced at Freddy, who tilted his head curiously. His dog didn't seem spooked. Perhaps that was a good thing.

Jeffrey unlocked the small safe at the foot of his bed. Once open, he retrieved the handgun and inserted the clip. Dad taught him how to use a gun – and Mom was okay with letting Jeffrey keep one in his room as long as it was locked in a safe. It was just Mom and him now – so it was up to him to protect her. Still, he thought it was odd she let him keep a gun in his room, but not his phone to dial 911. *I better talk to her about that.*

Every step betrayed his attempts of stealth with creaks and moans. Freddy remained behind, quiet except for his rapid panting and pattering feet. Reaching the bottom, Jeffrey felt a cool breeze dance across his skin. The front door was closed, but the breeze came from the kitchen. Mom would have turned on the lights.

Jeffrey's heart increased steadily as he turned towards the kitchen. The breeze, stronger, seemed to announce a presence. Heavy footsteps shuffled, although they sounded strange. He readied the gun, turning off the safety, but careful enough to not fire blindly. It could be Elise, and he didn't want to hurt her. If it was an intruder, though, he wanted to be ready. Freddy would be of little to no help in either situation. He'd always been afraid of Elise, and if it was an intruder, Freddy would most likely get a tennis ball to see if the thief might play "fetch," or beg the thief for a treat.

Jeffrey licked his lips and quietly sucked in a breath. Hopefully, a human intruder would not hear the small huffs through his nose. His hand reached for the light switch. Another loud thud ignited his heart to a panic mode. Jeffrey almost pulled the trigger. Fortunately, he held back as two or three deer dashed away from the outside back porch. Jeffrey whispered a laugh. He noticed the kitchen door slightly ajar, thinking either he or Mom hadn't shut it properly. After putting the safety back on, he removed the clip and set the gun on the table. Stepping outside, he noticed a couple of potted plants on the patio knocked over.

Jeffrey caught a shadowy glimpse of a doe and a fawn running away. He felt as if the two personified him and Mom: a mother and child, alone, trying to survive in the dark. He hoped they didn't leave behind any deer shit to clean up. Opening the kitchen door, he stepped onto the back porch.

The cool air bit his skin as he glanced out at the eerie night. He noticed the fog as it wafted off the pond, then spread across the ground. A few weak lights outlining the shed struggled against the blackness and gave the fog a spooky glow. He gasped, seeing a petite feminine silhouette in the fog. A dash of hope mixed with trepidation, forcing him to choose between taking a step forward or backwards. "Elise," he whispered, "is that you?"

The shadow changed. For a second, it grew taller, wider, with muscular arms, and a distorted head. The ears seemed long, twisted, and menacing. He heard sibilant laughter, although it did not float across the air, but rather through his mind. No, the image changed to the small stature of Elise once again. Instantly, it reformed to the ugly, wicked being.

Jeffrey retreated back inside, closed the door, and locked it. Glancing at the kitchen counter, he noticed the green bottle, empty, sat tilted to one side. Sauvignon? Although he was unsure of the language, he knew it was a popular wine Mom and Dad liked to drink with dinner. Mom, though, didn't have any wine with dinner.

He sighed, turned off the light, took the gun and clip, and started back to bed. No. He first glanced down the hallway towards Mom's bedroom. The darkness swallowed it. He walked lightly, finding a new prayer flooding his mind. *God, please help her stop drinking.* He repeated the thoughts endlessly. He didn't like seeing her drunk. In the past, before Dad died, it was rare - but it was happening more often lately. He knew it was stress: unable to find a job, the medical and legal bills piling up, along with the regular utilities, the loss of Dad, Elise's disappearance, and his own possession.

He glanced into the piano room when he passed by, realizing she hadn't played much of anything lately. A few more steps and he looked into the office. Usually neat, like the kitchen, it was now a mess with papers strewn everywhere.

Mom's phone lit up. She had forgotten it, leaving it in the office connected to the computer. The alert was for an email. Jeffrey unlocked it, then glanced at the message. Another job rejection. His own heart matched the blackness around him. He wondered if she'd cry just like him once she read the response.

Jeffrey went to Mom's contact list, scrolling through it to find someone for help. Beth McPherson? No. Aunt Beth was having enough problems, and Uncle Walt was worthless as a husband, father … and even an uncle. Unfortunately, Dad didn't have any other siblings, and both his parents had died.

One contact stood out: Janie and Dan Collins. That was Aunt Janet. He was surprised to see her in Mom's contact list. For some reason, Mom and Aunt Janet rarely talked to each other. He saw her and Uncle Dan at Dad's funeral late last year. The time before that was when Nana, Mom's mother, died. That was like … three years ago. He never saw Uncle Dan or Aunt Janet during the holidays or any other times. Mom hardly ever spoke about her. Maybe she could help? Jeffrey sent the contact to his own phone.

***

"Hello?"

Jeffrey wavered for a few seconds.

"Hello?"

"Aunt Janet … uh …" he didn't know what to say to an aunt he barely knew.

After a short silence, she blurted out, "Oh! Is this Jeffrey?"

"Yes, ma'am."

"Please, everyone calls me Janie."

Jeffrey smiled a bit. "Okay Aunt Janie."

"How's your mom and sister doing?"

"Well … uh …" he stammered a few more times. "Not very good. It's hard to explain over the phone, but … Mom really needs help." A strange blunt silence made Jeffrey recoil.

"Why didn't your mom call me?"

What was she doing? Playing mind games with him. She sounded so skeptical, or maybe angry. "Well … she doesn't know I've called you but … you're family," he flexed his eyelids to keep from crying, "… and I don't know who else to turn to. We …or rather I really need your help. Please?"

Chapter 8

Elise

"Once upon a midnight dreary – while I pondered weak and weary."

My favorite poem, "The Raven" by Edgar Allen Poe whispered in my ears, tickling them with a cool breeze. The dreary, dark night had dropped a blanket over the people and animals of the town. The little light around the house substantiated the horror – especially since a thick fog emerged from the pond, then rolled to land, billowing like transparent, ghostly figures. At the same time, I heard a quiet thunder to the east. It rumbled, like a murmur of angry students whispering under their breaths after the teacher assigned a pop quiz. A little light resonated off the security cameras outside the house.

I lay prone on the humid grass. I don't like the weather that acted as if Mother Nature could not make up her mind to deliver rain, keep us dry, or even what temperature to use. Although mid-July, this summer's heat and humidity had not been as fierce and strangling as with previous summers.

Looking up at the second floor, a lamp lit up the lonely room. Using my binoculars, I watched Jeffrey's silhouette standing and moving around. Stretching my neck higher, I watched the lower floor where the kitchen was located. It took a few minutes, but the light appeared subtly. I could see Jeffrey – although not very well. His hairstyle had changed a bit, now having a part that spread on the left side of his forehead. Did he grow more? He grinned at something.

Staying out of sight, I stood, then strode closer to the house. Still using the trees and shadows for cover, although nothing could hide the small noises I made walking on the grassy terrain. I jumped when a doe and its fawn bolted away from the house.

Should I try to talk to Jeffrey and Mom? Leave them a note? Unafraid, I stood and faced the darkened image of my brother. My twin. How could I leave him behind?

Fortunately, Victor slept. Occasionally, he'd disappear for a few hours, and on occasion he would be missing for a day or two. In the beginning, he would be gone for a week or two. Now, he whispered so much, he could annoy me. It was nice to have a respite from his presence. He also had an aura of dread, and it made me feel alone and helpless, and he did stink … a lot. When he was around, Victor and I talked about the things he saw, our opinions on Jeffrey, Mom, Dad, and Gunner. What I really liked was when he told me how wonderful I am.

Deciding to leave, I stood, took a deep breath and moved to the right near a few trees. I kept walking in slow metered steps, wanting to distance myself from Mom and Jeffrey. They wouldn't understand me making a friend like Victor. After walking for a half hour or so - I found myself in front of Gunner's house. It was far simpler than ours: one-story red brick, with a chain link fence and a gate. The porch light was out, so I stood on the sidewalk, staring at the thick door hidden in shadow. A slight breeze stirred the clicks and clings of a couple of wind chimes.

Falling to my right knee, my hands searched for the ugly green frog where they kept the spare key. Since they had no alarm, this would be easy. Although dark, my hands worked with precise measurements and turns. The bolt slid back quietly. My ears perked, hoping not to hear the doorknob lock release. With a silent breath, I pushed the door in carefully.

Walking through the short hallway, I found the living room. All of Uncle Walt's books were gone. The table was cluttered with papers surrounding Aunt Beth's laptop. The couch had magazines stacked on one end, and more were on the dingy brown easy rocking chair. Something dropped in the kitchen, but I realized it was the ice maker pushing out cubes.

Moving to the right, I entered the dark hallway. The posters of Halloween, Friday the 13th, Hellraiser, and Nightmare on Elm Street showed me the way to Gunner's room. On the door, he had a small metal poster that said, "You Can't Kill the Boogie Man." My hands glided across the wooden door, circling it softly, trying to detect any kind of brace. The doorknob did not turn, although I kept the pressure light to keep it from making too much noise. A couple of extra metal clamps suggested he had reinforced the door with extra deadbolts. *Smart, Gunner. Very smart.*

Pivoting my head, I placed my ear up to the door and listened intently. I did hear a couple of things – like the HVAC system kick in with a slight bit of air conditioning, and maybe the water tank. However, I could not hear Gunner at all. I'm sure he was asleep – hopefully having a nightmare of me completing the job I set out to do.

As I quietly hummed "The Addams Family" TV show theme, an idea came to mind. Slowly, quietly, I went back to the table in the living room. Sitting, I felt for a regular sized paper, and a writing utensil. Although I could not see incredibly well, I put the ballpoint on the paper and wrote my message.

Gunner,
Hello. I dropped by to see you. I miss you. I
hope to see you again soon.
Elise.

After sliding the paper underneath Gunner's door – I remained silent, left the room, locked the door, and put back the key. I can't wait for him to find my note.

Gunner

Gunner tried to turn over. His shoulders pivoted, trying to carry over his torso, but he could not move. Using more strength, he tried jostling his upper body and using his arm for leverage, but it held tight. Not even his head could move.

Fully stirred awake, his eyes snapped open. His insides flinched, locking his muscles, bones, and spirit in a vice-like grip. A frenzied heart rhythm seemed to crack his heart into several pieces as his eyes caught her: Elise!

Tall, with longer arms and taloned fingers, she loomed over him as her eyes glowed a scornful red. A malicious, blood-stained smile spread across her surgical mask.

"Good morning, Gunner." The low, hoarse voice dripped with a cold, sinister breath as she held a surgical tool that had a severed penis. "You're a new man ... sort of."

Although the strap dug into his forehead, he pivoted his head slightly, then looked down at his naked body. Nothing existed in his crotch area – except for pieces of flesh sutured together, stained in blood. Panic exploded into a swirling tornado, carrying horrid, terrifying emotions that acted like debris slamming on his insides – leaving bruises, cuts, and bludgeoning pain on his ribs, heart, lungs … and his soul.

Gunner's eyes opened as his body spasmed awake. His heart sped like galloping horses, and it hurt as if their hooves pounded on his chest. Gunner's hands quickly reached for his crotch, feeling for his penis and testicles. Even though his fingers were now covered in sweat, and possibly urine, he didn't care as he found those pieces of his manhood were still intact.

Shuddering, he grunted out his sobs as he turned on his side, trying to heave out the oppressive and onus terror. Unlike the stomach flu, these vomits never expunged all the horror that grew with every bellow. It took minutes for the icy tears to stop along with the sobbing. "Shit," he whispered – finally able to talk. It took several more minutes for his revved heart and hyper nerves to cool so he could take some breaths.

Looking around his darkened room, he was grateful for the fortress: the extra locks, and protective window shudders were strong enough to keep Elise out. The vents pushed out air conditioning, causing him to jump. Startled, he turned frantically as the ventilation caused the hanging crucifix to sway into the support on his low bunk bed. His fingers and toes still shook from the noises – helping him realize all the reinforcements did nothing to curb the horror that spread and attacked him from his inside.

Reaching for the old leather necklace with the crucifix he made a long time ago, his thumbs pressed onto the image of Christ and the cross. The touch alone helped him relax. Some light entered his mind, forcing the cold fear to retreat. At the same time, it reminded him of something that might halt the fear and possibly pulverize it into fine particles of sand. Putting the crucifix on his heart, he hoped God would listen to his weeping prayer.

Elise

It was the next day. I peered through the thick bush, eyeing the three boys who sat on a rock. What were they? 12, 13, 14, or 15? It was hard to tell as boys in this age had such a variety in height, weight, and voice. Their hats prevented me from seeing their eyes, but they were part of a Boy Scout Troop. Two wore cargo pants, one wore jeans, but they all had the traditional long-sleeved ecru shirt – but without the scarf. The one on the left was a bit overweight but not obese. He took his cap off for a second to wipe the sweat off his forehead allowing me to see his full, round face and dark, matted hair. He offered the other two a couple of snacks. "Here's my good deed for today," he said.

"My good deed will come when I meet a hot girl and we start the frickle-frack," said the skinny middle boy who stood and gyrated his hips.

"What the fuck is the frickle-frack, retard?" asked the Latino kid on the right.

"My mom and dad use that word when talking about sex. I gotta hard-on right now and don't know what to do with it."

I rolled my eyes as the boy made noises related to the "frickle-frack." Shaking my head, I wondered why boys were obsessed with sex.

"Keep it away from me, frickle-frackerer," said the kid on the left as he knocked the middle boy's hat off.

The kid on the right laughed. "Find a place alone to *hand*-le it, yourself," joked the other.

As they erupted in laughter, I focused on the middle boy. His long hair, somewhere between blonde and brown, fell to his shoulders. He was thin, lanky, and had little muscle. What I found deceptive were his innocent light-blue eyes. Also, his voice was on the bridge between a boy and man, not quite on the other side. From those two things, and his attitude, I knew he was perfect.

"What do you think, Victor?"

"What do you think, beautiful?"

Considering what the boy said, and what he was doing, I raised the left corner of my mouth, not into a full grin, but rather a sneer. *Victor – he certainly doesn't deserve to have his penis and testicles. I'll choose him. If only I would've acted faster on Gunner. Someday, when he least suspects me, I'll get my trophy from him.*

Staying behind, I tracked them back to their camp. Finding several trees and rocks to situate myself, I kept hidden but used binoculars to spy on them. I wonder how many others I could torture with the same punishment. Thinking back to my last incident with Gunner reminded me of the power and satisfaction I had during the moment. He was completely helpless and sealed in abject terror - which is what I want.

"Christ had power and came to serve people."

Father Matthew's words faded.

"It's fun to scare people, but it's more fun to talk with them."

"Sis – even Wednesday loved Gomez, Morticia, Cousin It, Thing and Lurch."

"Elise, quit it. I know you love us as we love you."

The memories of conversations with Dad, Jeffrey and Mom echoed a few times, then dissolved to nothing.

An annoying buzz erupted in my head, drowning out the past words of Mom, Dad, and Jeffrey. The sound jabbed me like a hot iron poker, stirring flames, logs, and ashes to fuel a fire. The flames burst wider, louder, flapping like wind to deliver an angry heat.

I thought of Gunner. Weak, naïve, nice, innocent. I hated him. He's stupid. He'll believe anything – even me when I want to torture and hurt him. He robbed me of Jeffrey's attention and love. Is that why I always wanted to hurt him?

My focus returned to the boy scout troop. They all pitched their tents, then ate the fish the scouts caught in the nearby stream. I had berries and beef jerky to eat while I watched them start their fires, clean their fish, cook and devour them. I almost smiled, remembering when Dad taught me and Jeffrey how to do those things. My dispassionate anger returned when I saw the scout cooking his fish and laughing with his friends.

How was I going to get him? I did have the anesthetic to knock him out, but with him in camp, it was too risky for me to invade his tent, jab him with the needle and drag him out. Yes, Victor gave me the needed strength to carry him back to the cabin and barn, but his troop would definitely capture me. It might be cruel, but maybe the taser Dad gave me for protection would be a good way to stun him. Still, I had to forge patience in order to find the right time.

Soon enough, the sun fell below the trees and horizon, stretching a blanket of darkness over the area. I crept out from hiding to get closer and listen – even more so when I saw him crawl into a tent with his buddy. Scooting closer, staying hidden in the tallgrass, I heard them whispering, finding the one boy who bragged about dominating women. It might be just 'boy-talk' Mom and Dad mentioned to me. Boys often brag about being the dominant sexual partner to impress their friends, but many do not really feel that way. Still, he shouldn't be saying such things. I crept closer, listening to the conversation.

"Judy's visage disappeared, mixing with the fog. A shadow emerged. Slish-Slash, Slish-Slash, Slish-Slash."

I recognized the boy's voice, and it triggered an acidic hatred that rushed through my mind. I knew why: he sounded just like Gunner. My hatred faded remembering when Dad told me that same story when I was younger. A vicious cold spiraled through my mind, chest, and finally, my belly. At first, the annoying ring erupted, but then quieted, allowing my ears to capture more of the conversation.

"Whoa! That's a wicked story. Cool."

"Do you have one?"

"Not as good as that one."

They muttered something indiscernible, forcing my ears to reach out in a vain attempt to catch the sounds. The words escaped the grasp of my earlobes. They laughed a bit, keeping their voices hidden from me.

"I said lights out!"

The angry adult voice startled me. It sounded like the voice of Mr. Clayton, my ninth-grade principal from last year. No, this black man had a deeper voice, possessing more authority.

"We got a lotta of ground to cover tomorrow," said the adult scout leader.

The boys laughed a little but did their best to stifle it and keep quiet. "I'll tell you another one," said the boy, "while we're on patrol together tomorrow at sunup."

I rolled on my back, staring up at the sky. The stars spread wider tonight as I was miles from any city. I wondered if the stars end somewhere? How cold is it in outer space? How far away were those stars? Far enough to go back to the beginning of time? Was Dad's spirit out there, flying to heaven? Did he get there? Or does it take a lot of time to reach heaven? What was heaven really like? Where is God in all this?

He never cared. He let your father die, said Victor. *Heaven is nothing. I've been there and left on my own volition.*

Were you the one in Jeffrey, too? Or was it someone else?

He was a friend. We lived and worked together ... until the Almighty cast us out.

Victor sounded angry – but it was a quiet anger, soft but ready to erupt violently. *He was jealous of us. He hated us – just as he hates you. Only I love you, Beautiful.*

That's what Dad called me. Please don't call me that, I thought. *Sometimes I miss him.*

He doesn't miss you.

Chapter 9

The video replayed Jeffrey's Exorcism. Father Matthew focused his attention on what he heard. His attention focused on the words and noises exploding from the speakers. The sounds resonated loudly, carrying a deep terror that felt like punches - especially from Jeffrey as the demon wailed loudly. It sounded unholy, full of hate and fear. It leveled profanities, both in English, Latin, and Greek. Other disembodied screams dug into his ears, dragging him back to those moments, and leaving behind an ominous dread.

Sister Regina gasped and cried as if both disgusted and traumatized by the experience. "I've never seen one before," she said. "I've read cases while in the convent, but I've never seen one."

Father Matthew remained calm, shushing her quietly. "Sister, please. I need to hear." Garbled voices emanated from the speakers, along with horrendous screams Jeffrey made when Father Bradly threw Holy Water on him while reciting the Exorcism prayer in Latin. His ears piqued, making out a little of the extra sounds and voices that lagged or jumped ahead of Jeffrey's voice. Silence erupted.

"Sister?"

"Father! I see it. I froze the video and backed up a few frames. It's … horrendous. Its arms look as if he's latching onto Jeffrey … and I think I see … an angel."

"Explain what you see."

She inhaled deeply. "It looks like … the demon is … ripping a wing off the angel."

A loud, thunderous screech stretched across Father Matthew's ears, reaching inside his head into his mind, freezing him from the inside-out. Although he covered his ears, it did nothing to block the horrendous noise that made him wince more than once. "Turn it off!" his voice trembled as his fingers shook. Father Matthew wondered if he heard the demon itself, or if it was part of the recording. "Thank you, sister," he said between a few breaths.

Sister Regina put her hands on his shoulders to help Father Matthew sit up in his chair. He repeated a Psalm he loved to use as a prayer:

> *How long, Lord? Will you forget me forever? How long will you hide your face from me? How long must I wrestle with my thoughts and day after day have sorrow in my heart? How long will my enemy triumph over me? Look on me and answer, Lord my God. Give light to my eyes, or I will sleep in death, and my enemy will say, "I have overcome him, and my foes will rejoice when I fall. But I trust in your unfailing love; my heart rejoices in your salvation. I will sing the Lord's praise for he has been good to me.*

The last few words were also spoken by the sister as both ended the prayer in unison. "Thank you, Father. I needed that, too," she said, clutching his hand. The tight, desperate grip conveyed a strong bond like a brother and sister might have, especially when counting on each other during a dire time.

"We all do," he said quietly, finding the peace that eluded him. He, too, returned the clutch, squeezing tight, then using his free hand to cross himself.

"Father …" Regina said strongly, "I really need to know something: who were Matteo and Luca?"

***

Matthew shook at the sight. Both boys' skins looked desiccated and were marred by black scars and darkened bruises. The gradual transformation began shortly after the family returned from Brazil. At first, the episodes were sporadic, and not threatening, but that changed heavily over the last six weeks.

Matteo and Luca's eyes looked up until they became an albino white as they bellowed a thunderous, deafening yell. Matthew could not cover his ears sufficiently to protect them. The room shook violently, almost knocking him off his feet, and nearly toppling his faith.

The heavy, moist air tried to choke him and added to the horrid stench of putrid meat. The environment changed to a freezing, dry ominous sense of dread. Matthew's nose and ears chilled as his breath emerged in a mist from his nostrils. It made no sense - which made sense to those accustomed to demonology. The disorder in the air reflected their chaotic evil and existence that mixed lies with truth, stirred a pot of insanity and logic, and combined holiness and depravity into a melee of massive confusion. Disoriented, befuddled, Matthew staggered between faith and doubt, fear and love, hope and dread. With no balance, he almost fell again.

A horrid memory returned to Matthew. He was only

11 on the day Officer Reed dropped to a knee and looked at him in the eye. Although the strong police officer was on the verge of tears, he managed to tell Matthew what happened. "The suspect grabbed Detective Barlow's gun and tried to shoot them," Officer Fields choked back his tears, "and a couple of bullets got your father in the neck. There wasn't anything we could do. I'm so sorry, Matty."

Mom bellowed loudly in the other room. She must have heard the same thing from Detective Goodman who helped serve the warrant as well. Her scream sent an icy spike through Matthew's chest, accompanying the one in his back that came from Officer Reed's words.

In the present, facing the demon twins, Matthew tried to focus on the boys, but all he heard inside his head was *"Your father left you and your mom, Matthew."* The voice had an eerie echo, starting with a deep bass and reverberating with a higher pitch. *"He could've found better work. He shouldn't have turned down being a detective."*

"Father Matthew – do not listen to its lies," said Father Samuel.

The voices, laced with icy and sinister whispers, repeated, shaking Matthew's faith and love. The immense humidity hanging in the air tried to strangle him. Malevolent eyes pierced through him, leaving behind a heavy, ghastly dread. Everything seemed darker and more sinister as shadows encroached. They made the room smaller, and strangely tilted the floor so much, Father Matthew almost stumbled.

Father Samuel threw the holy water at the demons and recited the Latin Prayer after calling out its name: Navidar. It was the demons' turn to cover their ears and wail from the Holy Prayers and Praises. Both priests crossed themselves and prayed again, casting their holy water at them.

Both boys levitated higher as their heads twisted and their arms contorted. The sounds of bones popping, stretched to their max, made Father Matthew cringe. He tried to focus on prayer and not let their torturous existence distract him. A foul stinking breath brushed across his face and hair, sickening Father Matthew. He wiped off the slobber and suppressed his gag reflex. Long cold fingers scraped his neck, his ears, and face. A strong hand felt his private area, causing him to panic and shudder - at least until the passage of II Thessalonians came to mind:

> *He will punish those who do not know God and do not obey the gospel of our Lord Jesus. They will be punished with everlasting destruction and shut out from the presence of the Lord and from the glory of his might on the day he comes to be glorified in his holy people and to be marveled at among all those who have believed. This includes you, because you believed our testimony to you.*

He saw it! Something with a faded, opaque reddish color emerged from Lucca's chest. At first, it was rolled in a ball, but after coming out, it slowly spread out its arms, legs, and wings. The entity screamed so loud, it felt as if Matthew's eardrums would rupture. A trumpet blast exploded as a light flashed brightly, taking the demon with it to the Abyss.

Father Matthew looked at Father Samuel. The old Jesuit's skin was flooded in sweat as his arms, legs, and jaw shook.

"One down, six more to go," Father Matthew muttered.

"They are weakening," said Father Samuel. His Italian accent teemed with authority and confidence. "We must cast another out before resting. Hold onto your faith. Don't listen. Focus on the Lord. Are you ready, Matthew?"

Although reticent, Father Matthew nodded, trying to find any bit of faith that drained from his heart and soul. Shaken, nervous, he felt overwhelmed by the thick dread that felt like a hot, humid day before a raging storm. For a split second, he wanted to beg for rest. Confused, scared, his nerves twitched under his skin - causing an electrical fire to spread. He perspired heavily as fear wrapped itself around his mind and body. Almost void of hope, Matthew said a silent prayer, asking for strength. He yelled out the next name: Severen.

The elder priest, repeated the prayers, cast the holy water as Father Matthew prayed. Both switched roles as Matthew cast the holy water while offering the Latin Sacrament as Father Samuel prayed. Again, the disfigured boys screamed. Matthew and Samuel switched roles again, hoping this might be the extraction they hoped for. It might be the strongest of them. It rolled out of Matteo's chest, spinning so fast it almost looked solid. It's squeal, so loud and high pitched, it felt like something stabbing at Matthew's brain. As it spread out, the demon used both arms to grab onto the twin boys. It pulled their necks as if using them as anchors to stay in this world.

The boys' necks snapped as their heads dropped lifelessly. The demon let their small bodies fall to the ground. The fallen angel lurched forward, grabbed Father Matthew by the neck and hurled him backwards into the stone wall. The back of his head cracked as warm blood spilled out, drenching his already sweat-soaked hair. He wanted to hold his head but couldn't as something cold and numbing spread through his arms and legs. Unable to feel them, Matthew panicked. Muffled screams could not overpower a ringing that pulsated in his ears. Some Nuns, a couple of Priests, and some medics started rendering first aid: a C-collar, an oxygen mask, blood pressure reading, and wound bandaging.

All the while, Father Matthew's world darkened. The fuzziness started far away but closed slowly, eating the light and visions he saw. Like dark storm clouds that blotted out the sun, they encroached, encircling his vision until his world turned completely dark.

Chapter 10

Jeffrey heard tires grinding the gravel on the driveway. Putting down the wrench, he wiped his hands on a dirty rag and went out to greet the black SUV that came to a stop. The driver's side door opened, and Aunt Janie stepped out of the vehicle. A refreshing smile spread across her face, waking up her tired eyes. "Jeffrey," she approached him – with arms open for a hug.

"Wait – I'm messy. I've got oil and grease on me from working on my minibike."

"Oh, it's no problem." She hugged him. "You've grown an inch or two since I last saw you."

He tensed a bit and kept his arms straight during the embrace since he was not too familiar with her.

"You remember the boys, right?"

Jeffrey noticed the taller one first. "You're Jason, right?" His sandy brown hair was cut short, almost military style, and he displayed the characteristics of someone rendered blind like Father Matthew wearing sunglasses - however Jason had a service dog that hopped out of the car.

Jason didn't extend his hand but held his cane close while smiling. "How are you doin' Jeffrey?"

"Fine," he replied. "Nice to see you ... uh ..." Embarrassed by using the word "see," he stepped back. "I'm sorry."

"It's okay," Jason.

"You should meet my priest, Father Matthew. He's blind, too," said Jeffrey. "He was the one who spoke at Dad's funeral."

"Hey, Jeffrey," said the shorter, yet more muscular boy. "I'm Justin," he said, offering a strong vice-like grip with his shake.

"Wow!" said Jeffrey, "that's one strong grip you have. You lift weights?"

"Trust me," smirked Jason, "his grip is strong because of his online porn addiction."

"Boys!" Aunt Janie said while shaking her head, "that's so inappropriate."

Justin and Jason tried to suppress a smirk as Aunt Janie rolled her eyes at them. Within a second, Jeffrey found himself trying to stop a grin – but he failed just like his cousins. He better change the subject. "Where's Uncle Dan?"

Aunt Janie shook her head. "He couldn't come because the State Department in DC had some meetings this week."

"Janie?"

Jeffrey tensed up and looked over his shoulder. Mom stood like a stone statue outside the front door. Arms crossed, head held high, she cast an icy stare. Her words were just as cold. "What are you doing here?"

Aunt Janie smiled. Although awkward, her brown eyes had a sincere and friendly aura. "Hi, Jenny. It's great to see you."

Jeffrey stiffened as Mom said nothing.

"Didn't Jeffrey tell you?" asked Aunt Janie. "He asked me to come."

"No. He didn't." Mom's words felt like knives directed at him - although he also sensed they were also meant for Aunt Janie. After a staring match between the two competing female alphas, Mom barely cracked a smile, although her eyes remained skeptical. "It's good to see you, Janie. Come on in, we'll talk." Her voice still resonated a strong defense. "And I'll deal with you later," she said to Jeffrey.

"Boys," said Aunt Janie, "keep the suitcases in the car. We might have to find a motel instead." Her head turned towards Jeffrey as she walked by. "You should have told her I was coming," she whispered sharply.

Jeffrey fidgeted, worried that he already made his Aunt Janie mad at him. "I'm in mega trouble," he whispered.

"That's weird," said Justin as he retrieved a bicycle from the SUV's bike rack. "Our mom's names are Jenny and Janie?"

Jeffrey let loose a slight laugh while helping Justin with the bicycle. "And what about us? Jason, Justin, and Jeffrey. It sounds like a cheesy movie."

Jason smiled but did not laugh. "And my brother's name was Jimmy."

"My dad's name was also Jason. Boy, God has a weird sense of humor," quipped Jeffrey.

***

"What are you doing here?" Jenny asked while preparing some coffee.

"Jeffrey called and said he didn't know who to turn to and that the both of you needed help."

She narrowed her eyes. "Do I look like I need help?" Although she did not yell, Jenny let her words become blunt, as if to leave behind a slight bruise or a scar. However, Janie's eyes widened in amusement and let loose a slight laugh as she looked around the house.

Jenny, realizing the kitchen was a huge mess, and that the living room was full of boxes, scattered magazines, and dust, she let a breath form a smile. She covered her eyes to regain her composure. "I don't want help from you," she said while crossing her arms. Knowing Janie had a wound, Jenny decided to poke at it. "I cannot forgive you. You got our baby brother killed … all for the sake of getting drunk."

Janie's mouth curled and her eyes flinched as a lone tear rushed out. "My God – that was twenty years ago, and I've been sober ever since." She dropped the last four words like angry steps across the floor. "I'm the one who has to live with that every day." Her hand shook, as if pleading with God just as much as her sister. "And I know, somehow, Bobby's forgiven me."

"I haven't." Jenny started to feel remorse for the last two things she said, but her anger retrenched itself, taking control of her mind and soul.

Shaking, Janie cried – although Jenny did not believe the faux guilt, the phony tears, or the empty repentance from her heart. She didn't want forgiveness. She wanted to be off the hook.

"Jenny, please. Despite all that, I do want to help you, Jeffrey and Elise."

The name struck a nerve that suffered damage. It throbbed like a burn on her skin, or perhaps a nasty bruise, or possibly a broken bone. Jenny cried, shuddering at the thought of Elise never coming back. Weak with no defenses, she sighed and sat at the kitchen table, covering her face. Unable to face her sister, she sobbed.

Sensing Janie sat across the table from her, Jenny lifted her head, then clasped a napkin to wipe her face. Finding a breath, and some words, she hesitated a split second but let them out. Looking directly at her sister's eyes for the first time in years, she hoped to trust her one last time. "I hope you believe me – but the last nine months have been a living hell." Her fingers drummed the table. "After Jason died, Jeffrey started acting weird. He was sick. He got into a huge fight and then he …" She paused again, hoping her sister might believe her. "Jeffrey was possessed by a demon."

Janie tilted her head as her brown eyes lost all emotion and her face lost color. No pity emanated from her, but rather a shocked aura that tried to mask her own terror.

"He was possessed for almost four months and went through so many exorcisms. I know it sounds crazy, but my priest, my sister and brother-in-law, my nephew, and Elise, all saw it." Jenny remained quiet, trying to get a feel from Janie. "And now Elise is missing. I think the demon went into her to hide and it tried to harm my nephew, Gunner." Embarrassed and afraid, she could not face Janie – until her sister gently squeezed her hand.

"Dan and I told you and Mom about the experience when we took Jason in after his parents and brother died. I believe you. I saw things that cannot be explained either."

Looking away from her sister, Jenny glanced out the kitchen window at the property: the shed, the field, and Jason's old truck. He used to joke that he wanted to be buried in it with her so they could ride the supernatural highways together forever. "And the insurance company has been balking at paying out his policy for the last several months."

"I want to help," Janie whispered. "So does Dan."

Jenny stood and walked to the coffee machine and poured a cup for each of them. After putting them on the table, she got some cream, and a little sugar for them, too. "Don't worry," said Jenny, "there's no Iocaine powder." They both laughed, remembering the connection to the old movie, "The Princess Bride."

Janie smiled while mixing some cream and sugar in her coffee. "Dan hates that movie."

"Inconceivable," whispered Jenny. They both laughed together again for the first time in over 20 years.

"Janie, part of me wants to forgive you, but another part of me wishes you died in that car wreck instead of Bobby."

Janie lost the brief happiness they shared. "I understand. Sometimes I feel the same way, too."

Jenny's pride and anger retrenched themselves. "While I need help to get my shit together, I have to be honest…" Jenny faltered, but blurted it out, "I still might not be able to forgive you."

Chapter 11

Eli Wilson rushed through the woods, following two of his scouts as the rest of the troop followed. Although frantic, he kept a cool head, wanting to be a confident example for his troop. Still, the thought of one of his boys missing left an empty feeling in his chest. The pain tried to instill fear, dread, and panic. Being a retired police officer, he reverted to his training to remain calm, think, and focus on the present problem. With each step, he felt he drew closer to something terrifyingly dire. His heartbeat squeezed tighter, causing his blood to bubble like a pot of chili. A cold dread circled his stomach. He hoped his scouts were wrong as a cold terror clutched his arms and smacked him in the face.

"Over here, sir," said Marco.

They broke through some trees to the open stream. Nathen's hat, scarf, and supplies were all in the mud. Slightly buried was his smart phone which had multiple cracks on it.

"Back up everyone," he told the troop. "We don't want to mess up any tracking." His heart sank, realizing this was not a scout who got lost or injured, but rather kidnapped.

"Mr. Devry, please take the troop back to camp, pack up and leave immediately. Once you're in a range of cell receptions, call the Sheriff's Office and tell them we have a missing camper. Give them the camp location. I'm going to track what I can and will call when I have cell phone reception, myself." A few boys resisted, wanting to help

Eli do some tracking. They begged him. "Look, I admire your dedication to another member of your troop, but I cannot put any of your lives at risk."

Eli knew he was putting his own life at risk, especially going without backup, but a boy's life was in danger of murder, possible rape, or human trafficking. He was a police officer and knew how to track in the woods, so he had a good chance to catch up. Moreover, he had known Nathen for four years. The thought of having to break the news of finding a dead boy to his parents felt like anticipating a knife jabbed into his chest.

Some resistance bubbled again, but eventually the boys relented and followed Mr. Devry.

***

Nathen squeezed his eyelids a couple of times. Unable to see, he tried flexing them again. He grunted and rolled on his back, but still unable to see anything, he wondered where he was, and how he got there.

An immediate pain throbbed in his testicles. In a guarded position, he grunted several times, hoping that would make the pain go away. It didn't. The dull, achy pain felt as if a horse kicked him in the balls. It also left a burning sensation. What happened?

The memory surfaced. He was taking a leak in the stream when someone came from behind and delivered an electric shock to his crotch. The fiery pain made him scream as he fell into the mud. The pain from the electric shock overwhelmed him, however he also felt a burning sting injected into his butt and within seconds, he passed out. He grunted many times, hoping it would help push out the pain in his balls. It didn't. The pain was beyond miserable, seeming to pulse with every heartbeat. He rolled from one side to the other, feeling hay straws scattered across a wooden floor. He cursed, then coughed, only causing the pain to flare even more, drifting into his stomach. What did the person use? A taser … a cattle prod?

Looking around, he saw nothing. In pitch black, he shuddered. Only in his boxer shorts, he felt chilly. He felt something cold and heavy on his naked chest and neck. A chain? It was wrapped around his neck – not enough to strangle him, but not loose enough to pull over his head. His hands found a lock on the chain links. Fortunately, he could stand, although he could only move so far until the chain tightened. His hands wrapped around his metal tether and followed it to a wooden beam. The link at the other end of the chain had been secured to a thick piece of wood with a metal bolt.

An awful dread sank through his chest and stomach. It dragged a hollow, empty feeling that chilled his ribcage and stomach. His heart seemed suspended between beats, as if waiting for something awful to happen. Nathen's mind went blank. When thoughts returned, they only focused on terrible, awful things that happen to a movie character victim – but not to him. Terrified, he gulped once as he stopped breathing. What would happen? Torture? Sexual abuse? Death?

Shit! This isn't happening. This isn't happening. This isn't happening! Reality refused to budge, and retrenched itself, rendering his thoughts irrelevant. An empty darkness pressed heavily against him, paralyzing his breathing. It blotted out any hope or anticipation of rescue. The horrid reality sent a cold shock that crushed his bones … and even his spirit. This was like some serial killer series on Netflix, except this was real - and it was happening to him! Weeping, shaking, he kept telling himself this wasn't real. Nothing altered his present reality that refused to give way like an onus weight.

Wait! Maybe this place might have cell reception! Although he doubted it, it seemed to be the only way to escape the pitch blackness. He moved to the left, spreading out his arms and hands to find his phone. *Where is it? I need to text Mom and Dad. Or should I call 911? Shit! I gotta find my phone first. Where is it, where is it, where is it?* His hands and fingers worked as sensors, meticulously searching the immediate area. As he moved back to the right. The tiny spark of hope faded as he realized he was unlikely to find it.

A painful moan emanated from the ceiling, as a steady military-like gait walked across. More beams creaked and whimpered – snuffing out the small bit of hope that quickly imploded into a deeper sense of horror. Nathen shook, expecting the worst. Thuds descended from above. They sounded like heavy footsteps in a measured, military-like gait. Terror dripped with every step, falling on him like frigid water, stilling him into a frozen statue.

A door opened, allowing a dim light to spread from above. Surrounding blackness blocked most of the brightness of above. A dark shadow descended the stairs. Both images and sounds felt like a cold knife stabbing Nathen's hope. Dust circled around the small amount of light and surrounded the intimidating shadow. Its head, surrounded by muscular shoulders, was huge. Its legs and arms appeared to lengthen, increasing the foe's reach and height. It couldn't be real!

"Oh, God," Nathen whispered.

"God's not here." The voice, a deep bass, had subtle grunts as if it snored in its awakened state. "I'm here, but nothing good is in me. NOTHING!"

Nathen lost his breath as his skin, muscles, tendons,

and bones all spasmed at the harsh voice. The shaking started in his lungs, stomach, heart and spread into the nerve endings in his fingertips and toes. Nathen's teeth dug into his lower lip in a futile attempt to find control of his mind and body. Weak, tired, hurting, his breaths shot in and out of his nostrils. Finding an iota of reason, he tried the only thing that came to mind. "Please," he stammered, "let me go. I promise I won't tell anyone; I swear to God. Please. I wanna go home. I wanna see my mom and dad. Please?"

After it descended halfway downstairs, it set the lantern on a hook. Nathen's eyes widened seeing the long fingers. They did not look human. No. He was seeing things. That had to be it. Fear magnified his perception and harrowing terror. Again, he stuttered out his thoughts. "What … are you going … to do … to me?"

He … or rather it kept quiet. The large chest flexed in and out as it inhaled and exhaled. Nathen's nose caught a sulfurous smell that made his eyes water. A ringing erupted in his ears.

"I'll let you imagine it," the monster said, leaving a sibilance in its words. "I'll send my assistant to take care of you until your time. Sleep well." It walked back up the steps and let the heavy door fall into its brace.

Nathen looked up as it … or maybe he … walked heavily on the upstairs floor. Every step was a huge thud that sent an ominous vibration which penetrated Nathen's body and soul. He shuddered with every sound.

The noise stopped. Nathen stared at the small lantern that emitted a limited scope of light. He stood and tried to reach it, but he maxed out the tautness of the chain. Only able to stare at the small illumination, Nathen cried. The terror froze his skin, muscles, organs, mind, and spirit.

Unable to move, all he could do was stare at the bleak reality surrounding him. His thoughts became a prayer, which escaped from his lips. "Oh God, please let me out of here. I promise I won't lie anymore and be nice to my brother and sister. Please God, I want my mom and dad."

Chapter 12

Elise

I stood outside amidst the trees, cabin, and barn. My flashlight illuminated a path away from the barn and cellar door I secured with a latch. There was no way Nathen would escape - much less remove the chain from his neck for that matter. It was around his throat tight enough so he could not get it over his head, but loose enough so he could breathe. The other end was secured to a two-by-four with a one-fourth sized round screw. Fortunately, I had some tools, and Victor gave me strength to do it.

Victor suggested I strip Nathen completely, but I thought it would be best to let him keep his boxers. It would be humiliating enough and deter him from escaping during nighttime. I might give him a blanket to help him sleep at night – and I burned his scout uniform to create a small fire for my warmth and meals. My trap caught a rabbit, so I skinned it and cooked it. I had some berries that were safe to eat, and some beef jerky. In fact, the boy had some in his pockets – along with a few Snickers bars.

"Hello, Beautiful."

"Stop calling me that," I whispered out loud.

I felt his dry hand and long fingers running through my hair. Although his fingers were cold, I liked his attention and affection. Still, sometimes it made me nervous. "Please stop that," I said. "You act like you're grooming me."

I felt the sting of my hair yanking an instant before my head jerked back. With his fingers in control of my head, I felt a dry, coarse fingernail draw across my skin close to my carotid artery. Breaths poured out in short puffs, dissolving from fine mist to nothing in the cool, humid air. His rancid huffs stank so bad, it was like salt poured on rotten meat.

"Don't talk to me that way. Or you'll go back to the cage."

The voice, accompanied by a subtle ring, tickled my right ear … but not in a good way. Terror dug into the tunnels of my ears, leaving behind a frozen sensation. "I'm sorry," I stuttered between huffs.

My head jerked forward as Victor let me go. After a minute, I calmed down, finding a little peace. My thoughts turned to Jeffrey and Mom. I wondered what they were doing right now. What was Gunner doing? Were Victor and I going to return for him and issue the punishment we wanted to levy against him. I hope so. It'd be fun.

"Victor," I murmured, "when are we going to castrate that boy in the cellar? After a day? Two days? What?"

"What do you think?"

My mind turned on itself like gears in a machine. "Two, three, but no more than four days. He'll panic every time one of us goes down to torment him, give him food. Every visit will have him wondering if that will be the last time. He'll wonder if this is the time he's going to lose his life, or his testicles." A light went on in her mind. "What if we … did it over three days? After one day we remove one testicle, then the next day, he wakes up without another one. Then the last day we would … no, we don't have enough horse anesthetic for three operations."

"But … we could do one without an anesthetic,"

whispered Victor.

I thought about it, shaking my head. "No. All that screaming he'd be doing would get annoying." I drew my knees up to my chest and tilted my jaw on the right knee. "I'll sleep on it. I just wanted him to be continuously terrified"

Was that my thought? Or Victor's?

Chapter 13

"I'm sorry our guest room has too much junk in it," said Jeffrey as he led his cousins up the stairs. "You can stay in Elise's room." Jeffrey had to haul a couple of suitcases while Justin guided Jason up the steps.

"What happened to your sister?" asked Jason.

Jeffrey used the usual, and mostly true explanation. "She ran away. She took a bunch of camping equipment and is hiding out in the forests somewhere."

"I lost my twin, too," said Jason. "I know what that's like. I'm sorry. And I'm sorry about your dad because mine died, too."

Although he didn't feel any tears, Jeffrey's memories reminded him of losing Dad … and now Elise. He tried to figure out a way to change the subject. "So, what's it like being blind?"

"Dark."

Jeffrey snorted out a laugh. "I'm sorry. I'm mega stupid."

"He's mega-smart," Justin said, pointing to Jason. "He's always reading a book."

Jason grinned. "I need a good hobby to pass the time. What's weird is that I never was a reader until after I went blind."

Jeffrey squinted his whole face and tilted his head. "Really?"

"He plows through two or three in a week," said Justin.

"Reading by touch is much more engaging," said Jason.

Reaching the door, Jeffrey dropped the suitcases in front of Elise's door and opened it. "Here you go. You'll love her room … that is if you can see it."

The door hinge creaked as it opened. "Holy shit! I'm not sleeping in here!" said Justin as he looked at the contents.

"What is it?" asked Jason.

"His sister," said Justin, "has a very weird doll collection … and they're freaking me out."

"They're just dolls, shithead," quipped Jason.

"But you can't see them. They're freaky, scary, and ugly. There's Chucky, and Pennywise – and I don't know what those others are."

Jeffrey smiled but didn't laugh. "Chucky is signed by Edan Gross who did his voice in the first Child's Play movie. Pennywise is autographed by Bill Sarsgaard. The other doll is a Talky Tina doll from an old Twilight Zone episode, as well as He Who Kills, which was a Zuni doll from an old TV Horror Movie, Trilogy of Terror."

"Shit," said Justin, "that's an Annabelle doll."

"It's signed by Vera Farmiga from The Conjuring Movies," said Jeffrey. "Sis collected evil looking dolls."

"This is too freaky. What about those other dolls?" he asked, pointing to the ones in the far back corner to the right.

"Just various evil looking dolls she found at garage sales and collector stores."

Justin took a step back. "I can't sleep in here."

"Justin - get over it." said Jason.

"Well," stammered Justin, " … do you hear anything or … smell anything?"

Jason kept his hand on the inside of Justin's arm as he moved to the middle of the room. Jason turned his head to the left, then to the right, and back to the left. Using his cane, he navigated closer to the bed, then stepped to the left. "I don't smell anything."

Curious, Jeffrey's eyes narrowed. "What's going …"

Justin shushed him.

Jason turned his head and spun around slowly. His head turned up, then pivoted down. His jaw was tightly formed, and his nose was lean and straight, but he had a few vertical scars on his face, and part of his left lower ear was missing. Still, he looked more like a man. Jeffrey hoped he would be just as good-looking as he grew more. "What are you listening for?"

Jason faced him, pausing, sighing, and shaking his head. "I … uh …" He cleared his throat before speaking. "Well … after going blind, my senses heightened so much … and please don't think I'm crazy … that I can hear and sometimes smell … the supernatural: ghosts, and other things."

Jeffrey, although dumbfounded, believed him. He could tell by his cousin's confident voice that also resonated with humility. "My dad said you guys experienced something supernatural. What was it?"

"We," said Justin, "… don't really like to talk about it outside our family and one friend. We don't want anyone to think we're nuts."

"I don't think you're crazy," Jeffrey said emphatically. "I believe you. Really."

"Right, dipshit," said Justin, letting the sarcasm drip like acid.

Jeffrey felt slighted and backed away, as if guilty or embarrassed. "No. I promise you. We've experienced …

something, too. Especially … me."

"What?" asked Jason.

Jeffrey sat on Elise's bed. Something begged to come out, but he was afraid of their reaction. Would they think he's crazy, or some sort of conman. Jeffrey faltered, still debating the quandary in his mind. His mouth dropped open, he hesitated, then said it quietly. "I was …" he took a huge breath, then let it out. "I was possessed by a demon," he said, afraid to look at them.

"Seriously possessed?"

"No," said Jeffrey as he snapped. "I was humorously possessed. It made me dance, make funny speeches and make jokes." He instantly regretted his derision. "I'm sorry, but the worst thing is that … I remember everything." He closed his eyes for a second. "It tortured me in my mind, taunted me, terrorized me in a … never ending nightmare that went on for days and weeks." He wept. "And I hurt Mom, Elise, and Father Matthew and Sister Regina." He shook his head. "It was terrifying. I had no control. I forgot who I was. I wanted it out, but it refused. I hated being around it and wanted it to leave because it felt so … sickening and … horrific." His fingers, trembling with fear, sent a chill through the deepest part of his soul. Why was he telling this to two cousins he barely knew? It begged to come out. "I started to," he thought for the right words to describe his strong, menacing fears. "I was losing my … identity."

Both his cousins sat on opposite sides of him. "I believe you," muttered Justin.

"Have you talked to anyone else about this?" asked Jason. "I went through counseling after my parents and brother were killed. That was tough, but I can't begin to imagine what that was like."

"It was like," Jeffrey cried as the memories returned. "Nothing was left of me. There was no love or hope but just … a cold terror within me … growing and growing. Removing everything about me: my memories of Dad, Mom, my sister …" He sobbed for a while, hoping his tears would wash out the horrifying memories. Justin and Jason each patted a shoulder until he could take breath. "Thanks for listening," he muttered.

"Damn," said Jason, "... and I thought I was traumatized."

Jeffrey let out a heavy sigh. "And now," he paused - needing another huge breath. "Now we think it fled me and went into Elise. That's why she's missing. She tried to cut off Gunner's dick and balls - but then fled."

Justin jumped and clutched his private area. "Holy shit! She's not coming back, is she?"

"How the fuck would I know?" snapped Jeffrey. "I just know if we wait too long, it'll be harder for us to get it out of her. The longer it stayed with me, the more control it had and the more stubborn it was in leaving. That's what worries me."

Two familiar shadows came up behind them. Jeffrey turned, already smiling, knowing who they were. "Father Matthew, Sister Regina! These are my cousins, Justin …"

"Hello, Sister," Justin said politely while extending his hand. "Hi, Father. Nice to meet you." Once Father Matthew extended his hand Justin took it. He then made a point to shake the sister's hand and then helped Jason find Father Matthew.

"Jason," said Jeffrey, "Father Matthew is blind, too."

"Really? Wow. When did you go blind, sir?"

Father Matthew turned to Jason. "It was 22 years ago while I was in Italy. And you, young man?"

Jason smiled, although it appeared marginally. "I was in a car wreck about a year ago. My parents and brother died, too. I live with my Uncle Dan and Aunt Janie now."

Somehow, Father Matthew found Jason's shoulder and offered a quick innocuous, yet sincere, hug. "I'm terribly sorry."

"How did you go blind, Father?" asked Justin.

It seemed like Father Matthew balked at the question. He sighed, backed up a step, and appeared to fake a cough. "It's a long story and it was very traumatic. Perhaps we can discuss it some other time."

"That's okay."

A few more pleasantries, and the whole squad descended the stairs, with Sister Regina and Justin guiding Father Matthew and Jason, respectively.

At the bottom, the wonderful aroma of food tempted Jeffrey's palate. He licked his lips smelling the lemon chicken, the mashed potatoes, and the butter-basted rolls. Even better, the kitchen was full of light, and he heard Mom and Aunt Janie talking – even laughing together. He smiled, feeling as if he accomplished something to help both his mom and aunt.

Jeffrey got Justin to help insert a leaf in the table so they could all sit and eat together. Many conversations started among the guests until Mom lightly tapped her wine glass, stood, and beamed widely. "I must say – this is something I've long missed: a huge dinner with close friends and family." She leaned to kiss her sister.

"I'm glad to be here, too," said Aunt Janie. She seemed reserved, or perhaps uncomfortable with the kiss, but managed to emit a smile. "Thank you, Sis. It's been a while since I got to spend some quality time with you."

"Mom, did you call Aunt Beth and invite her and

Gunner?" Jeffrey asked.

"Are you kidding?" she laughed. "You think Gunner is going to leave his fortress of solitude?"

Jeffrey nodded until Justin poked him. "Whose Gunner?" he said between bites.

"He's my cousin on my dad's side," whispered Jeffrey. "He's the one Elise wanted to castrate."

Everyone passed the food and soon their plates were filled, and more conversation started. Mom poured some red wine into her goblet. Aunt Janie flinched, dropped her fork and glared at Mom.

"What is that?"

"It's called a glass of wine," she said while lifting her eyebrows. "You should know all too well."

More of the guests quieted, hearing Mom's subtle, yet not so subtle, comment.

"How dare you do that in front of me!" said Aunt Janie.

Jeffrey knew everyone else noticed Mom's blunt words – as if trying to cause damage.

"I'm being an example of how to hold my liquor," Mom said - adding a hint of pomp to it.

"I've been holding my liquor for 20 years now. If you'd bother to call and talk regularly, you would have known that!"

"Ladies," Father Matthew's calm voice tried to seize the hostility, "… the sister and I would like to offer …"

Mom raised her hand as well as her voice. "Father Matthew – please stay out of this."

"Why shouldn't he?" asked Aunt Janie. "You're the one who can't offer any kind of olive branch. Maybe you should listen to him."

"Maybe you should've learned to control your liquor

before you got Bobby killed!"

Both of them slammed their napkins down.

"I knew this was a mistake," whispered Aunt Janie. "I just knew you wanted to rub this in my face – and in front of my boys!"

Mom faced Jason and Justin and took another sip. "Boys – your mother's drinking got our brother killed. He was only 11."

"Aunt Jenny," whispered Justin, "it's rude to stare at a blind person who cannot face you eye to eye."

"Mom," interjected Jeffrey, "stop it! Please." He retreated when her usual glare sliced at him, freezing his heart.

She sipped some more wine.

"Oh, shit, sure. Drink it like that in front of me. You're no better than I am. You've been drowning your sorrows over your husband's loss. I can tell. I see it. Who knows alcoholism better than someone who's been through recovery?"

"I didn't get someone else killed!"

Aunt Janie somehow let out a silent explosion with one breath. "This was a mistake," she said quietly. "I can't do this." Shaking her head, it seemed she tried to stifle some tears. "Boys, pack your bags. We'll stay at a motel, and head back tomorrow."

Chapter 14

"Mom … what the fuck are you doing?"

"Hey," she said, pointing her finger at Jeffrey. "Don't you dare talk to me that way, young man. I am your mother." Her angry eyes were much larger than usual, showing more color. Also, her forehead vein bulged – almost throbbing. "If you take that tone with me, you'll be off your minibike for six months. Understand?"

All the angst burst out of Jeffrey's chest. "No!" He no longer cared that Aunt Janie, Justin, Jason, Father Mathew and Sister Regina could hear them in the kitchen.

Her hard slap left his cheek stinging. but had no comparison to the painful angst in his chest. Over the last three months, the hurt, confusion, and pain built slowly, gathering strength like an approaching thunderstorm, or a giant boulder rolling down a cliff. Unable to scream, he cried through his words. "Mom, I miss Elise and Dad, too. But I can't live like this anymore. I'm tired of coming home and seeing you drunk. I can remember everything during the possession, but I can't talk to you about it because you're not here."

"Of all the people," Mom's face relaxed and her voice calmed, "you called my sister?" Tears gushed, somehow wetting her brunette hair. "You know what she did now, right? It's unforgiveable … at least for me."

This time, his tears hurt coming out, stinging like scalding water or acids leaving burns in their wake. "Mom, I felt awful when that demon was inside me. But it hurts so much more when I come home and see you drunk, asleep in the office or in your bed. Aunt Beth gave up trying to help you. You refused help from Father Matthew. Aunt Janie's been sober for over 20 years and wants to help — but the way you treated her was cruel. Mom, I love you, but I can't live like this anymore. I can't rely on you anymore."

Mom curled her lips tightly while incessant tears flowed through her eyes.

"Mom …" Jeffrey heaved a few times to find the strength to tell her how he felt. He faltered twice, then blurted it out. "If you don't get help, I'm going to live with Aunt Beth. I don't want to live like this anymore."

Her voice got caught in her throat. She gulped a few times, as if having a spasm. Tears belted out with each move, as if panicking. She pulled Jeffrey tight, squeezing him as hard as she could, but not to hurt him — but rather save herself from falling. "Please don't go, please. You're all I have left. I can't afford to lose you."

"Then let somebody help you."

"I'll do anything you want," she said between sobs. "Please don't leave me alone."

***

Jenny glanced at the circle of people around her: Beth sat on her right, Janie on her left. Beth was the sister she wanted. Her dark hair complimented her rich brown eyes that swelled with concern, sadness, and love. She was slow to speak and preferred the listening role, but she voiced her own pain and regret. She filled the void for the last 20 years.

Jenny's eyes turned towards Janie, afraid of her. Her blue eyes were full of empathy and love but possessed a tint of uncertainty and regret. Janie's hands also had

84

folded, and her lips kept pursing. Did she want to say something? Or did she try to hide her constant fear of judgment? Jenny took a deep breath, trying to find some anger, but embarrassed, she let a few tears escape. *"How can I be weaker than my sister? I'm the oldest. I'm responsible."* While she told herself those lies, they lost veracity within a few seconds.

Now she looked at Father Matthew and Sister Regina. They were the two most Christian people Jenny knew: selfless, kind, loving, giving no judgment or self-righteousness. Regina was not wearing her habit – as she did most of the time because she didn't want people to feel uncomfortable as if they had to put on a show for her. When she wasn't assisting Father Matthew, she sought ways to serve others – whether it was making a meal for a shut-in, visiting them, starting up a reading tutoring program for children, and simply being a good friend. Her contagious laugh found humor in the most trivial things – often saying things like "I'm not wearing my habit again, so don't tell Father Matthew."

Father Matthew, although, insisted on wearing his collar – wanting people to know he was an agent of God. Despite having a deep, bass voice, he never yelled but remained quiet and reserved, full of patience. His hair was somewhere between blonde and a slight red, and he often joked that's why he did not have the typical Irish temper. His smile radiated so much confidence, and it highlighted his handsome face that displayed strength and confidence.

Embarrassed, unable to look at them, her eyes fell to the floor.

"What's wrong, Jenny?" asked sister Regina.

She paused, shook her head in regret, then barely glanced at them. "You've all been so good to me. And I've been too blind to see it." Sniffing, she tried to retract the tears. "I certainly don't deserve your kindness."

"Grace," said Father Matthew, "is very embarrassing … almost humiliating – isn't it?"

Janie and Beth moved closer, putting their arms around her torso, providing the warmth she wanted so much since her husband, Jason died. She tried to fuel flames to keep her warm with anger, resentment, and guilt. Those flames never found the oxygen needed to provide relief from the cold loneliness in a half-empty bed. Janie kissed her on the cheek.

"What do you want me to do?" she asked.

Unable to look at her, she let out a huge sigh and thought about the question. Glancing at Beth, Jenny bit her lip and laid her head on Beth's shoulder. Considering her problems so mountainous, she did not know where to take priority – or even begin. One thought came to mind. "First … toss out all the wine." She looked fully at her sister. "Next, explain to me how you got sober. I need to know."

"As you wish," said Janie.

Jenny noticed her sister smiling. She smiled too, especially hearing "The Princess Bride" quote her husband, Jason, used so many times when he was alive.

Sister Regina stood, taking charge. "Beth, Janie, let's start cleaning this place up and getting it organized. We'll start with the kitchen. It is the heart of a home."

Left with Father Matthew, she sat next to him and started to cry. It kept coming more, refusing to stop like a raging river after flooding storms. Putting one arm around her and clasping her shoulder, he whispered some Psalms to her, then offered prayers to forge strength in weakness, and faith amidst doubt. She lost track of time as her arms shriveled, her nose dripped of mucus, and her eyes became red and sore from crying. Taking a deep breath, she wondered if she truly let her husband, Jason, go. No, she hadn't.

"Father Matthew," she whispered, "it's so hard to say goodbye to my husband. At night in bed, when I was scared of a nightmare, uncertain of the future, or seeing nothing but obstacles, he kept me warm and promised we would get through this together. Sometimes, I'm angry at him for dying – and I shouldn't be. I'm afraid that the demon will come back to take my son from me again. And now I keep wondering if Elise will ever come home. Why am I suddenly dealing with all these demons?"

"Jenny," he paused, "I can try to explain, I can try to say something, but what I do best is listen. Since going blind, it's become the best skill I've acquired."

A brief laugh opened a short grin on her face. "Maybe we should all go blind to learn how to do that."

He let out a subtle laugh, then rubbed her back. She liked the strong grip but really savored the warm massage to her back. It made her feel safe. As her head dropped to his shoulder, she caught Jeffrey in her sight. He leaned against the wall, dressed in jeans, a Friday the 13th T-Shirt, covered with a flannel shirt that acted like a jacket. His long hair now parted high on his forehead, making it much easier to see his eyes now. Strangely, his eyes radiated confidence and insecurity, as well as bravery and fear. partial smile broke across his face, making him even more handsome in her biased eyes. Pride forced a huge smile as she stood, walked over to him, and embraced him tightly. She recognized his sigh that indicated he felt delivered from anxiety.

"I am so proud of you," she whispered after kissing him on his brow, "for being the strong one – and doing what needed to be done to help your mother. I can't express how much I love you."

"I love you, too, Mom."

Chapter 15

A squeal and a thud echoed in the basement. Awakened, Nathen wished he remained in his dream where he was with Mom, Dad, Ethan, and Leslie. Pain in his groin flared, making him grunt several times. At least the vicious affliction stopped radiating into his stomach. His resting heart jolted into a rapid staccato as footsteps pounded above his head. Dread fell with dust and wood particles from the ceiling. It must be that big, scary guy again. Was he coming to kill Nathen? His eyes clamped tight as a horrid shudder rushed through his body at a single question: is he going to force himself sexually on me? His thought sent a shock that made his heart run faster like a stampede of horses. It also put his breathing out of a proper measure, and made his skin feel like thousands of freezing needles jabbing him. He whispered another prayer: "God, please don't let him molest me." Terror ran so deep, he felt his fingers, toes, hands, feet – and even his soul shake uncontrollably.

A shadowy figure descended the steps – although this stature was shorter, thinner, and much less intimidating. A rancid stench did not accompany the figure carrying a few things. He heard her humming something … somewhat familiar, but too soft to really identify.

"Hello," said a demure feminine voice. She turned up the light on one lantern and lit another to its brightest. It hurt Nathen's eyes, so he had to squint to make her out.

He recognized her – but from where? Dark hair, large

over-sized glasses, very white skin, and … wait … he knew now. "You're that girl who went missing a month ago. I remember seeing it on the news." He struggled, trying to recall her name, hoping to make a connection with her. Surely, she was kidnapped and if he could forge a friendship with her, they could both escape. "Elise! Your name's Elise, right?"

Unfazed, she remained emotionless while sitting on a chair and putting a blanket and a tray on a table. "Here," she said, tossing him a blanket. "This'll help keep you warm." She stood, took only a few more steps and put the tray on the floor. "Here's some food for you," she said, backing up to a table.

His eyes widened at the food. Nathen's belly surged with anticipation as he took the beef jerky, the apple, a Snickers, and a bottle of water. Wanting to scarf all of it, he tried to keep himself from devouring every last crumb. He overcame his ravenous appetite and ate slowly to keep from getting sick. "Thank you," he said between a few bites.

She didn't smile or even acknowledge his "thank you." Her emotionless eyes just stared at him, scanning him up and down, making Nathen feel nervous and awkward – especially only being in his boxer shorts. Embarrassed, he focused on eating. Her silence perplexed him, and her eyes cut at his skin. No – they attacked him like someone throwing a rock at him.

Feeling discomfort in his groin again, he grunted and squeezed his eyelids shut. His body circled in a guarded position. Embarrassed more, he turned away from her.

"Do they still hurt?" she asked.

"Yes," he grunted. Two groans followed. "What'd you use on me?"

"A taser," she said. "Then I jabbed a few CCs of horse anesthetic in your butt."

Fear encroached, making the room seem darker and more compacted. Elise's deadly silence returned, making her seem menacing. Terror left hot jabs on his skin, especially near his head, shoulder, and chest. Dread pushed through his body deeply, making the light dimmer, and the room colder. He stammered. "Why are you doing this?"

She nodded. "I'm helping my friend."

His eyes darted around, hoping to see her friend. "You mean that big dude I saw earlier?"

Elise nodded again. "His name is Victor. He's my best friend."

"So, you weren't kidnapped like me?"

She shook her head, reiterating her answer. "No." Her silence, only a few seconds … seemed like a minute or longer. "I went with him willingly … on my own."

Taking a huge breath, Nathen held it to calm himself. However, he stammered out his next question. "So … what's Victor, planning to do to me? Kill me?"

"No," she said while shaking her head.

Nathen shuddered, wondering if this was some sort of mind game. Did they have another sinister plan? Maybe they planned to abuse him or sell him into some sort of child sex ring.

"You'll be going home within three or four days."

Nathen's fear dissipated, although it never fully vanished. "Really? When?"

"After we cut off your penis and testicles."

Nathen felt his skin turn pure white as blood left his face. Was this a joke? No. She looked dead serious. He gulped hard as his thoughts froze his bones. This time, his tears felt ice cold, shedding terror instead of sadness. "I think," his whispers stammered, "… I'd rather be killed." She remained deathly quiet, which propelled his panic to a higher level. "You got your joke," he managed to say between stutters. "It's gotta be a joke – right? Please tell me it's a prank."

She shook her head.

Panic swirled in his chest like the cold waters of the Great Lakes in a storm. Cold, paralyzing, he had no idea of what to say or do. Stuttering, crying, he tried to beg her for some reprieve. "Look, I'm sorry for whatever I did and I'll never do it again - I promise! Please let me go and I won't tell anyone. I just want my mom and dad. Please let me go."

"No."

His fingers seized the chain around his neck. Two links were shackled with a padlock. Nathen again pulled it up, unable to get it around his chin or lower jaw. Its opposite end had been tethered to a flattened bolt secured to thick beams. At full length, he probably was still several feet short of the wooden stairs leading upstairs. The door over the steps looked to be thick, heavy oak, probably suspended with a thick rope or another chain. A scant light emanated from above, not offering much hope.

Icy tears flushed through his eyes again. "Please let me go. I'll take you with me, and I'll lie to protect you. I won't say I saw you or him or tell anyone – I promise. I just wanna go home. I wanna see Mom and Dad. Please … help me." His voice devolved into sobs.

Unemotionally, she stood and went to one lantern and shut it off while lowering the other to a small level that emitted a small bit of light. Nathen could see his faint reflection in her large glasses. "Finish your food," she said coldly. "And you might want to play with your dick as much as you can – because you're not going to have it much longer. Soon, you'll see a pretty, sexy girl - and nothing … will … happen."

It felt as if his throat violently shrank. "Please," he begged. "I'll do whatever you want. Just don't let him …" He couldn't finish his words as the thoughts burrowed deep in his mind - terrorizing him to his core. The thought of losing that part of him sent his whole body into a panic - unable to think. Fear rolled over him like heavy ocean surf, pushing him deeper. Unable to find a breath in this frantic state, he couldn't breathe and even thought he might drown.

Standing, he followed, reaching for her, desperate for any help for liberation from impending dread. The cold floor pinched the soles of his feet, and bits of wood, hay, and gravel poked his toes. His chain reached maximum length, stopping him in his tracks. "Please don't leave me," he begged. "Let me go and I won't tell anyone - I promise!"

Her indifference and lack of emotion chilled his soul to a hard block of ice. Nathen moaned lightly in his throat, but noises grew as he pulled on the chain around his neck. He looked for anything to bargain with. "I … I can help you against this guy. If you help me, I'll help you. I promise… " No longer able to speak his words, his chest fired fast with erratic breaths.

Horrified about unwanted surgery and taking the things that defined him of his sexuality and even his identity, his teeth bit his lower lip. Everything twitched violently: fingers, toes, limbs, and even his heart. Wailing, he found it impossible to speak - or even think. He kept yanking the chain violently, hoping to find superhuman strength to break free. Icy tears dripped incessantly. She wouldn't even turn to acknowledge him. Realizing he was so unimportant to deserve her eyes, all his horror escaped in violent convulsions. He could only think of one thing to do.

"Help! Somebody, anybody - please HELP!" His voice strained so much, he felt it scratch as if gravel was poured into his throat. He lengthened his screams and took huge breaths - trying anything to increase his volume so somebody might hear him. "I'm down here if you can hear me! Please help!" At this point, his strained, stretched vocal cords had maxed out, leaving beyond a rough, dry feeling in his trachea and mouth. All out of breath, he dropped to his knees and sobbed.

She turned to face him and sighed. "Nobody knows where you are. Nobody is looking for you. And nobody will hear you. And nothing will change Victor's mind."

Terror iced his heart and lungs still. His breaths stammered as she turned and walked up the last few steps. Slamming shut, the door blocked out the little light from above, tightly sealing him in blackness, and blocking out his final yell. "Somebody help me - PLEASE!"

Chapter 16

Jason smiled while talking on his phone. "I love you, too, Robyn."

"Hey, Robbie … Jason's naked and playing with his dick…"

"Justin!" Jason's voice erupted with anger. "You shithead!" His voice returned to his phone. "Robyn, I'll call you back tomorrow after I kill my cousin and attend his funeral."

Anger did not resonate in Jason's eyes, but rather in his stature, steps, and taut face. He tripped on something, almost stumbling while trying to unfold his cane. "Where the fuck are you – shithead?"

"I'm over here," Justin said tauntingly before shuffling left of Jason.

Jason swung his cane but hit nothing. "Where are you?"

Jeffrey smiled, entering the fray. "To the right." Jason's cane pegged Jeffrey's jaw and ear. "Ow! I meant your left."

Jason swiveled his cane the opposite way, barely missing Justin. He obviously heard him laugh and lunged forward, trying to pelt him with his cane again. Instead, Jason lost his balance and fell down.

Aunt Janie poked her head through the door, "What the hell is going on in here?"

Jeffrey helped Jason stand while Justin kept laughing.

"Aunt Janie," said Jason, "I was talking to Robyn on

my phone and Justin yells that I'm naked and playing with my … you know."

Her angry voice knocked Justin backwards to sit on the bed. He stopped laughing and shrank from her presence. He fidgeted, as if afraid to look his mom in her eyes.

"Young man," Aunt Janie hesitated, and lowered her voice. "We have talked about this over and over. If he's on his phone with his girlfriend, you can't say inappropriate things like that."

Justin tried to suppress a smile by curling his lips. However, his mom's stare made him squirm, sigh, and hunch his shoulders. "I was just kidding."

His mom shrugged her shoulders, batted her eyes angrily, and sighed. "Well, I'm not. Give me your phone."

"Jesus, Mom," he said while relinquishing his phone.

"And I don't want any more horseplay from either of you shitheads tonight. Got it?" Justin's mom hesitated as she glanced at his phone. "Oh Justin, you just received a text from Robyn. It says she's going to staple your balls to the floor." His mom's glare got angrier. "I might help her."

Jeffrey smiled a bit as Justin fidgeted more. Once Aunt Janie left, he stood to help Jason get re-established. "So," he said, "what's your girlfriend look like?"

His face felt red as Jason and Justin slowly turned their heads at him, gawking with confused eyes and furrowed brows. Feeling dumb, Jeffrey felt as if he lost an inch off his height. "I'm mega-stupid," he whispered after clearing his throat. "Sorry. Maybe I can get you guys a Pepsi?"

"Sure," said Jason.

"Not me," said Justin. "Sugar is poison to the body. I'm in training."

"He's a health nut," said Jason.

"I'm in training, shithead. You know that." Justin turned to Jeffrey. "I'm in training for an iron man competition." He peeled off his shirt, revealing sculpted shoulders, arms, and abs.

"Wow," said Jeffrey. " You do all that for cosplay?"

"What?"

"I mean," said Jeffrey, "you do all that weightlifting to be Iron Man at a fan convention?"

Justin shook his head disdainfully. "No, dipshit. Not cosplay for Iron Man. I don't do that nerdy shit. I'm training for an iron man competition that includes running, swimming, and bicycling."

"He bikes 10 miles a day, runs another 10 the next day, and swims a mile the next day," said Jason.

"It helps keep my mind off sex," quipped Justin.

"Obviously not enough compared to the time you spend looking at online porn and jacking off."

Justin rolled his eyes. "I have to practice, EVERYTHING. I want to be ready when Peri McFarland wants to ride my dick. That's why I'm sculpting a perfect body."

"Oh, my God," said Jason as he laughed. "You're so disgustingly rude, shithead."

Shocked, Jeffrey squinted his whole face at Justin - unable to say anything for a minute. "Who's Peri … who?"

"She's some poor retarded girl," said Jason, "who has a crush on him for some bizarre reason."

Justin returned the judgment with laughter. "I can't help it if she loves me for my body," he said smugly.

Jeffrey cringed at Justin's comment, but he couldn't help wondering if his cousins had sex - or were just talking like a lot of other boys do. He did admire Justin's physique, wishing he had one like that so girls would be interested in him.

"Anyway," said Justin, "she will be mine. She will be!"

"She won't be once she sees how puny your dick is!" quipped Jason.

"How would you know since you can't SEE it?"

Jason laughed. "Okay, shithead, you got me." He paused and changed his tone. "Hey, dipshit, where's that Pepsi?"

"Whoops - I'm mega-sorry." Jeffrey rushed downstairs and brought up two bottled ones for he and Jason, and a water bottle for Justin. Back upstairs, he saw them on their knees as Justin rifled through some papers in a box.

"Look what we found," said Justin. "Jason tripped over this box near your sister's bed, and we found a whole bunch of papers.

Jeffrey set the drinks down and dropped to his knees, mesmerized by all her weird drawings Justin had found. He cringed at ugly images and their sinister colors. They sent strange, threatening vibes that pulsated through his chest. Jeffrey wondered if Jason and Justin felt the same thing. He knew Justin was disturbed but couldn't read Jason's eyes. Images of the dark, heinous pictures made him lose a breath, cowering at the sights. At the top, in red crayon, Elise had written, "Elise and Victor." Below left was a crude drawing of Elise with dark hair, glasses, and a face with small eyes and no smile. To her left was a devil-like creature with massive wings, a long snout, horns, and yellow eyes surrounded in red. Both held hands with stick-figure fingers.

Another one was a poem she had written, with another

crayon drawing of Victor and Elise holding hands. Jeffrey froze, reading the dark poem.

He's cold and he stinks
He's a friend and he thinks
That I am beautiful, wonderful, just as I am
I'm his heart, his love, and his little lamb
At night he whispers in my ears, chilling my soul like no other
Although he doesn't like Mom, Dad, and my brother
I cannot wait to release all the hate
Against my cousin 'cause he masturbates
I will instill terror and fear
To complete my mission which is why I'm here.

"Holy shit," whispered Jeffrey.

"Look at this one," said Justin. He showed Jeffrey a crude, dark drawing of Elise performing surgery on Gunner. Graphic pictures included a horrified boy dripping with blood and sweat.

"We better show these to Father Matthew," said Jeffrey.

"How are you going to show these to a blind priest?" asked Jason.

"He can sense evil. It's kinda like how you can hear supernatural things except he feels it with touch. Also, we can tell him what they look like, and Sister Regina can examine them, too."

Jason seemed to shudder. "Wait …" he said nervously. "What the fuck?"

Everyone shook as a swathe of cold, stinking air fell on them. They tightened their eyes and crinkled their noses in an attempt to block a horrid, putrid stench. Even Samson and Freddy shook, and their warm breaths misted.

Jason flung his cane while backing up as if something

approached him. Although invisible, it cast a subtle, yet definite shadow. "Get away from me!" he yelled. Immediately, he fell backwards, dropped his cane, bellowed, and covered his ears. "Ahhhh! Stop it! Stop it! Stop it!" His shoulders spasmed, his jaw opened wide and rolled to his stomach. "Make it stop. Make it stop! Please!"

Samson was pushed away by some invisible force. He let out a yelp but then tried to attack again while Freddy bolted out the door.

Terrified by Jason's screams, Jeffrey and Justin froze, not knowing what to do. They flinched and covered their faces as Elise's doll collection flew across the room directly at them. Other things followed, books, decorations, memorabilia. Jeffrey and Justin yelled as some of those items pelted them.

The huge, stinking cold disappeared.

Justin, Jeffrey, and Jason all jumped as Mom and Aunt Janie burst into the room. Aunt Janie rushed to comfort Jason who had curled into a fetal position. "Jason, honey … what's wrong?"

Shaking, stammering, and shocked, Jason reached around his body, locating his dark glasses so he could put them on. His breaths raged, and even his teeth chattered. "It was, it was … something that … screamed at me. Did you guys hear it?"

Justin's brown eyes widened as confusion as fright filled them. "No," he whispered. "I didn't hear a thing." Jaw quivering, he grunted. "But those dolls flew across the room by themselves."

Jeffrey shook his head. "I didn't," he stammered, "hear anything either." He pointed to the dolls scattered on the floor. "Justin's right. They just flew across the room."

"Sweetie," said Mom as he pushed his hair back some. "You're bleeding."

His fingers found warm blood dripping down his forehead. A tender bruise on his forehead radiated a sharp pain. Mom already had a warm, moist washcloth to clean his wound. He tried to think, but his terror had left behind confusion and anticipation that something else might happen. Rapid breaths made his chest hurt.

At this point, Aunt Janie tended to Justin to see if he was okay. "I'm okay, Mom," he said. "I'm just … so …" his voice stammered every word, "scared. I … can't … stop … shaking."

Jeffrey saw his mom close her eyes. "This can't be happening again." Her breaths raged faster like waves following a Tsunami. "Please … not again!" she snapped. "We need … to move … out of here."

"It won't help," said Aunt Janie.

"It won't hurt much, either," said Justin. "I thought we were through with this shit. I can't go through this again. Please, let's leave."

Jeffrey's mom cried and fell to her knees. She sobbed for a few seconds, then her furious eyes looked up as if releasing a barrage of bullets or lightning. "What the fuck do you want from me?" Jeffrey stepped back, listening to her furious prayer. "Why are you letting this happen to MY children?" As if embarrassed, she dropped her face to her hands while sobbing.

Aunt Janie dropped to her knees. Mom clutched her tightly. "Don't leave me. Please don't go. Please don't go."

"Jenny, Jenny – listen. I'm not leaving. I'm not leaving you. I just got you back and I'm not leaving you. I'm going to be here for you. I promise. I've been through something like this, myself."

Jeffrey cried as Mom sobbed.

"Sis, I'm here for you. In fact, let's go get that wine out of the trash, have one last round." Both let a laugh escape in a single breath. "Then WE'LL both go through rehab together." The laughter loudened for a split second but quieted with their gentle crying.

Jeffrey smiled for a moment, until Justin poked him, pointing at the wall where Elise's dolls once were. Three horizontal cuts that looked like claw marks stretched across the wall. Probably an inch wide, they spread evenly about five feet across. Left of the slashes was a water stain that formed a hideous creature. Its large, crazed eyes cast a piercing glare at them. Beads of stinking water sweated from the wall, darkening its face with stains that dripped terror. An ominous low, yet thin noise found Jeffrey's ears and left a subtle vibration that pounded through his ribs. It triggered a dread that fell on him, making it hard to breathe. Its mouth did not stretch wide but frowned as mold stained its teeth a disgusting color. Uneven, chipped fangs jutted up from the lower jaw. A rancid stench rolled from its mouth as if it exhaled a rank breath. Although silent, it seemed to scream at everyone. Flames somehow flapped from the despicable image, casting cold shadows, and a terrifying dread that dropped on all of them. Everyone took a few steps back, terrified and mesmerized by the brazen, despicable image.

Chapter 17

Exhausted, Eli leaned against a tree. Sweating profusely, he used his sleeve to wipe it off, hoping that it might put his pounding heart at ease. Offering a prayer to God, he begged for some mystical or supernatural revelation as to where Nathen was. As of now, he could only go by spread and broken branches – some thin, others thick. It had gone on for four miles.

Glancing at his phone, he smiled seeing a little bit of reception. However, no texts or emails. Surely Eli's troop had contacted the Sheriff's department by now. Tall trees and hills had already provided a shield from some daylight, although the sun was nowhere near setting.

Again, he almost cried thinking about Nathen: the boyish charm, blue eyes, and his long hair. His quiet and determined confidence was always carried with a smile. He not only knew character but lived it in every aspect of his life with kindness, being helpful, and thinking less of himself. He tried so hard to do everything correctly and always did his best.

Eli's fond memories of Nathen faded – as he caught sight of a cabin resting 100 feet below him where the bases of three hills met. A prominent stream rushed through, providing life in the plants, grass, and animals. Nearby, rocky formations likely had caves and crevices for animals – and possibly people – to hide. Tall trees jutted up, spread around the stream and provided a canopy that offered heavy shade for the cabin and barn.

A slight wind whispered, beckoning him to explore the cabin. It blew again, goading him on, and saying Nathen was held within the structure. Eli hesitated for a minute, wondering if he should wait for backup, or perhaps try a text or a call. Spotty reception, however, ruled out that possibility. Something seemed to pull him by his stomach – to find out.

Seeing a few shadowy figures gawk at him, a breath exploded from Eli's chest. After a few seconds, he realized they were deer. The larger ones, bucks, turned their heads towards the cabin, as if telling him they saw Nathen there.

His steps remained slow and measured to keep from falling down the steep hill. One stone retreated from his weight and dislodged, as if trying to stop his search. He regained his footing, staying still to get his flashlight going. Although small, it had a powerful beam that showed a path. He scanned the rocks, mostly fearing they waited to trip him either as a joke or as sinister players in this whole scheme.

Darkness gave the cabin a sinister aura – reminding Eli of his visit at Castle Dracula about ten years ago. His light beam scanned what was left of the outside walls and partial roof. For some reason, it seemed much larger than it really was. It was two stories tall, and it had a good amount of space, likely comparable to a modern two-story, four-bedroom house.

Much sturdier, though, was a huge barn next to the cabin. The upper doors were open, and gentle winds pushed them, emanating long squeaks and moans. The main entrance was shut. Eli tried to open them, but they would not budge.

Circling to his left, he found a standard door around the corner. Slightly ajar, he hesitated to enter, wondering if someone was inside. Nathen? The kidnapper? Both? The darkness amidst the crack either teased him or urged him to check inside. Hesitant, he feared something dreadful waited behind it. Now he regretted not bringing his firearm with him. For years, though, he feared a boy's curiosity might find it and play with it instead of respecting the weapon as they should. It seemed as if something was whispered to him, telling Eli what he sought was inside.

The still air inside the barn carried something unholy. Eli sensed it penetrating his mind, his skin, and bones. Hairs on his arms, legs, and head stiffened as a terrifying electricity enveloped him. His training took over and he focused on his breathing, balance, and bravery. Although terror was present, he kept it far enough away to think and act.

His head jerked towards a whisper. Turning around fast, his flashlight lit up the area around him, revealing a fog that apparently came from the stream, pouring into the barn. Another whisper taunted him as a vicious cold jumped from the fog.

"My place!"

A hideous creature with large, black, and hateful eyes appeared in the beam of light – glaring at him with a vile hate. Its breath pushed a horrible, reeking stench across his face as its mouth opened, revealing serrated, bloody teeth. Eli fell backwards as it scrambled on four legs – snapping at him like a dog – yet this was no dog, but rather a monster something from the black pit of his subconscious. Someone appeared in the visage of the beast, but his arms tried to protect his head, shielding him from whatever it was. A hard, honed, and heavy object slammed into his skull. He felt it protrude through his head, lodging deep into his brain. His nerves fired, his fingers, legs, and jaw shook and spasmed. Within seconds, images flashed of his parents, his sister, her kids, his wife, and his own children. A cold darkness circled his mind, faster and faster until everything became black.

***

Nathen felt a wet, sloppy tongue lick his nose, face, and even his lips. His head turned and he grinned, realizing Woody, his Jack Russel Terrier, licked his face to wake him up. After twitching from his dog's breath, a wide yawn stretched around his mouth for the first breath of a new day. Mom entered his bedroom, smiled at him and opened the blinds. Sunlight broke through his night, calling him to wake up. "Be downstairs in ten minutes," she said. Sitting up, he remained in bed, keeping his sheets and blankets over his waist, not wanting Mom to see his morning erection.

Abruptly, darkness dropped and surrounded him, blocking any warm light. A cold fell through his blanket, robbing him of warmth. His neck, his shoulders, and spine were all sore. Rolling on his back, feeling a hard wooden floor littered with straw, he suddenly remembered his dilemma. Darkness and pain bludgeoned his head. Nathen closed his eyes, then opened them – hoping they might revert to his dream that he mistook for reality. Despondent, he grunted while his eyes cracked – letting loose a few tears.

He was surprised he slept at all. Last night, all he could think about were horrible things that could be done to him. Crying alone with nobody to talk to in a pitch-black setting added to his fear - and his misery. Terror had him sobbing until he fell asleep, and it returned with a mighty force. His stomach sank, and his heart followed. "Oh, God – please. Please tell me my troop is looking for me and that they'll find me. Please."

The moaning door alerted him. Lifting out of the cut rectangle and locked at an angle, dust crept from upstairs, outlined in a faint shaft of light that tried to bore in and provide some sort of comfort. It was that girl again. She had a tray for him, although the food was hidden by a large cloth. His stomach, already begging for sustenance, growled with heavy anticipation of eating. Nathen even licked his lips.

It took a minute, but he finally remembered her name: Elise. Was she humming the theme to The Addams Family TV show? She stopped, increasing the illumination provided by two lamps. Although brighter, she somehow tamed it, so it wouldn't fill the entire room.

"Thank God," he said as another wave of anticipation surged. "I'm starving."

Elise put the tray down and backed away to - sitting on the steps. "Enjoy your meal," she said quietly.

Leery, Nathen tried to see her face and eyes, but light from above drowned it in her shadow.

"Please let me go. Please let me go. I won't tell anyone – I swear."

"Stop being a pussy." She sounded irritated. "Eat your food. You need strength for your upcoming surgery."

Nathen flinched as she reminded him of his fate. Although they still felt a little blistered, at least his private area didn't throb like the previous night. Several breaths rocked his chest into many desperate heaves that devolved to heavy tears. He cried for three, maybe five minutes. At that point, his desperate hunger became more prominent than abject terror.

However, now, a curious dread grew in his belly – driving away the pangs of hunger. Looking at the tray, he noticed a covering that hid his food. Although roundish, it was taller than wide. Its oval shape had him tilting his head left, then right, and back left, trying to figure out what it could be. He could not smell anything. He glanced at Elise who remained seated. She stared at him, offering no empathy or concern. Her taught mouth, blank facial expression, and emotionless dark eyes reminded him of that girl in that "Wednesday" series on Netflix

Looking back at the tray, Nathen felt anxiety surge, bubbling like a boiling pot of chili, or a vegetable stew. Remnants of it spread to his arms and legs, causing his fingers and toes to tremble. He took two steps forward. Something on the floor pinched his dry sole on his right foot. Examining it, it looked like a small wood pellet that latched to his naked foot. He inhaled deeply to stave off his edginess. Nathen glanced at Elise, then at the covered item. He took two more steps, then stooped to examine it again.

Eying the covered item, he kept glancing at Elise to see if she might give a hint as to what this covering hid. She sat quietly, hands folded, never blinking, nor giving off any emotion. Nathen took two more steps, then dropped to his knees and gently clasped the cloth's edge. An eerie sense signaled that the covering hid something frightfully dreadful. Instinct ruled over rational thought, and terror held reins of a cold, blunt reality.

Lifting the cover, Nathen's panicked soul erupted into a yell as he scurried away. His own wailing left a stab in his ears, and its sight froze his mind into a hard ball of ice. Although terrified, he kept staring at it. The severed head had a deep crevice above its left eye which had been knocked out of place. Dried blood stained the man's horrified face. A thinly manicured goatee sprinkled with gray looked familiar – along with this man's wide, lifeless eyes that still held the terror of dying. It was Scoutmaster Eli!

Soon, Nathen's terror swelled into a surging sadness of tears gushing up from underground rivers and dripping like raging falls of a snow-capped mountain. Floods drowned all remaining hope he had – along with rational thinking. All he had left was pure terror that darkened his thoughts. "You killed my friend! You killed him," he repeated amidst his sobs. "I hate you! I hate you!" he said between his raging and lamentable breaths.

The light dimmed. He turned towards Elise's measured footsteps that marched out of the pit. Within seconds, the horizontal door slammed shut, trapping him in darkness.

Chapter 18

Jason's fingers clasped the helmet in his hands. He tried to imagine what it might look like based on his tactile information. The hard plastic surface curved but did not form a perfectly round shape. Oval, one opening stretched about three inches wide and spread 10 to 12 inches to opposite curvatures. A larger opening with a rounder shape probably about 14 to 16 inches with straps on opposite sides.

"Here," said Jeffrey, "let me help you."

Jason let his cousin put his helmet on and snapped both straps together.

"Now, let's get on my minibike. Justin, get his hands on my arm pits."

A familiar tension tingled in his stomach as Jason clutched Jeffrey's upper torso. Taking a deep breath and holding it, Jason hoped to calm his uneasy feeling of gnats or butterflies flapping their wings inside his belly.

"Step high to the right," said Justin. "I'll help you."

"Shit." Jason winced and put his foot back down after it got caught on part of Jeffrey's minibike.

"Higher," Justin said.

Jason lifted his foot higher and straddled Jeffrey's minibike. The seat had worn out padding underneath some plastic. Those flying insects in his stomach seemed to multiply in number. He kept telling himself he could do this, taking deep breaths over and over, hoping to shield his anxiety from Justin and Jeffrey.

The motor woke up as power erupted, letting loose a loud wail like a morning rooster. Jason laughed as his heart, lungs, and spirit all jumped from the unexpected sound that quieted to a rumbling grind. Vibrations rattled his groin, thighs, and hips – rising to his guts. The tension felt good, providing a sense of dangerous energy. It sounded as if it breathed in short, rhythmic huffs to prepare for a run. His own breath tried to keep pace with the small motorcycle. Sure, Jason jogged, often tethered to Justin when he ran but this type of movement still scared him. This was not in a car, but an open bike with no seat belts, walls, or airbags. Of course, surfing was the same - although seawater would have a much softer impact than hard asphalt.

"Okay," Jeffrey yelled, "…hold on tight. I'll start off slow and make turns light so you can get used to moving with it, okay?"

Unable to speak, Jason let go with one hand, reached underneath Jeffrey's arm pit, and gave him a thumbs up. He wrapped his arms around Jeffrey's chest and locked his hands together.

"Whoa, dude," Jeffrey yelled. "Not so tight. And move your arms down closer to my waist."

Jason followed instructions.

"And keep your hands off my dick!"

Jason, barely hearing Jeffrey's last remark, smirked. "Don't worry," he yelled, "it's probably way too short to hold onto if I fall off." Jason's body twitched in a panic as Jeffrey's minibike took off fast. Within a couple of seconds, he held tighter as the rear wheel lurched forward, causing the front wheel to jump off the ground. Scared, Jason kept a tight grip, realizing Jeffrey did that on purpose. His arms relaxed a little when the front wheel returned to the asphalt for a more stable ride.

"Sorry!" yelled Jeffrey. "I shifted too fast."

"Don't do that again, dipshit." Jason took a few breaths, hoping oxygen would relax his heart.

"Never insult your driver." Jeffrey did slow down by shifting his gears and using his brakes to make turns. A few times he yelled "left" or "right" when adjusting his lane position. Jason leaned and counter-leaned with each adjustment to keep his minibike steady. After a few minutes, Jason acclimated and started to feel a rush. It felt similar to his surfing 'high.' A flow of adrenaline coursed through his blood, making his heart rev higher in a steady fashion. His breathing adjusted, triggering endorphins to spread from his brain to his muscles. His subtle excitement kept him in tune with this particular moment and second.

Jason's rush faded when they stopped, and the minibike's rumbling breath ceased. The noise slightly echoed from corners of a thick, tall wall that felt wrapped in shadow. "Is this your church?"

"Yep. St. Patrick's." Jeffrey guided Jason off the bike. While Jason unfolded his cane, he clasped Jeffrey's arm to be guided through the large doors. Their footsteps resounded softly, matching the whispered awe of a few parishioners with the cathedral. A few spoke quiet confessions, but most spoke solemn, whispered prayers. He thought he heard something else - other voices.

"Be not afraid."

"He is here."

"Have faith."

"He loves you."

Actually, they were spoken in another language — probably Latin. He knew some. These quiet voices echoed strangely, moving around without resounding off the church walls or stained-glass windows. He smiled.

"What is it?" asked Jeffrey.

Jason hesitated, wondering if he should tell him. "I can hear two, maybe three angels in here."

"Seriously?"

"No, humorously. They were telling jokes and doing impressions." He regretted his smart-ass answer but softened it with a grin. "It's not the first time I've heard them – but it's not often."

"What are they saying?"

"Things like 'have faith,' or 'he loves you.'"

"But it's not like what you heard last night – right?"

Jason perfectly remembered the demon's howling wail overloading his mind. Covering his ears did not help, and its sinister voice sent a shiver through his mind and spirit. Its unholy sound cut him, leaving behind a cold remnant that injured part of his essence. Shuddering, Jason shook his head. "I … don't want to talk about that." Jason shook off his uneasy feeling and focused on keeping a tandem with Jeffrey.

Jeffrey's knock resounded on Father Matthew's thick, heavy wooden door.

"Father Matthew? It's me, Jeffrey."

The door opened almost immediately. "Jeffrey. I just heard your message. Come on in so we can visit."

Jeffrey guided Jason to a chair.

"Who's that with you," asked Father Matthew. "Jason?"

"Yes, sir. We had some things we wanted to bring you."

"Father Matthew," said Jeffrey, "… we found these pictures in a box in Elise's room last night. They're really scary and disturbing. She drew them. And then, we found a water stain drawing on the wall. Her doll collection covered it. We took a picture of it and printed it for you to … feel, I guess. You said you could sense evil presences, right?"

"Whoa," said Jason. "Are you shitting me?" Immediately, he regretted his profanity, flinched, and turned his head. "I … I'm sorry, Father. I didn't mean …"

"It's okay," Father Matthew said. "I say 'shit' too … sometimes." He paused. "Jeffrey, please put the pictures in front of me."

"I'll start with the first one. There are dates on them. The earliest one goes back to 2018."

Father Matthew

Although hesitant, Father Matthew let Jeffrey place his hands on the drawings in front of him. Nervous, he wondered what he might feel this time. He had more experience with people who had unholy spirits as opposed to cursed objects. He wondered what they might feel like. Cold? Prickly? Coarse or hot? The first one did emanate a chill, especially as his fingers felt a large mass of crayon markings. The next one sent a wave of uneasy tension, feeling like a slight surge of electricity at his fingertips. He made sure to cover every paper, from edge to edge and corner to corner in order to find the proper sensation. The next one jabbed something sharp and painful, and it left a dull ache in his wrist – especially over a large uneven mass of crayon. "Jeffrey, what color is underneath my right hand? And what does it look like?"

"It's black and misshapen."

As Father Matthew continued, his hands shook more. The feeling dug deeper, moving through his arms, shoulders, chest, and neck. Something like snakes slithered, leaving behind a repulsive, slinky feeling. A cold tingling awareness vibrated from his skin, even making his jaw quiver. His hands, although reticent, moved to the next paper. His voice quavered, only emitting small grunts as an uncomfortably warm presence tried to burn his hands. A rancid stench reminded him of visiting a slaughterhouse in Ireland.

"Father-"

"Yes, Jason."

"I can hear them."

"Her who?"

Jason's voice balked with a gasp. "I can hear a couple of angels. They want you to be careful."

Matthew stood, facing Jason. Astonished, his mouth opened, his joints locked, and his muscles stiffened. "You can hear them?"

"Yes, sir." His voice stammered – sending out a deeper sensation of fear. "Last night, I heard a demon when we found the water-stained picture."

Amazed, Father Matthew carefully returned to his chair and continued his search. Remembering the caution angels had sent him, Matthew moved his hands further right to feel the next drawn image. A weighty dread filled his mind so much, it darkened memories and obscured the truth of Scripture. He forgot the words of God, finding no hope. A lone, warm tear streaked down his left cheek. "Jeffrey," he whispered, "…what is this?

"That's an ugly one, Father Matthew," said Jeffrey. "It's Elise carving up Gunner, showing blood and guts."

Father Matthew found light returning to his mind once his hands left the unseen drawing. Already feeling an icy presence, his fingers hovered over the next one. Tiny, hot spikes pierced his fingers and palm, although he had no full contact.

"Father! Don't ..."

Too late, both hands clutched the picture. A horrid stench, accompanied by a heavy dread, and frigid temperatures thrust his soul into panic. Forgetting the triumph of Christ, and his power in his resurrection, he bellowed loudly, begging for help. His fingers had wrapped around ice cubes – yet a fiery stinging pain jabbed his back, chest, neck and face. Convulsing, he tried to let go but could not release this beacon of evil. It had been years since he could see in his dreams, but somehow, memories of Matteo and Luca emerged as the demon killed them.

Everything retreated at once after Jeffrey and someone else yanked his arms away from the picture he touched.

Realizing the other presence was Sister Regina, he sat back in his chair, huffing, trying to get his heart and lungs back to proper timing and rhythm. Huffing, his hands covered his eyes as he wept. "Sister Regina," he said between breaths, "please shut the door."

"Father," said Jason, "I'm sorry, but I didn't understand them in time. The angels said 'don't touch the picture."

"What was it?"

"The stained demonic image," said Jeffrey. "We snapped a picture of it last night and printed it this morning."

The room's deathly silence returned to a peaceful flow of air as if something whisked through, removing the horror, ignorance, and dread with it. How long did that take? A minute? Five minutes? An hour? Unsure, Matthew sensed others around him, staring, stupefied, and uncertain. Not liking his shattered confidence in God and the Word, his ego tried to regain its position but could not find proper footing. Embarrassed, he feared his abiding faith and servanthood had yielded to his ugly sin of pride. It dwelled so deep and was the most difficult to discard.

"I must tell you all of something in the strictest confidence," he whispered quietly. "I participated in a botched exorcism in Italy 22 years ago that resulted in two deaths. It also attacked me and … rendered me blind. It challenged my faith," His head tilted down, embarrassed to cast blind eyes towards the heavens.

Father Matthew continued. "When I tried to exorcise the demon out of Elise a month or so ago, I am almost certain it was the same demon I encountered all those years ago. It is very powerful, and I admit it scares me. We need to find your sister." He hesitated, not liking to be this vulnerable to people. Yes – the pride stayed alive, desperately clawing to rise up and take over. The room filled with a strange and uneasy heaviness, keeping everyone quiet for a minute … another minute – and another.

The whole room flinched when their smart phones sounded an emergency alert.

Chapter 19

Sister Regina peeked at Jeffrey's phone. He let her read it. A fright filled her body, making it colder, heavier, and confused. Again, the old dilemma whirled in her mind: how can a good, loving, and powerful God allow such things? Why did the hearts of people seek such wicked things on innocent victims? Her despair made her eyes close and pray silently to God as to why he would let a boy suffer so much.

"Sister," said Father Matthew, "what does the alert say?"

She put on her reading glasses to read it and perhaps get greater insight. "It says the Butler County Sheriff's Department and Pennsylvania State Police are in search of a missing scout named Nathen Rhoades. The 14-year-old was separated from his troop and preliminary investigations suggest he might have been abducted. If you recognize him with anyone, please contact your local police department or the Pennsylvania State Police."

Sister Regina wept as she traced the young boy's image. Such a sincere smile, and angelic eyes. No boy or girl was immune from mischief and sin, but her first impression put a heavy burden on her heart. How could she help him?

Jeffrey took his phone. "Could … could it be Elise that abducted him?"

"How could she carry him by herself?" asked Jason.

"If there is a demon in her, it would give her added

strength," said Father Matthew.

"Something tells me she does have him," said Jeffrey. "I just know it," he whispered. "However … I don't have any idea if she'll kill him, or … do to him what she tried to do to Gunner? We gotta find her."

"How?" said Jason. "Where would we begin and where would we go?"

Jeffrey's eyes lit brightly. "Samson! He could track her down by scent. Maybe Freddy could, too."

"Samson's not a tracking dog, but a seeing-eye dog," Jason countered.

"And you …" added Jeffrey, " you can hear demons. You could help."

"Oh, HELL NO! I can hear them, but I sure don't wanna be near them."

"I had a demon in me, but I want to find her."

Sister Regina clasped Jeffrey's hand, sharing her deep concern. Her brown eyes radiated fear, concern, and deep desperation. She gently clasped Jeffrey by his chin to face him in hopes to reason with him. "Jeffrey, let the police handle this. When they find this boy, they'll find your sister."

"But they'll shoot her. Or put her in prison and put her on trial for kidnapping and maybe murder." Shaking his head angrily, he fell to a chair and pounded an armrest. "I can't let that happen to her. She's not just my sister, but also my twin." He looked at Father Matthew. "And you can get rid of the demon, and we can prove it."

Sister Regina watched Father Matthew drop his head and sigh. She knew him better than her own siblings and parents. For ten years, she had been at his side, assisting him with meals, driving him places, and helping him with counseling. She knew when he felt confident or steady –

but now he resided in defeat. Strangely, while he could not see light of any form, he radiated it with confidence and surety. Yet now, his face and posture suggested his faith wavered amidst an onslaught of doubt.

"Jeffrey," said Father Matthew, "… please understand that courts do not recognize demonic possession as an excuse. There was a case in Connecticut that dealt with it back in the early 1980s that ruled against such defense. Also, I cannot be authorized to do an exorcism on my own. A Jesuit is involved as well as a Bishop and the Vatican. It took me almost six weeks to get your exorcism approved."

"And I hated you for that!"

Sister Regina, startled by Jeffrey's outburst, noticed Father Matthew's dejected look. His head dropped as if embarrassed, and his broad shoulders dropped as if losing confidence.

She tried to hug Jeffrey, but for the first time she could remember, he pushed her away. Falling to a chair, he hung his head, casting several heavy sighs until he regained his breath. Her empathy and love felt hurt from his rejection, but she put her own insecurity aside and rubbed his back with a loving touch. He leaned into her.

"Father Matthew," he said, "… I'm sorry but I hated you for leaving me like that for so long. If you had done something earlier, maybe I wouldn't have been stuck in that nightmare that went on for weeks. You don't know what that agony was like. Its psychological games, the torture it did to me, losing myself to it. I thought I would've been … erased … from existence. It was like an ongoing nightmare – and it seemed like forever. I had no sense of … time or … place. I asked God to help me … and I asked him to help you help me. And I hate remembering everything that happened."

Sister Regina hoped a long quiet might ease Jeffrey's feelings. He kept sighing hard, as if trying to expel his awful memories, emotions, and pain that acted like a burdensome weight. She rubbed his arms and whispered. "Just let it out. It's okay."

Jeffrey, becoming calm, lifted his head to face Father Matthew. She knew he was ashamed, embarrassed, and sad. Strangely, Father Mattew always seemed to know the right words to say but now sat at a loss. His head lifted and faced Jeffrey. "I'm so sorry. I wanted to help you so badly. But when you're part of an organization, one that has ordained me and …"

"I don't wanna hear it!"

Sister Regina, startled, stepped away from Jeffrey's explosion. Never seeing or hearing him respond with such anger, she wept. After waiting several seconds, she stepped closer, clasped his shoulder, and hugged him.

"I needed help immediately," he said. "So does Elise," his volume lowered a bit, "and I'm not going to sit and wait for the right moment to help my sister." He looked back at Jason. "Come on, dude. We gotta find her." Both boys exited Father Matthew's office.

Sister Regina and Father Matthew both sighed then remained still amidst an oppressive and unfamiliar silence. Regina hesitated, then softly whispered her thoughts. "Matthew … when will you tell Jeffrey what you discovered? When will you tell him why he remembers everything about his possession?"

Father Matthew let loose a slight grunt, then let his head fall back on his chair. His hands rubbed his forehead and eyes. He always did that during heavy thought, and great doubt. His elbows found his desk, and his hands cradled his chin. "Now's not the time. He's so young and vulnerable … and he isn't ready."

"When will he be ready?" Her words got a bit louder, harder, and direct. She knew he waited for the wrong reasons and needed to be forthcoming.

"Besides," said Matthew, "… I don't know how he'll take it. He's the closest thing I've ever had as a son."

"Fathers must be honest with their sons and not dance around the truth."

He kept quiet for a minute, as if trying to find a proper answer. "I know you're right – but I'll tell him in my own time."

Jason

"Hey, man." Jason had to use his cane since Jeffrey wouldn't be a guide for him. The echo of Jeffrey's footsteps provided some location ability however he could not keep pace. "Wait up. Calm down. Should you be driving your minibike while you're like this?"

"Look dude," Jeffrey turned to face him. "I'm mega scared. She's my sister. My twin. You understand that, right?"

Jason felt a remnant of pain chip at his heart, opening up his painful wound of losing Jimmy, Mom, and Dad. He had not felt such hurt since his birthday … which also was Jimmy's birthday. It was his first birthday since Jimmy died. It stirred his familiar pain so much more. For years, he and Jimmy would both wake up excited for each other's birthday, and for Mom and Dad's plans they made for them. His parents' birthdays also triggered the same feelings … along with special times like Christmas, Thanksgiving, and other holidays. He always tried to go back to what his friend, Roger, told him. *The only things you have control over are your emotions, your thoughts, your actions, and reactions.* Should he tell Jeffrey that?

No. Jason doubted it would help his cousin he barely knew. Jeffrey was very passionate about his emotions, seeming to ignore logic. Besides, Jason still struggled with his emotions.

"Look, Jeffrey …" he tried to think of anything to possibly help, "…think this through: you don't know where she is, and you have no idea where to look for her."

Jason heard Jeffrey sit down and sighed. Using his hands, he guided himself into a padded pew next to Jeffrey. "Calm down, man," he said quietly. "Take a few deep breaths and listen to the stillness."

"Listen to what?"

Jason raised his voice above a whisper, letting it climb to be heard. "The stillness. Remember when Elijah went to the mountains? There was a fire, and an earthquake, but God wasn't in them. Then a stillness arrived, that's when Elijah heard God." His voice lowered back to a whisper to emphasize his point. "So, listen. What's the stillness telling you?"

Jason waited, isolating sounds: a woman praying for her child, and soft voices and weeping in the confession booth. At least two people dropped to their knees and whispered their desperate prayers.

"Jeffrey … what's it telling you?"

A long quiet settled in the air around them. It felt peaceful, having a calming effect on Jason's body and spirit – similar to how he felt while surfing. His heart, mind, emotions, and thoughts all stirred together in a soft eddy, mixing together perfectly into a lagoon of contentment.

"It's telling me," he whispered, "… that I gotta go pee."

Jason's chest erupted into laughter that bounced off

church walls in a gentle, comforting manner. Soon, Jeffrey's chuckling mixed with his. Their laughs, slightly out of rhythm, almost sounded like a musical round with one giggle following right after another one. Jason put his head on top of his cane, then put his hand on his chest in a vain attempt to stop the frivolity. Not working, their erratic laughter continued for the longest time. Strangely, it didn't asphyxiate him but offered condolence and a new energy that provided strength to stop his chuckling. He burst out laughing again for another minute until it worked out of his stomach, chest, and mouth a second time. Tired, he let loose a few heavy sighs, finally finding new energy and hope.

"By the way," Jason managed to say, "this kid who was kidnapped - what's his name?"

"Uh," said Jeffrey, "Nathen."

Jason's face stiffened at hearing the name.

Chapter 20

Freddy barked at Samson, challenging him. The German Shepherd looked at Justin as if asking to have the service dog uniform removed. With that signature vest on, Samson always remained a sentry and guide for Jason, never socializing with other dogs - nor playing "fetch" with anyone else in the family. Justin smiled and winked at Samson. "Okay boy, show that puny dog who's in charge," he whispered while unzipping Samson's service dog uniform.

Once removed from the vest, Samson took a defensive posture with Freddy who snapped again, as if daring the larger dog. Their barks, yips, and growls resonated as friendly insults and dares like boys who wrestled outside during recess. The dogs wrestled with their jaws and paws, and rolled on the ground, each trying to find dominance. Both of them bolted into a run, spreading out close to the fence like kids playing tag in a playground. Justin grinned wider, imagining Samson winked back to thank him so he could play with another dog.

Stepping inside Aunt Beth's house, he heard Jason beg. "Please, Aunt Janie. When I heard this boy's name, I could not help thinking of Rabbi Nathan who helped us. I felt really bad that he died getting rid of that demon. We need to look for this kid."

"Yeah, Mom," added Justin, "we can use Samson and Freddy to find this kid's scent."

"No! The police already have dogs, but more

importantly, I don't want my son and blind nephew out in the woods where bears and wildcats can get you. You are not going out to find this missing boy!"

Aunt Beth interrupted. "Guys, I know you want to help this boy, but you don't even know where to begin to look."

"Come on, Mom," said Jeffrey. "I know how to survive out there. You and Dad taught me, and I can teach …"

"No!" Jeffrey's mom raised her hand and repeated herself with more volume. "NO!"

Father Matthew's calm voice and gentle spirit put everyone at ease. "Boys, listen to your mothers. They're right. And they know what's best. You'll put yourself in danger and one of the first rules in helping others is not to put yourself in a position where you have to be rescued as well."

Everyone sighed. Janie, Jenny, and Beth appeared exasperated, cradling their foreheads. "Boys," said Aunt Beth, "…why don't you visit with Gunner so we can figure out how to arrange Jenny's rehab and me taking in Jeffrey during that time."

Justin stood, clutched Jason's arm, then followed Jeffrey to the mystery room. According to Jeffrey, it was usually closed and locked with six latches and bolts. He couldn't believe someone willingly hid in their room for a month.

Jeffrey knocked. "Open up, dude. It's me."

A small section of the door slid open, revealing a lean face with ashen skin and two scared, blue eyes. "Who are they?"

"They're my other cousins, dude. Open the damn door."

Justin counted. Three bolts turned, and three latches sounded before the door opened. Gunner stood with his lean frame blocking them from entering his room. His eyes, riddled with fear, darted around in every direction multiple times.

"This is Justin," Jeffrey said while Gunner's weak grip offered a limp handshake.

"And the blind one is Jason."

"How are you doing today?" Gunner's volume exploded, causing Jason and Justin to flinch.

"Damnit," said Jason, "I'm not deaf, you dipshit. I'm blind."

"Sorry," with his volume still loud, Gunner stopped, then lowered his voice. "Sorry. I'm really sorry."

"And why are you locked up in here?" asked Jason. "Did you not eat all your broccoli or cauliflower?"

"My cousin, Elise, tried to castrate me … twice. And I'm not coming out until she's in jail or a mental hospital."

"Whoa," said Jeffrey. "Look at this!" He noticed a paper on the floor and stooped to pick it up. He read it out loud:

Gunner,

Hello. I dropped by to see you. I miss you. I hope to see you again soon.

Elise

Gunner's eyes exploded as he grabbed the note and read it. Within a few seconds, he pulled everyone inside, locking all the deadbolts and latches.

"Dude," said Jeffrey, "you gotta calm down."

Gunner retreated a few steps back. "Shit, shit, shit, shit, shit. She's gonna get me. She's gonna get me."

Justin noticed Gunner's twitching eyes, indicating he did not sleep well. His fingers, voice, and arms shook intensely, almost keeping time with his relentless breath. Justin grabbed Gunner's hand, sensing the intense anxiety that manifested to cold, shaking skin. "Man," said Justin, "cooping yourself up in here is making you an emotional wreck. You need to get outside."

"No. No." Gunner shook his head. "She'll get me. She'll get me."

Justin tried to stop grinning as Jason shook his head and rolled his dilated eyes.

"Calm down," said Jason. "You're safe here. But you gotta face your fears. I almost got attacked by a shark while surfing and I went back out."

"I'm sure the shark wasn't going for your balls."

Justin examined Gunner's room, noticing bunk beds against the wall, next to a window that had been nailed shut. Also, a metal shutter, probably half an inch thick, provided another protective barrier. About three feet from Gunner's bed was a messy desk that had a laptop, some headphones, and a bunch of papers that had drawings which slightly covered his smartphone that was connected to a charger.

Three or four feet left of Gunner's desk had a bookcase with schoolbooks, some paperback books, and many swimming trophies which interested Justin. Another four or five feet to the left was a door to a bathroom which was messy as well. It stank a little – but not of urine or crap, but more like a mildew stain that triggered irritation instead of revulsion. Next to the bathroom door, a bifold closet door did its best to hold back a bunch of junk like trash, shoes, and clothes. In the far corner opposite Gunner's bunk beds and desk was a flat screen TV connected to an Xbox. "This is awesome," said Justin, "you have everything you need." He turned his voice into a whisper. "Except freedom.".

"I have to stay in here," Gunner emphasized every word, "or she'll get me."

"You know there's someone out there who's about to lose their balls, too, right?" quipped Jason.

Gunner scoffed and shook his head violently. "At least it's not me."

Jeffrey put his arm on Gunner's shoulder. "Come, on, dude, let's get out of here."

Gunner balked, dug in his heels, and resisted. Justin tried to coax Gunner as well. "Come on, dipshit. There's a whole world out there just waiting for us. Waiting for you. You can't get it in here." Justin turned aside to Jason. "Step back, we don't wanna knock you down."

Turning bolts and unlocking latches, Jeffrey opened Gunner's door, then grabbed his cousin by his shoulders to drag him out. Although he tried to back away, Justin kept Gunner in check to get him outside. Fortunately, all the weightlifting and bicycle training helped his physique be strong. Once Jeffrey pushed all the junk aside, he helped pull Gunner outside his room.

"No! No!" yelled Gunner. "Please. No. I'm not safe. Let me …"

"Quit being a weenie, you little dipshit," yelled Justin.

Jeffrey, not having a built physique, grunted a lot more and struggled in coaxing him out. At this point Gunner hyperventilated, twitched, spasmed, and shook. "No. Please. She's going to get me." He cried. "She's going to get me. Stop it. Please."

"Jesus," grunted Justin, "she must've really traumatized him."

"I can't …" Gunner's breath shot like rapid machine gun fire. "I can't … I can't … breathe."

"That's all you're doing, dude. Calm down and take slow breaths." said Jeffrey.

Justin heard Mom yelling. "Boys! What are you doing?"

"We're trying to …" Jeffrey grunted, "… get him outside. He's mega … paranoid."

Justin struggled pulling on Gunner along, hoping sunlight might coax him outside and to break free from his self-imprisonment.

Gunner

Gunner panicked as Jeffrey pushed open the door. Light fell on Gunner's face, his breathing decelerated, falling into a slow meter. Still, his arms flexed more, as well as his legs, trying desperately to return inside away from danger. His whole body shook as his mind raced with terror of Elise sneaking up on them, stabbing him in the groin repeatedly.

Gunner flinched when a dog barked. Terrified, he wobbled, got his feet tangled, and he toppled to the grass. A German Shepherd, along with Freddy came up to him, licked his ear and sniffed his head. Gunner, realizing he hadn't seen Freddy in a while, smiled and started petting him. Freddy, excited, rolled to his back and lolled out his tongue as if telling Gunner to rub his belly. The German Shepherd, with his tongue hanging out, seemed to grin at him. He inserted his nose and head to introduce himself, even letting loose a playful bark.

Smiling, Gunner's right hand rubbed Freddy's belly and his left hand petted the strange dog's majestic fur. Gunner's fear gave way, retreating and fading into nothing. Freddy jumped up and ran away, disappointing Gunner, although the friendly German Shepherd wouldn't leave. "Whose dog is this? What's his name?"

"That's Samson," said Jason. "He's my service dog. Feeling better yet?"

Nodding, Gunner found laughter emerging from his chest and stomach - along with a warm feeling that filled his body. Freddy returned, dropping a ball from his mouth. Grinning wider, Gunner picked it up, stood, and hurled the ball as hard as he could. It bounced about 20 feet from his backyard fence and then rolled. Samson raced Freddy to find the ball first, however Freddy's head start and small frame out-maneuvered Samson.

Jeffrey smiled and extended his hand. "Awesome, dude. Come on – let me look at your minibike. It hasn't been ridden in over a month."

Gunner stood with the aid of his cousin – or rather his best friend. When Jeffrey was possessed, he hurt Gunner a few times, but he knew that truly wasn't Jeffrey but instead an evil being using his cousin.

"You gotta minibike, too?" asked Jason.

"Yeah. But it's not built for racing like his. And I'm not nearly as good a racer as Jeffrey."

After getting it out of the garage, Jeffrey looked it over.

Gunner smiled, reliving a simple joy of starting his bike roaring back to life. His grin spread as the engine bellowed a loud roar but kept still as it remained neutral. Walking it outside, his hands gripped his handlebar tight, hoping it did not forget Gunner's touch. He pushed his accelerator forward, letting loose an explosive power. Its noise re-introduced him with life - just like the dogs, trees, grass, Jeffrey and his two new cousins. Putting on his helmet, he straddled it for the first time in … he forgot when. He had been cooped up inside for almost five weeks. Quiet, he thought about his freedom, although his

131

stomach rumbled with worry. He closed his eyes and inhaled deeply.

"Come on," yelled Justin as he straddled the seat and held onto Gunner. "I haven't ridden yet, so take me on a ride, wimp."

Irritated, Gunner cast a slight scowl towards his left, although he never really faced Justin and his taunt. Angry, Gunner hit the accelerator while shifting to a high gear almost instantly, popping his front wheel to a 45-degree angle.

"Holy shit!" yelled Justin as he clutched Gunner tightly.

Take that, asshole, Gunner thought as he lowered his gear and put his front wheel down. He took pride and pleasure frightening Justin. Not through, Gunner leaned to right – almost getting the bike to a 40-degree angle, then making a hard left to straighten it up for a second, then tilting it to the same degree in the opposite.

"Fuck," yelled Justin, "slow down!"

Gunner, still angry, ignored Justin's request and pulled more on the accelerator, hurling it faster. Gunner savored the speed as well as Justin's panic mode.

"Let me off!" yelled Justin, as his grip latched tighter to Gunner.

Gunner headed towards an open field towards some trees. He downshifted, hit his bakes, and turned his front wheel right - slinging the bike around 180 degrees. Immediately, he accelerated to a higher speed and shot across the bouncy terrain.

"Stop it! Stop it!" yelled Justin.

Gunner downshifted and braked hard, bringing the minibike to a stop a few feet in front of Jason and Jeffrey. The engine shut off, and he pushed down the kickstand.

"What the fuck is your problem, dipshit?" yelled Justin.

Gunner dismounted his bike, turned to face this guy and closed the distance between the two of them. Although Justin had a muscular build, and a height advantage, he pushed this kid in his chest. "Who's the wimp, now, asshole!"

"I was just kidding."

"That's always your excuse, Justin," Jason said calmly.

"Whose side are you on, shithead?"

Jason, who was a head taller than Justin, pushed him backwards a couple of feet. "I'm on the side against you," Jason said. "You run your mouth too much. You embarrassed me in front of Robyn and then embarrass this poor kid who's been traumatized."

"Guys!" said Jeffrey, "cool it, okay?" He turned to Justin. "You barely know him so shut the fuck up."

Gunner exploded. "Dude! I don't need your help. I'm tired of you always trying to keep people away from me. You treat me like a little brother who needs protection at school and everywhere else. Now everyone there thinks I'm a pussy!" Everyone got quiet. "I can fight my own battles, you know." Gunner fell to the ground and leaned back against a tree as tears dripped from his eyes. He was envious of his cousins who were at least five feet and six or eight inches tall. He hadn't grown since sixth grade. It seemed like Jeffrey hung around close to Gunner's height for a couple of years until he sprouted in the last few months. Jeffrey's voice also deepened a bit - as if to leave Gunner behind.

"Jeffrey and I have always been pals – or like brothers. He was always looking out for me, and I wanted Elise to be like a sister, but she was always trying to hurt me somehow … and I never understood why."

"It was part of her personality," said Jeffrey, "… and that …"

"That's only part of it." Gunner shook his head and wept a bit more, thinking of Uncle Jason. "God, I really miss your dad – much more than you'll ever know. He would listen to me, talk to me, and treat me with respect. I never got that with my dad." Gunner told them of a memory he had kept to himself.

***

Mom and Dad sat across the table from each other.

"Walt," said Mom, "we need to discuss one more thing about our divorce: joint custody. I don't want to keep you from your son, so I think it's best …"

Dad sniffed a breath through his nose and lifted it up high. "It's best if you just keep him. I don't want to be around him because he's too much like his uncle. He's an embarrassment to me."

Gunner's heart stopped between beats, and his stomach shriveled. It did not react from hunger or fear, but from Dad's harsh words. His spine cracked, causing him to shrink another inch or two, and his throat pressed hard on itself. Gulping, he tried to find a thought, however his mind shuffled for some sort of reasonable answer for Dad's rejection. His soul felt as if an avalanche of boulders had fallen and crushed it. Shocked, no words came to mind except one: "Dad?"

His father kept his eyes away, as if ashamed. Gunner realized Dad rarely looked at him directly, and when he did it displayed nothing but disdain. He never softened his voice, nor did he offer much affection – not even so much a tap on Gunner's back or shoulder. Stiff, pompous, he

134

could only discuss things he taught college kids – usually material that eluded Gunner's thinking and comprehension. It was always the same criticism:

Stop slouching.

Speak clearly.

Leave me alone, I'm reading.

Quit whining.

Gunner realized Dad's reddish, neatly trimmed beard, lean jaw, and blue eyes all served as a mask that hid something vile and disgusting. It was not hatred or as if Dad ever antagonized him – but rather detached. Dad's ambivalence towards him hurt far worse than any anger or punch. His gut had been slammed not by a fist, but by indifferent actions and hurtful words Dad threw at him over the years. Why didn't Dad like him? Gunner wasn't hated, but he did not sense any love or acceptance, either. Indifference hurt far worse than anger or hate - and his dad's carved a large hole in his spirit, leaving it empty and void of anything.

He missed Uncle Jason so much. He would always face him when talking, offering a hug or a pat on the shoulder or back. He'd play tag and catch - and he taught Gunner how to fix motors just like he did for Jeffrey. The kindest man he'd ever known was taken from him.

***

Everyone appeared ashamed to look at Gunner. He hoped they would not use this weakness against him. He wiped his tears and sniffed to pull his emotions back.

Jeffrey, Jason and Justin all took a deep breath and hesitated. Jeffrey stammered as if searching for the right words to say. "Dude," he whispered, "I wish you would've told me." He shook his head. "I'm so sorry."

"I'm," Justin faltered for a minute "so sorry for being

an asshole to you." He looked at Jason. "And I'm sorry for being such a shithead to you, Jason."

Gunner's eyes and cheeks wrenched so tightly, they almost hurt. Tears gushed more for another minute. His fingers wiped them. Suddenly, Samson and Freddy surrounded Gunner, sniffing, whimpering, and licking his hands, his cheeks, and ears. It tickled, making Gunner laugh. Both dogs lapped his tears, as if trying to clean his wound.

Justin, Jason, and Jeffrey's hands reached for Gunner to help him stand.

Chapter 21

Nathen's tongue tried to find any moisture on his lips. So thirsty, he'd even settle for a tear to fall from his eye into his mouth. Feeling his own lips shake, he pressed his fingers on them to keep them still. Or did he do that to stop his fingers from shaking?

Looking around again, only having dim lights from two lanterns, he struggled once more with despair. Totally losing his discernment on time, he had no idea if he spent two or three days in this prison. Or had it been four? He wanted to get out. Longing for freedom, movement, sunshine, and seeking company of things other than darkness, coldness, and loneliness, he … wanted … out.

He stood, getting off the latrine – at least that's what he thought it was. The bench-like structure had a hole that acted like a toilet seat. Nathen surmised a stream ran underneath to keep this place from stinking even worse. Pulling up his boxers, he cringed.

Again, he wondered what this place was for? Imprisoning British Soldiers during the Revolutionary War, or rebel soldiers during the Civil War … or maybe it was a stop for runaway slaves? Where was this place? Underneath a cabin, a barn, or a church?

His eyes scanned the room, catching sight of Eli's severed head. Nathen's eyes clamped tightly, and he turned his head, but the image of his scoutmaster's wide opened and shocked eyes and mouth terrified him. Maybe he could get it and hide it under something. No! He didn't want to touch it. It resonated with his scoutmaster's mind and thoughts, and his blank, dead eyes radiated a ghastly fear.

"What are you going to do, son?"

Nathen fidgeted and glanced at Eli's disembodied head. The eyes did not blink, the mouth did not move, but somehow, he heard his voice. No – it did not come from his dead mouth, but he did hear it. Could it be Eli's ghost?

"You've been in my troop for three years. Have you forgotten everything I taught you?"

"What?" While Nathen spoke, he could not understand who he talked to. Did he really hear Eli's voice – or did he hear his scoutmaster's thoughts trapped in a dead head?

"If you wanna escape, you have to work for it. Nobody's gonna come along and set you free. Use your mind. It's a weapon. Scout your environment. Think your way through. Imagine a way to free yourself."

Although unsure where Eli's voice came from, Nathen realized it was correct. He needed to think his way out. Standing, he examined his prison. About 20 feet in front of him were steps leading out of his cell. Although unsure, he thought he could see a latch. However, the chain around his neck ended his mobility at six or seven feet.

At his feet was Scoutmaster Eli's head. Nathen almost picked it up but stopped himself and looked for that cloth Elise used to cover his head. Finding it, he turned away from the decapitated face and somehow dropped the covering over the head.

"Sorry, Eli," he whispered, "but you're freaking me out."

Behind him, it was much darker. Yet, he could still see an opening that looked like a huge fireplace. Using his sense of smell, he realized it might be during very cold months - however, feeling a draft Nathen imagined it was more for ventilation. Maybe he could crawl up. Yet, the chain stopped him about four or five feet away from the huge opening. Trying to stretch his body, the metal links dug into his neck.

Nathen backed up, then took off his boxer shorts and ran them between his neck and the chain. Maybe that would allow better comfort. After stretching out a little, he tried to get closer while pulling. The strain pinched his skin, his joints, and his hair. Maybe he should cut it like Mom keeps suggesting. Catching a whiff of his boxers, his nose and eyes cringed at the disgusting smell. *"Always wear clean boxers"* Mom always said.

"Don't think about your mama right now," said Eli. *"You gotta think your way out."*

Nathen nodded while putting his boxers back on. "Yes, sir." Looking up into pitch darkness, his eyes rolled. "I can't believe I'm talking to a severed head." He waited for a moment, wondering if someone else might also be also kept as a prisoner nearby. Perhaps there might be a search party outside. "Help!" he yelled – trying to push his pleas up the shaft. He waited a few seconds but heard nothing. "Help! Somebody help me, please!" Every word got louder – however all he heard were echoes. They weren't long and drawn out as if in a cave, but rather short and muffled like in a church building. "I'm going to guess," he talked to himself to help think, process, and create a plan, "if I hear echoes … that probably means my voice can't escape and nobody can hear me." The thought scared him, but at least his rational thought answered an important question.

The cold, heavy chain slapped his chest as he turned

towards steps. "This chain is my first problem," Nathen whispered, again to provide thinking and comfort. He was trying something instead of waiting to be dead … or rather castrated which to him was far worse. His body twitched in terror at the thought. What if she doesn't have an anesthetic? Nathen's breaths shortened thinking of horrible pain, humiliation, and total horror. Dread set in like a heavy weight on his shoulders that forced him to his knees.

"Son, just calm down." Eli's voice wasn't rough or mean, but soothing. *"Take a deep breath to get it deep into your lungs."*

Nathen followed instructions, closing his eyes to concentrate on his breathing.

"Now, let it out slowly."

Again, he listened for more advice from his … dead scoutmaster. "I can't believe I'm taking orders from a dead person's ghost," he whispered, trying to find some humor to alleviate his fear. He continued breathing, hoping to rid the horror from his head, chest, and limbs.

Studying his chain, he noticed it had been bolted to an oak beam with a round screw that had no standard or Phillips notches. "Maybe the beam has a weakness?" he muttered.

"That's it. Think it through, son."

Hard to see in dim light, Nathen ran his fingers near the beam surrounding the screw. He found a deformity on the back corner. Something had whittled it to a mushy decay – perhaps a rat gnawing it, as well as water rotting the wood.

Finding a bit of hope, anticipation swelled in his chest, and a brief smile spread across his face. He circled on himself a few times, trying to think of something to help him scrape away the rotting, decaying wood. For a change, excitement overpowered his persistent, darkening dread. It seemed brighter for a few seconds, allowing him to search for a useful tool.

Moving towards the steps, his eyes focused on the floor. On his hands and knees, his fingers, hands, and toes probed the area for something – preferably something metal. Reaching its maximum length, Nathen moved left, then back right. His arms reached out so he could measure his maximum reach of both arms and fingers. His excitement faded while moving again, but he refused to give up hope.

"Mom," he said quietly, "just to let you know," he cringed thinking, "I am sorry for embarrassing you last summer at your bridge club. I was being stupid for taking a dare to jump off the diving board naked." He started moving right, still at the chain's maximum pull. "And Dad, I'm sorry for trying to cover up that dent I made on your car with my bike. I was being dumb. And Ethan, I'm sorry for convincing you to help me trick Dad and getting you in trouble."

Nathen could think of more sins and wrongs he had done in thought and deed. Could he list them all? Manipulating his grandparents to undermine his parents to get what he wanted, scaring his little brother and sister, hurting Heather Delacroix when he lied to his friends about hating her "ugly, dumb smile."

Hope for atonement faded when he reached his maximum pull to the left so much that his shoulder bumped a wall. Leaning against it, he flexed his eyelids and inhaled deeply, choking back his tears to keep them from snuffing out the dim and weak flame of hope.

"Fuck!" He kept a whisper, not wanting Mom, Dad,

or God to hear him say that one word he swore he'd never utter. Sure, he thought about it many times, but he could never bring himself to say it. He had to be a good example for Ethan and Leslie, and he didn't want to embarrass his parents, Scoutmaster Eli, or Pastor Andrew.

A few heavy sighs caused his head to fall, deflating any hope of escaping this stubborn darkness around him, and his horror within. Elise and Victor's terror filled the room, keeping a thick, palpable sense of fright that closed in tightly. It tried to asphyxiate him, rob him of a single breath, and snuff any bit of his anticipation.

Something glistened in the dim light. Although it caught his attention, he lost it amidst a closing darkness. Moving his eyes back and forth, up and down, closer and farther away, he tried to catch its wink once more. It flirted with him, but he had to catch its glint to find it and play the game.

He gasped, catching sight of it several feet to his right, just a foot out of reach. Crawling on his hands and knees, his eyes remained fixed on that item so he would not lose it again. Stretching out as far as he could, he tried to reach it, but the heavy chain dug deep into skin and neck. His heart raced into a gallop as he strained his muscles, tendons, and bones. Every vibration and thud in his chest became louder with each pump. Something had to give, or he might pass out. His blood could not find any more oxygen to keep him going, and his chain constricted tighter around his carotid arteries.

Pulling back, he huffed for a minute … maybe two so his heart could replenish oxygen needed for his limbs, skin, muscles … and even his spirit. Finding a normal pace of breathing, he tried again – this time pushing fingers between the chain and his neck. Grunting, he stretched further, hoping to find just a few more inches needed to obtain the elusive object that rested so near, and yet so far away. Unable to bear his stress, he coughed, retreated from the tautness, and huffed to catch his breath one more time.

Leaning against the wall, he glanced at Eli's covered head. "Any more advice, Eli? Shit!"

"I'd advise you to wash that mouth out with soap. After that, find longer arms."

Nathen smiled and even managed to laugh as he imagined Eli's snide bit of counsel. The small light of anticipation in his mind grew – not too much to blind him but not too little to be of no use. The tray Elise used to serve him Eli's head! It rested within reach. Elated once again, he scurried to get it, turned it upside down, and returned to the maximum chain length. Taking a deep breath, Nathen stretched and reached out with his tray. His chain pressed against his neck, pulling his arteries and veins tighter. Retreating, Nathen waited for his breath to replenish an ample supply of oxygen, and a normal rhythm for his heart and lungs. Reaching out again, his tray barely missed to the left. Adjusting its position, Nathen reached again while begging God to help him snag it.

"Patience, boy. Be patient … and you'll get it. Don't rush it."

Still desperate, he took a huge breath, stretched his whole body out, eyed the object, and brought his tray down on top of it. Dragging it closer, he hoped he captured whatever that thing was. Having enough slack, his mouth widened to a smile, then took in a heavy sigh. Wrapping his fingers around a screw - one that had a fine point and perfect grooves. Elise must have dropped it. Despite dust, dirt, and a bit of hay, Nathen kissed it, then returned to the board that anchored his chain.

Furiously, he chipped at the rotting decay. He cringed when the screw dropped from his fingers. A light sound clinked, revealing its location. Reclaiming his lost tool, he started chipping away again.

"That's it, son, I knew you could think your way through."

"Eli," said Nathen, "… if that's really your ghost, I wish you'd go tell a psychic or someone else where the fuck I am."

Chapter 22

An icy sensation made its way into Jason's ears. It tickled at first but quickly became painful and uncomfortable. Barely awake, and barely asleep, he wished his state of consciousness would choose one or the other. Preferring the slumber, he turned on his side, hoping to dive lower into comfort and rest.

His mind still bubbled with ideas, conversations, smells, and other echoes from the day. First were lyrics from one of his favorite songs on his Spotify list. Next was his conversation with Gunner. Jason's pity resonated stronger, along with a hatred for a man Jason never met. How could a father say something so horrible to his son? It made Jason appreciate his own father, even more. He thought of Nathan, the kind Rabbi who sought them out to help. A split second later, he hated Justin for embarrassing him in front of Robyn - but then felt so much love and loyalty to his cousin for all his help - especially in finding the blind surfing school.

Jason heard it: a whisper that called him subtly – just below the threshold of audibility. At first, he felt a strong annoyance, hating this "gift" of hearing the supernatural. It was not a loud wailing dissonant scream or a mixture of hurtful sounds that jammed his ears like spikes. Fully awake, he sat up in bed, barely remembering the faint images of his dream.

It had been almost a year since he went blind. He

noticed the sights in his dreams had faded more to a grainy picture that seemed more and more transparent to darkness. The blackness poked small holes in the visages and expanded out. How much longer? Three, four … maybe five years at most. He knew that darkness in his dreams would grow, overshadowing the diminishing imagery during his slumber. Eventually, his nightscapes would vanish, and his dreams would become only what he heard, felt, smelled, and tasted.

A slight chill pierced the skin of his ears and nose. Something was here – but it was not malevolent or hurtful. He heard Justin grunt in his sleep. The voice surged a little. What did it say? He concentrated, wondering who this might be. Jeffrey's dad? He concentrated, hoping the voice might get a little louder to decipher it.

Robyn's father, Roger, was blind as well and could hear the supernatural. He said to relax, focus, and try to coax the spirit to speak a little louder. Roger's guess was that the ghost did not have enough power for its voice since speaking was something that occurred in the physical world. A voice existed with vocal cords, and aided with air flow, and the moving of the throat, tongue, and lips. Without the body to do that, the ghost had to learn to speak in the metaphysical realm.

Jason cast aside the thoughts of theory and tried to elicit the voice.

I'm listening, he thought. *What are you trying to tell me?*

The words, murky, tried to make their way without soundwaves, volume, and pitch. They repeated a few times, then faded. Repeated again with a little more volume and faded again. Jason piqued his ears, finally understanding the message. The words, faint, came together, barely becoming audible, cohesive, and clear. *"I know where he is."*

The voice barely echoed … once, twice, a third time. Jason listened intently hoping whatever and whomever it was would speak again. Trying to be patient, he didn't repeat the question, realizing the spirit probably needed to regain strength. How long had it been? A few seconds? A minute?

"I know where he is."

"Who?"

"Nathen."

Jason felt a surge of anticipation swell, almost like a whirlpool spiraling up after a rush of water flooded a tub.

"Where is he?" Jason's thoughts almost passed to his voice.

"Her favorite place."

"Whose favorite place? Elise's?"

"Yes."

"Who is this?"

"Eli."

Jason shuddered, wondering who that might be? Wait! He remembered the last news report said Nathen's scoutmaster, Eli, was reported missing. What was his last name? Was this him trying to make contact? It must be.

"Can you help?"

Jason cringed as the anticipation that swelled earlier in his rib cage cooled and sank. Was that his connection? The anemic voice whispered again.

"No. Something has her. I can't speak or even think of it. Too strong for me."

"What?"

A low-pitched howl erupted violently, jumping into Jason's ears, and surging through his brains. He covered his ears to no avail as it yelled louder, penetrating deeper, sending his heart and breath at a rapid pace. It carried hideous, cold tendrils that mapped his body, mind and spirit. They burrowed their way into his neck, arms, and legs. The sensation turned so hot, sweat spewed like lava, drenching his sheets and sleeping shorts.

"What is it?" yelled Justin.

Jason's respiration slowed to a normal pace after the wail passed through his mind. His heart slowed as the onus anxiety diminished. It surged like a bolt of lightning for a split second when the door opened and the sound of Jeffrey's voice startled him.

"What's going on? You okay?"

Jason's shoulders spasmed at the sound, but he found the calm that he had lost. Tears welled in his eyes as he sniffed and sighed. "I heard that demon again." Clamping his eyelids, it felt as if a random wave crashed on him, knocking him off balance and into the sea. "God, how I hate this. I thought I was done with this shit."

Warm hands clutched his shoulders. Although Jeffrey and Justin's body odors meshed into a stench that irked Jason more, the comforting touch helped him forget about it. Helping him move away from the smell even more, his mind clung to the voice he heard before the demon.

"Wait," he said in a whisper. "I … I heard something … before the demon." His mind tried to sift through memory, hoping to recount what it said. "He said his name was Eli. Wasn't that the name of his scoutmaster? Anyway, it said he knew where Nathen was."

"Where?" Desperation dripped from Jeffrey's voice.

Jason's brow wrinkled as the conversation returned again. "He's at Elise's favorite place." Feeling their anticipation mixed with his own, tension spread like wildfire on parched land. "He said something else was with her and it was too strong for him."

"I guess it killed him," said Justin, "or he couldn't talk to you."

"Elise's favorite place?" Jeffrey's words were laced in confusion and worry. "She's not here in her room. She couldn't be in the library … or in the shed. Jeffrey gasped. "Wait … I think I know where she is."

Chapter 23

Nathen grunted while his body shed heavy perspiration, greasing his skin, hands, and feet. It mixed along with the soot that had gathered in the vent. He huffed, coughed, and put his forehead on a rock. His own rancid stench nauseated him. Not able to see very well, he relied on the draft that fell on him. Painful scrapes on his arms, chest, thighs, shins, and feet sent sirens of pain through his skin. At the same time, his shoulders, elbows, knees and neck radiated a dull and achy pain.

Because he had fallen three times already, he worried about falling again. First, he worried another fall would dash his hopes and strength and he wouldn't be able to try again. More troubling was that he was much higher up, somewhere between 15 to 20 feet, so any injuries could be serious - perhaps fatal.

"Don't fall again. Don't fall again. Almost there. Almost there." He repeated his words in a whispered rhythm, then found new words to inspire him out of exhaustion. "God, please help me." He repeated them in a new whispered rhythm – like fast taps of a drum that added cadence and tension.

He worried about his chain dangling below him. He freed it by using that screw he found and chipping the board's weak corner. Hearing that screw fall loose was his first victory. To him, it was the sweetest sound - better than his favorite song. His fingers, swollen, raw, and bleeding did hurt, although calluses provided some numbing.

Climbing up the shaft, though, was the most difficult challenge. His biggest worry was the chain that dangled below him. It got heavier as he climbed and lifted it off the floor. Even worse, if Elise or that big guy, Victor, came in, it would be easy for either to grab his loose chain and yank him back down.

Ready to let go with one hand, he reached up another three or four inches, found a bit of rock to cling to, then lifted his foot up to a small hold. It slipped. He flinched, almost falling, but his fingers refused to give up. His toes, also callused and in pain, lodged onto a small foothold, getting closer to the opening. Another reach, another hoist with his foot.

"Almost there, almost there. Don't fall, don't fall," he said while keeping his anticipation in check. He gritted his teeth as a sensation in his shoulders, arms, and legs burned like a raging inferno. Reaching up again, his knuckles grazed something hard … something metal. Panicked, his fingers shut tightly on a small brick that barely jutted out the shaft frame. Sweat poured down his forehead and into his eyes, leaving a stinging burn. Wanting to wipe his perspiration off his face, Nathen endured his discomfort, afraid he'd fall again if he let go. His boxers felt gross as they were drenched in sweat. Hopefully, he could break free and then take a long, cleansing shower when he got home.

Reaching up, he felt the grate again. It was not solid but had openings like a colander or a sieve so air could flow up and down. His fingers poked through some openings, grabbed the metal and tried to push it up and over. A loud scraping sound shot through his ears like a pickaxe.

"Come on," he whispered to himself. "Don't give up, don't give up. You're almost out, you're almost out. Don't fall again, don't fall." Only able to use one hand, he tried to push it up and over, hoping it might push through or flip it on its side. However, not well-anchored on the wall, he had little leverage. The cover moved slightly but refused to budge. He jerked it side to side, front and back, and side to side again - all while trying to push it up. It scraped a couple of inches up as its back half of it descended down at an angle. So close to freedom, he refused to let go and tried to push up again, then jostled it side to side. It descended behind him while the part directly above him pivoted vertically. Vexed, he remained still, huffing as his chest flared with burning pain, while his rapid thudding heartbeat resounded in his ears. "One more time, one more time," he told himself. "Don't let go, don't let go. And don't fall." His foot stepped up to a tiny ledge as he thrusted upwards, pushing it more.

The blockage turned, and fell sideways, but got caught in the shaft's corners. Although jammed, the opening was just enough to reach through and grab the shaft's rim. After his hand latched solidly, he smiled for a split second, then batted his eyelids a few times to keep the burning sweat from his eyes. He had to reach up one more time. As his left hand planted firmly gripped the rim, hopeful tears flushed through his eyes. He wished he had more shoulder and chest strength, but those eluded him right now. Using his feet, he tried to press them against the brick, rock, and adobe used to construct the shaft's inner walls.

His sweaty toes could not find a good holding, but they landed on a small foothold and pushed up. Nathen grunted, realizing the grate still blocked enough of the opening to prevent his torso from escaping. So close, he pulled harder with his hands and feet and wriggled his way through the metal covering. It grazed his back, leaving scratches and scrapes. His injuries stung violently as sweat dripped into fresh wounds. The aperture now tore away his boxer shorts, leaving scrapes on his butt, with the same stinging sensation.

Once his rear end cleared the opening, he flexed his arms straight and his legs easily cleared his prison. Nathen fell over and landed on cold, wet grass and dirt. Exhausted, he huffed endlessly for several minutes, trying to get some strength back to his stiffened, sore, and aching muscles that had reached their breaking point. His hair was totally drenched in perspiration which also clung to leaves and blades of grass. A weak yet refreshing wind hit him, giving Nathen a slight chill.

Nathen realized a bigger dilemma. Although nobody could see him, he was naked. The temperatures weren't cold, but rocks, roots, plants, would hurt his feet. It was like that reality tv show, "Naked and Afraid," except he had no camera crew to get him out of this situation. Where was he? Even if he knew, he couldn't navigate his way without sunlight. While he could use stars at night, too many trees prevented him from seeing them. Maybe he could find a spot to hide and sleep for the night, then try to find his way back tomorrow morning. No. If he did that, Elise or Victor could find him out here. Nathen also had to haul the heavy chain with him … although he could use it as a weapon.

The chain! His eyes opened wide as his body jolted. He stood and quickly pulled it up from the shaft and dropped it next to him. Falling back on the cold ground, his stings on his back flared. Worried about infections, Nathen realized the importance of clothes beyond modesty. Dull aches in his joints and muscles, and bruises on his skin also reminded him of his weariness. Having no energy, he realized his best option was to hide and rest until morning. His hunger pangs had a life of their own – feeling like two squirrels rumbling inside his stomach as they battled for food. In the morning, he could find some berries.

Nathen noticed sounds in the forest: crickets chirping, owl noises, and … the rushing of a stream. His ears fixated on the last sound and moved towards the water. Using his hands, he cupped the water and drank several scoops.

Footsteps came close. Nathen cursed silently and remained still. A huge sigh helped him relax – seeing silhouettes of a family of deer drinking from the stream, he smiled. One was a huge buck – probably at least an eight or ten point.

Some other steps followed. Lower to the ground, precise, they walked in a measure as if stalking prey. With his eyes adjusted to darkness, Nathen saw low shadowy figures approaching the deer. high grass. They scuttled closer, as if coordinating and planning an attack. Realizing they were coyotes, he thought of yelling to warn the deer – but remembered he was an escaped prisoner.

Inhaling deeply, Nathen looked up, stretching his arms high, realizing what it was like in that movie his parents loved, "The Saw-something Redemption."

Something hard walloped him on his head as everything went dark.

Elise

I watched Nathen sleeping. Victor helped me bring him back down to the hideaway, then I secured a fresh bolt through a chain link and into a two-by-four beam. This time, I made sure to center it, and not to put it close to the beam's corner.

He looked peaceful – although he had scrapes and bruises all over his skin. If he had escaped, Victor would have been very angry with me – so I'm glad I caught him. At first, I thought of sharing the pain medication from my first aid kit – but realized he needed punishment for trying to escape. Maybe I should jab his dick and balls with my taser again.

He was kinda cute. Although his eyes were closed, his face was pleasant to look at – although his ears stuck out just a little bit. His long, blondish-brown hair framed his face – although it needed to be washed and cut. He sniffed, turned more on his back, opened his mouth and eyes and stared at the ceiling. His eyelids clenched tightly as if trying to shield him from reality. Tears seeped from the outside corners as he sat up and dropped his face into his hands.

"Oh, God – no!" he said while crying. Yanking on his chain, he discovered I reset the link with another bolt. "No," he moaned again. "I was out. I was out."

"You tried to escape," I whispered. "I had to bring you back, or Victor would have been very angry. I should punish you somehow"

Nathen's head jerked towards me, then he pulled the blanket tighter.

"Your boxers were torn to shreds," I said quietly, "so I had nothing to dress you with. But don't bother. I'll see everything when I help Victor castrate you."

Nathen buried his face deeper in his hands, sobbing violently. "Why are you doing this? What'd I ever do to you?"

Relishing the despair he displayed, I tried to think of the best words to instill more terror, and the cadence to modify it. "Nothing. We just needed someone and … we chose you … randomly."

"I … I just wanna go home. Please let me go home."

At first, I felt some pity for him. Maybe I just should have kidnapped Gunner, brought him out here, and finished the job. No. I do need to practice. At least that's what Victor kept telling me. I have to practice to get better at this punishment – although I have not done it … yet.

"No," I said back to him. "Don't worry. You'll be home soon. You'll just be a freak for the rest of your life."

"What the fuck is your problem?"

While his voice startled me, I kept all emotions away from my face as well as my mind.

"Were you brainwashed by this guy? Or are you a complete bat-shit crazy psycho?"

I brought down his tray for a meal: a fish I caught, cleaned and cooked, along with some berries and a canteen of water.

"Please let me go. I won't tell anyone – I promise. I just wanna go home."

Getting tired of his incessant whining, crying, and begging, I went upstairs, closed the door, and latched it shut. I went over to my table and turned down the lantern. The sun had come up, providing enough light for me to have my own food.

"Very good, Beautiful," Victor said as the salty odor returned. *"You are a master at instilling fear and terror."*

After a few bites, I thought openly. "Victor, maybe we shouldn't do this. I mean … he's kinda cute and I sort of like him. Yeah – he's annoying, but just like so many other boys. Maybe we could castrate Casey Righetti, instead."

I could always tell when Victor was angry: his smell went from something annoying like too much salt in diesel fuel, to something rancid like a dumpster behind a restaurant. The temperatures also became frigid, making my breath misty and visible. More than anything, I felt his rage attach to my soul, making me shiver with terror. The heavy blanket of dread enveloped me, making things darker – blacker, and bleak.

Strangely, it felt as if Victor was inside me, and outside me as well. His inner dwelling made me queasy, unbalanced, and confused. The confusion ebbed, replaced with sharp and keen awareness, analyzing everything like the temperature, the barn structure, and animals that were nearby. Victor's outer essence pressed against me, keeping me alert, but also constrained. Although his strength surged through me, it also kept me cold and restrained - feeling as if heavy chains wrapped around my wrists and ankles. It seemed he made things darker, scarier, filling me with terrifying dread. Unable to hear anything, I lost control as my arms, hands, and legs all worked under his volition – not mine.

The feeling was somewhat familiar. I had been like this a few times before. The first one … when I played "Circus" with Gunner. The second one was playing "William Tell" with him. The most recent one was when I was going to castrate Gunner.

Victor's cage emerged around me. Naked, I shivered, covering myself as best as I could with not just my arms, but also trying to use the hay around me. Very little light emanated from above. Seeing a mirror embedded in the cage, I stood and looked into it. It seemed as if I peered from the inside of my mind at the table. My hands surveyed the surgical blades, the scalpels, the sutures and needles. My eyes scanned the directions for the anesthetic as I wrote the proper numbers for mathematical calculations: Nathen's weight, the proportion of the drug to the weight. A sneer spread across my face as I thought of taking away Gunner's … I mean Nathen's genitals.

Wait. Was that my thought … or Victor's? I did hate Gunner for taking Jeffrey's attention away from me, but this boy had done nothing to me. *What am I doing?* I thought. *What are we doing?*

"*We are doing what I want to happen.*"

"*Victor, I thought it was my choice.*"

"*It always was, Beautiful.*"

"*I just suggested it.*"

His prickly voice reached a pitch that hurt my ears - like a high squeak of railroad brakes. I twitched, feeling as if a cold blade stabbed my brain.

Chapter 24

Father Matthew stepped into the Confession Booth. Of all the duties he had, he found this the most taxing. It drained his soul to hear confessions from people in his parish. It never ceased to surprise him how so many good people struggled with sin deeply embedded within them. Even more troubling was their burdensome guilt that refused to budge and give up despite the sacrifice of Christ and his miracle over death. Much of that guilt stemmed more from sinful thoughts as opposed to action.

So many people led double lives, looking holy and pious in the pews, but once in the darkness of the confessional booth, confessions stripped away their masks. They laid naked, desperate for forgiveness and exoneration for their sins. True, some were imagined, or they made too much out of innocuous thoughts, but the confessional booth, although dark, cast light on the despair stemming from their inability to save themselves from their own destructive behavior, and a stubborn belief that no forgiveness existed.

The door closed.

"Forgive me, Father for I have sinned."

Matthew smiled. "Gunner! It's been so long since I heard your voice. It's good to hear from you."

"It's nice to hear you, too, Father."

Matthew smiled, somehow hearing Gunner do the same.

"It has been six weeks since my last confession. In that time, I have committed the sins of lust at least 10 times but more hating my brothers and sisters in Christ and beyond. I've been afraid …" Subtle sobs and stammers indicated Gunner's emotions seized hold of him, making him wretch, moan, and weep. "I've turned my back on Jeffrey, hated him, hated Elise, hated my dad, and even hated … God." Heaving, sniffing, it seemed as if he tried to retract all his crying and confession. "And I've locked myself in a room for over a month, keeping Jeffrey, Mom, and Aunt Jenny away."

Hearing Gunner's confession punctured Matthew's heart so much, it seemed to open a hole for his own tears to cry though. Sighing, he had to find the right words for empathy, counsel, and love. "My son … you felt betrayed by your cousins – and you have a strong reason to – especially with Elise. And your father's rejection hurt the most … didn't it?"

Gunner continued crying, sniffling, and grunting. Somehow, he managed a "yes, sir."

"Gunner … it's perfectly natural to feel that way. Betrayal is something that hurts probably more than anything else because they come from people we trust and love. But far, far worse, are those who plan revenge and to repay evil with evil. Someone who doesn't recognize their own hate … those are the ones who are truly lost … who are not in repentance. Be grateful you are feeling such guilt." After a short pause, Matthew heard Gunner sigh a few times, somehow regaining his composure. "And if I know Jeffrey," Father Matthew added, "he's already forgiven you. Ask him."

The silence worried the priest, but he remained quiet himself, hoping the boy's own thoughts and spirit would take their time in finding a solution to his dilemma. "What about …" his long pause seemed to tease Father Matthew. "What about my dad?"

"All you can do is hope he will return. He might … he might not." Matthew fought hard to keep his own composure. "However, you are the one with the good intentions. You have shown your contrition and penance in your honesty, and in that I offer you absolution. In the name of the Father, Son, and the Holy Spirit."

Father Matthew somehow knew Gunner crossed himself just before saying his prayer. "God, I thank you for your mercy. Your forgiveness has restored my soul to friendship with you. Thank you for loving me even when my actions show that I do not love you fully. Amen."

Gunner left but immediately following him were three familiar voices.

"All three of us can't fit in here," said Jeffrey.

"Move over, dipshit," said Justin. "Oh, sorry Father."

"Ow," said Jason as he grunted and fell with a thud. "Which one of you tripped me?"

"Relax, dude," said Jeffrey. "It was an accident."

Father Matthew laughed in his throat, looking up, and thanking God for the amusement the three boys gave him. "Gentlemen," he said while shaking his head, "confession is not a group activity."

"We're sorry, Father," said Jeffrey, "but we all have a serious question."

Matthew's voice became stern and direct. "Okay," he said, "what is it?

"Father …" said Jason, "we need forgiveness for what we're about to do."

The priest cleared his throat. "It doesn't work that way boys. If you intend to commit a sin, there is no repentance and no absolution."

"But we gotta do this, Father," Jeffrey said.

"Hey! Jason whispered, "I'm the oldest, I'll speak for us."

"But he's MY priest," countered Jeffrey.

They taxed Father Matthew's patience – and he became stern. "Boys … please tell me what this is about."

"We think we know where Elise and that boy are," said Jeffrey. "Jason heard a ghost last night – and we think it's Nathen's scoutmaster who was reported missing. We need to go get them – and we need you to exorcise the demon out of her."

Father Matthew sighed and shook his head. "Jeffrey, I am not a Jesuit Priest. They do the exorcisms – and it must be sanctioned through the Diocese and the Vatican."

"You helped me, you can help her! I know you can."

Even though the boys couldn't see him, Matthew shook his head. "Boys, I can't do that without sanction from the Church. It's a process we must respect and adhere to."

"That's ridiculous!" said Jason. "The Rabbi who helped us didn't need time for approval. He came back within a few days."

"Jason," Matthew reminded himself to remain calm and soft. He learned a long time ago his deep bass voice could easily sound angry when it wasn't. He also knew an angry voice turns people away from listening. "Jason, please let me finish. Your friend was a Rabbi. That's of the Jewish Faith and they have their own rules and requirements for such things. They're more autonomous and …"

"Stop making excuses," Jason said. On the verge of tears, his voice squeaked as it begged. "Please. Rabbi

Nathan died to help us. He lived his faith to help. Why can't you?"

Torn, wanting to help, but remembering the rules he promised to live by, Matthew sighed. "Boys, I can't … I just …"

Jeffrey cut in. "Father, remember the first night you met Elise's demon. It knew you. What are you not telling me? What are you not telling us? What's going on?"

Father Matthew sighed and waited. Almost speaking, he stopped, wondering if he should tell them something he had kept to himself for ages. It left him with regret laced with doubt, fear, and anger. All the prayers he shouted to God seemed empty and lacked answers. He tried not to let it affect his faith and courage, but the stained memory taunted him, regurgitating awful memories of the demon tormenting him as a young priest. Guilt seized him by the shoulders, regret knocked him down, and fear tried to drag him into an underground prison. He almost cried.

After a long silence, a sigh burst forth – followed by the pain he had only shared with only three other people. Would the boys speak of it to others? They were young and might not understand the vows of confidentiality. They might break that with friends or family. Jeffrey, though, was the son he never had. Jason shared the journey of being broken after losing his sight and rebounding just as Matthew did. He recalled the struggle of learning Braille, navigating with a cane, using his hands as a guide and clapping to provide echo location. He had to give up watching basketball games, boxing matches, and driving. Sister Regina had to help him make meals, be his chauffeur, and assist him with the Eucharist.

"Jeffrey … boys, please understand the vows of the Confession Booth. It is in the strictest confidentiality. I do not discuss my parishioner's confessions with anyone. It is a vow of confidentiality – like a doctor with his patent, or a lawyer with his client. So what I'm about to tell you is something you must keep to yourself." He heard them all let out a huge breath. "Can I trust you?"

They all responded within a second after each other.

"Yes, Father."

"Yes, sir."

"I promise."

Despite Father Matthew's distance from his memory, it was easy to find. It occupied his mind like a huge desk in a small office, obtrusive, invasive, and painful as if accidentally hitting it with his knees. Maybe it might help the guilt, regret, and pain that came with it. "The other day I mentioned a botched exorcism. I'd like you to know the full truth. I've only shared this with two other priests, and Sister Regina." Taking a deep breath, he hesitated, realizing his story was about to enter the boys' ears. "I was a young priest, paired with a Jesuit to perform an exorcism in Florence, Italy in 2003. Two boys, ten-year-old twins, were possessed by seven demons."

"Seven?" Jeffrey's shocked voice felt like a sharp icicle plowing through Father Matthew's mind.

Just behind Jeffrey's voice was Jason's. "Twins?"

"We had … exorcised one demon out. Father Samuel wanted to get one more out before we sought some rest and more fasting and prayers. I was tired, impatient, and angry as those vile creatures tormented the boys. Their voices were so many, it was hard to tell which was which." Matthew felt a warm tear stream down his cheek and curve under his jaw. "They taunted me. Used old memories, guilt, and fear to torment me. I tried to talk back, which took my attention away from God. Up to that point, I had never witnessed possessions or exorcisms but only studied them in seminary.

"I wanted to rest – and even run away. The experience was terrifying and I … found my faith faltering. The dread of seven demons is very onus and taxing. Instead of telling Father Samuel how I felt, I continued. After a few minutes, another one was pulled out. It was hideous, frightening, and especially spiteful – more so than most demons. Seeing it, I lost my faith for a split second." His eyelid flexed once to let out another tear. "In that doubt, I tried a prayer, but it was empty and carried no weight to it. The demon resisting snapped both of the boys' necks – killing them both.

"Shocked, I couldn't think of anything to do. Angry, afraid, I stared at the creature – then it threw me into the back of the temple wall. I hit my head on the stone – and I became blind."

Hearing only the boys' silence, Father Matthew felt ashamed. Would they lose their faith because of his doubt and fear? Their three breaths fell into sync as if they all shared the same heartbeat, respiration, and thoughts.

"Well," said Jeffrey, "can you help us, then? Please."

"I cannot let …" he stopped his stern, impatient voice – then tried to soften it. "I am bound by Church doctrine, law, and orders. I want to help – but I cannot under these circumstances."

"Well, then we're going to do it on our own."

Justin's whisper felt like a cold, sharp knife slicing into Father Matthew's chest.

"Boys, please … listen to me. You don't know the rituals, prayers, procedures …"

"We got the prayers online," Jeffrey said louder. "I know Latin. I gotta save my sister."

"And we gotta help that kid Nathen," added Jason.

"Boys," he said louder, "you're in over your head. Please, please don't go there."

"We're going and we're going to try," said Justin. "You may have lost your faith, but we haven't lost ours."

Matthew rushed to the door as he heard the hasty exit the boys made. "Boys, please." Their footsteps faded as they bolted out the door.

Father Matthew rubbed his forehead. He had to stop them. His instinct was to get Sister Regina to call their mothers but realized it would violate the sanctity of confession. Confused, upset, and anxious, he tried to think of a way to dissuade them. His hand moved to the right, found his cane and pursued them. Realizing a few other people waited at the Confession Booth, he apologized to them. "Please wait. I'll be back in a couple of minutes."

After a few steps, he realized the boys were in front of him.

"Father," said Jason, "those twins who were killed in Italy … by any chance did they visit Sao Paulo, Brazil?"

Shocked, Father Matthew's breath froze. "How did you know that?"

Chapter 25

Elise

I examined everything: the scalpels, artery clips, and sutures, and anesthetics. Using pen and paper, I re-checked the proper amount of horse anesthetic for Nathen. I swiped it when we took Freddy to the veterinarian's office. I ordered medical equipment online - which is also where I found instructions on how to perform this operation. If people don't want others to do these things, then why are they on the Internet?

On the other hand, I sneered about the horrible thing I was about to do to him? Finally, my dream of castrating a boy would be complete. Or was it Victor's dream? Either way, this would give me such a deep feeling of satisfaction and fulfillment.

Reading the instructions in my composition book, I looked through the steps again – even though I read them a hundred times. I wanted to do this right, so he'd have a nice long, miserable life without his dick and balls.

Wait – maybe this was too cruel? If I was a boy … how would I feel? Shit. I don't want to be wishy-washy like Gunner. I know I could follow through if it was him. I actually hated him. He certainly doesn't deserve happiness. He should go through life without his genitals. Gunner took Jeffrey – my brother and my twin – away from me. Gunner had no idea of the connection he broke between Jeffrey and me. I'd rather do this to him than Nathen - but I had him and thought it best to practice on him first.

I thought a sedative in Nathen's food would be best to initially put him out cold. After that – then I'd use the anesthetic. That would be best to keep him paralyzed during the procedure. Then he'd wake up as a new and deformed freak. My ultimate prank. Victor suggested doing surgery without an anesthetic – but I'm sure that his endless screaming would get annoying.

Nathen

Nathen sat against the wall of his dungeon. Eyes down, his head shook. Although he wanted to cry – no tears fell. His reserve was empty, void of anything to expunge. Not only was it drained of tears but also his emotions. Stale, not sad, not angry, nor happy, he felt nothing … except resignation. No thoughts entered his mind. Blank, his brain found no plans of actions, no ideas of escape, nor any hope to try.

Why was she and that big guy waiting? To torture him? Ironically, it failed to add any anxiety or terror anymore. Resigned, Nathen had yielded any anticipation of escape or rescue, snuffing the subtle flames of a dying fire. Nobody could hear him, and nobody was coming to help him.

A flash of anger lit up like a malfunctioning firework spread, but it lasted not even a full second. He was free – and was almost able to get away. Although his headache dissipated, and a small amount of blood from the blow had dried on his left temple, he had not felt any effects of a head injury.

All he had to show for that hard work was sore muscles, joints, hands, and his scraped and bruised skin. His pain was worthless like a participation trophy. He understood why Mom and Dad never wanted him or his siblings to get one of those things. They, like his sore and injured body, made him feel cheated or short-changed, giving no value, nor fulfillment for all his dedication, discipline, and hard work.

Feeling his stomach vibrate with every heartbeat, he thought of one way out of the awaiting torture of unwanted surgery: wrapping his chain tightly around his neck to end his own life. Perhaps he could go out on his terms instead of those two psychopaths damaging him physically and psychologically for the remainder of his life. Taking a deep breath, he clasped a couple of chain links, wondering how to wrap them snugly enough to cut off his oxygen flow from his heart and lungs to his brain. He hesitated, wondering how painful and frightening it would be. Was it wrong to do this? Did he have enough courage and determination to follow through? What would his parents think when they found out he ended his own life? Would they be angry at him for giving up? What would Pastor Andrew think of him? Or his friends?

He glanced over at Eli's covered and severed head. The tattered covering still hid his face. It had started to really stink. Should he toss it into that hole he had been using as a latrine? Or would Mrs. Wilson, or his kids or grandkids not like that and be angry with him? Or would they even know?

All his plans: ending his life, getting rid of Eli's head had zero motivation, leaving behind a hollow shell full of nothing. No. It was full of apathy and defeat, as if a fire had combusted all thinking, innovation, and even hope for the future. This dungeon would be a tomb – or at least a torture chamber that rendered him into a freak.

Tired and weak, his eyelids fell – trying to drag him asleep. No. He wanted to stay awake. Nathen had drifted to sleep several times with hope of waking up in his room. Every time he woke up in this pit, it killed a little bit of hope until there was little to nothing was left – just like a bucket of water losing volume under a burning sun.

Although Elise always kept her distance from him, he hoped for a chance to get ahold of her and knock her out cold, find the key to the padlock, and run. He longed to turn the tables on her but knew he lacked the gumption to inflict such damage on her. Besides, he just wanted to get away.

His hands, having a mind of their own, clutched his chain, ready to pull it as tight as he could, and lock them in place. Or perhaps he could figure out a way to lock the links on each other to finish himself off. His fingers, knuckles, and wrists throbbed in pain. They strained during the climb. Losing agency, or rather power, his hands relaxed, falling on both sides of his body. However, right now, this seems best. He wanted to get this over with.

What were they waiting for?

Chapter 26

"Guys," said Justin as he guided Jason along, "hold up, will ya?"

Jeffrey turned to face his cousins. Even Gunner lagged behind. "I'm pretty sure I know where she is. It's a place where the whole family went camping two or three years ago."

"You can't be serious," quipped Jason. "If she's possessed, who knows what she's capable of? And Father Matthew said he can't help you."

"I gotta help her."

"Dude," interjected Gunner, "what's wrong with you? She's gone. She's stalking me – you know that."

"I understand why you're afraid, Gunner, but I gotta try."

"Besides," said Jason, "how are we going to get there? We can't drive."

"I've got my minibike," said Jeffrey as he continued his determined strides.

"And how are you going to get the kid AND your sister back to town on a fucking minibike?" said Justin. He finally stopped Jeffrey by blocking his path. "Think about it. Do you even have SOME sort of plan."

"Think, Jeffrey, think." said Jason. "You're letting your emotions get the best of you. Justin's right. You have no plan."

Frustrated, angry, he fell to the ground and sat on some grass near a sidewalk. "Shit!" he said as his head dropped. His blood had been simmering as all the stressors ate his soul, attacked him, weakening his spirit. "I can't take it. I can't take it." His angry words weren't able to vent his overwhelming stress. It felt like a bubbling cauldron of water that would not cool. "Damnit! Why am I the only one trying to keep what's left of my family together? Shit!" All the stress had worn him to nothing, and he had no idea where to send his anger.

Jason dropped and sat next to Jeffrey, then poked him with his elbow. "Okay. We understand. We want to help you, shithead."

The comment triggered a spark that lit an explosion of rage. "Stop calling me shithead!"

"Hey," Justin said quietly, "from us – 'shithead' is a compliment."

Gunner, who had already sat on the pavement with Jeffrey, hunched his shoulders and squinted his eyes. "Calling him a shithead is a compliment?"

Jason and Justin grinned. "It is for us," said Jason. "And I understand. Losing a twin is …" his voice faded a bit, "one of the hardest things I had to deal with."

Gunner glanced at Justin and Jason. "So, am I shithead, too?"

"No," quipped Justin, "you're still a dipshit."

Jason stood, as if he took command. "Let's try this. I'll ride with Jeffrey out to this place. Hopefully I can hear this demon at a distance. If so, we'll call or text you and drop a pin. Then you guys can come out on Gunner's minibike."

Gunner's mouth dropped open. "Me? Can't I just teach Justin how to drive a minibike?"

"This is why you're still a dipshit," said Justin. "Besides, you'll need a navigator to hold the phone, okay."

Gunner sighed. "Okay. But you won't let Elise get me, right?"

"We'll protect you," said Jason.

Gunner scoffed. "That's really comforting coming from a blind dude."

Jason slapped him. "Respect your elders, dipshit."

"How'd you do that?" asked Gunner.

Jason pointed at his ears. "I hear everything."

"Okay," said Jeffrey. "We have a plan. Let's go."

"We'll be at my house," said Gunner. "In my room!"

***

Jenny smiled as Freddy and Samson followed her and Janie through the house. Like shadows, they never let her and Janie out of their sight. Freddy seemed like the comforter, while Samson was akin to a guardian. Freddy's barks begged the girls to stop and pet him. Often, when they sat, he jumped up to sit next to them and snuggle, as if trying to help them through a difficult time. Samson liked attention but was quieter – keeping his growls and barks to a minimum. He didn't need to do those things like Freddy. They were saved for serious threats.

"Remember our dog, Buttercup?" The memories of their yellow lab shuffled through her mind, thinking of all the times Buttercup would nestle between Jenny and Janie, or find a ball to play "fetch" with, or finding their socks or gloves to chew.

Janie laughed through her nose. "Oh, I miss her so much. I remember when Mom and Dad brought Bobby home and Buttercup thought he was her baby. She sniffed him, licked him, and snuggled near him – and even growled at people who got near her baby."

Jenny flinched, recalling all the memories with Bobby: helping Mom feed him, changing diapers, rocking

173

him to sleep, and reading to him. Her heart flexed, as if in a fight or flight mode, ready to strike back. No. Janie was trying to help her.

Only to cover up her horrible mistake.

No, she's legitimately sorry.

No, she's not. She has you where she wants you so she can exploit you.

Janie clasped Jenny's shoulder. It felt cold, and Jenny wanted to retreat. As her eyes closed, she focused on her thoughts. *"I need to forgive her. I need to forgive her."*

"Are you okay?" asked Janie.

Jenny hoped her smile appeared genuine, although her breath signaled stress. "I'm …" she searched for the right words to say. "I'm okay … just scared." She hoped Janie wouldn't notice the smile that masked insecurity, embarrassment, and depression. Jenny did need help – but her stubborn pride kept her from trusting a sister who once killed …

"Hey," said Janie. "I can tell you're thinking. Tell me, please."

No. She would mention her resentment, hurt pride, and anger that remained for all these years. However, she had an inkling to say what was on her mind: *"Hello, my name is Jennifer Cook, you killed my brother. Prepare to die."* Unable to say it like Inigo Montoya, Jenny inhaled holding it back out of sheer desperation.

Janie (and Derek's) lawyer was working with the insurance company to get Jason's policy taken care of. Janie also knew people who could work with the hospital for all of Jeffrey's medical bills, and the lawyer fees. She had arranged a plan with her own family insurance to help pay for the rehab Jenny had to go through.

Why is it so hard to forgive? Why does she silently

resent her sister for trying to help? Jenny was the first born. She was the responsible one – not her. Her pride lost to reality. Janie was the one giving herself right now, and the one being responsible. "I hate you," her voice erupted quietly, "but it's not for getting Bobby killed." That was lie number one. She wiped a trickle that escaped her right eye. "You're doing so much for me, and I do appreciate it." A second lie. "I'm really worried about being separated from Jeffrey," she said – finally finding some truth.

Janie sat next to her. Although she reached out, Jenny retreated. "Stop lying, Sis." Janie pursed her lips.

Afraid, Jenny's eyes darted away.

"You're about to go to rehab – and if you can't be honest with me, how can you be honest with yourself? Those counselors and other alcoholics will see right through you. You confronted the demon in Jeffrey – but not the ones you're dealing with."

"Don't preach to me." Jenny stood, giving glimpses of her anger in her words. "I just hate feeling … out of control." Another lie dripped from her tongue. When did she get like this? Was she afraid of the truth about her own pride and anger? Did she cook up the falsehoods to alleviate her pain or hide it?

Jenny slightly recoiled from Janie's touch. It felt cold … or rather invasive. The touch of a relative she knew well for the first part of her life. They shared a bed. They told each other their deepest secrets … until Janie started drinking. Her weakness added to more and more bad choices and lies she never thought Janie would say to her … as well as Mom and Dad. Now the lies and frailty both sat before Jenny's feet.

The funeral was rainy, adding more to the misery of watching their … or rather Jenny's eleven-year-old brother buried. The baby of the family was gone, the Cook name ending at that moment in time. She finally blurted out a truth begging to be released. "I want to forgive you … but it's so hard." Unable to face her sister, Jenny's cheeks, eyes, and mouth all wrinkled.

Janie whispered, enunciating every word, and adding a second pause between each of them. "Imagine … trying … to … forgive … yourself. That was the hardest part for me."

The door opened, whisking Jenny and Janie away from their private world, as well as their dance around the truth. Beth walked in with some groceries. Jenny helped her with the bags, hoping to move away from the guilt and embarrassment she felt around her sister.

"Have either of you seen Gunner?" asked Beth.

"No. We haven't seen the boys since this morning after breakfast," said Janie. "I'm surprised they haven't returned for lunch."

Jenny texted her son. "Where are you boys?"

Within a minute, Jeffrey texted back. "Just left St. Patrick's." Another text soon followed. "We're going to Laurie's Diner for lunch."

Jenny texted back. "Is Gunner with you?"

"Yes."

Jenny relayed the news to Beth and Janie.

Beth sighed hard. "I'm so glad they got him out of his room. I need to get him into counseling. Of all the things in the world – being a mother is the hardest."

Jenny faltered at what she wanted to say, hoping it would not upset either sister or sister-in-law. "Uh, Beth … I'd rather Jeffrey stay with you and Gunner." She quickly turned to Janie. "That way you won't be overwhelmed, and Jeffrey can remain in his school." Jenny coughed, although it was more like a stifled laugh. "Of course, he'll have to repeat the ninth grade."

Beth and Janie nodded – until the dogs started whimpering. Having already walked Freddy and fed him, Jenny messaged Jeffrey. "After lunch, get back, and take care of Freddy." After a few seconds, she added another message. "And tell Jason and Justin they need to take care of Samson." Both texts got a "thumbs up" from Jeffrey.

***

Jason burped. Jeffrey burped louder and stretched it out for a few extra seconds. Gunner's burp, short and weak, did not impress anyone. They all "booed" his belch. Justin's burp exploded as the loudest and longest – declaring victory. The boys clapped, although a few customers at the diner seemed agitated.

"Okay," said Jeffrey. "We better get going."

"But our moms want us home," said Justin.

"Okay – you and Gunner wait at his house. If Aunt Beth or our moms show up, don't tell them where Jason and I are going. We'll text you if we find Elise and this kid."

"Then what?" asked Justin.

"Then get out there so we can get the demon out of her."

Jason shook his head. "No way, dipshit. You don't know how to do it. And I certainly don't. Neither do these guys. We need Father Matthew."

Jeffrey sighed hard. "Okay – so we'll go out to this place and see if they're where I think they are. Then text them, drop a pin, and they get Father Matthew."

"He's not coming, shithead. You heard him."

Jeffrey sighed. "I thought I could count on you guys." He turned to Gunner. "Come on, dude."

177

Eyes widened, Gunner shook his head. "No fucking way. If she's there, I'm heading in the other direction."

"Come on, dipshit," said Justin, "show some balls, will you. Or did she already cut them off."

Gunner pushed Justin in the chest. "Fuck you!"

Justin rushed towards him, grabbing Gunner by his collar.

"Cool it, shitheads!" Jason's voice took command as his cane went up – dividing Justin and Gunner.

"Yeah! You're mega annoying, dudes." Jeffrey scowled at them.

Jason took the lead again. "Okay – Jeffrey and I'll head to the location. If they're out there, we try to rescue the kid and get him out of there."

"Three on a minibike?" asked Gunner.

Jason's forehead wrinkled, indicating his mind processed the information they had. "Okay … if we find him, we'll text you for back up. Then Gunner can come out on his minibike and Justin can get Father Matthew and Sister Regina to drive out there and get Nathen and Elise."

"Oh, no," said Gunner. "No way. Justin can do it."

"I don't know how to drive a minibike," said Justin. "Mom let me bring my bicycle, so I can haul ass over to the parsonage and tell Father Matthew and Sister Regina where to go once you find him."

"Sounds good," said Jeffrey. He put on his helmet and a jean jacket for protection. Jason folded his cane, put it in his inside jacket pocket, and received help to get his helmet on. Jeffrey, about to kick-start his minibike, hesitated, feeling an old fear return. The memories of his possession burst forth like several bolts of lightning from an explosive thunderstorm.

"What is it?" asked Gunner.

Jeffrey leaned close to him. "Dude – I'm mega scared. I need prayers."

Gunner and Jeffrey's hands locked into a tight grip, then used their free hands to hit each other on the opposite shoulder. It was their private salute to each other. Jeffrey, along with his cousins, bowed their heads.

"God," said Gunner, "please don't let us fuck this up." He crossed himself.

"Amen," they said collectively.

Finding the added power he needed, Jeffrey kickstarted his minibike and sped east with Jason.

Chapter 27

Jason did not like the bumpy ride. His cousin, Jeffrey, had no problem with going fast over the paved roads, but they disappeared several miles back and now they bounced over an uneven, grassy and rocky terrain. Not only the noise from the bike grated on his nerves, but the tires and shock absorbers bouncing off the natural ground agitated his back, shoulders, and neck. It also agitated something else that needed immediate attention.

"Stop for a minute."

Jeffrey turned his head.

"I said stop, shithead!"

The motor silenced, but before the minibike stopped rolling, Jason swiveled off the seat, almost falling as he pivoted his body, took off his helmet and tried to unfold his cane as he sprinted a few feet.

"Wait, dude. Stop"

Jason had his cane unfolded, took three steps, and almost stumbled. Keeping his balance, his body came to an abrupt stop as his shoulder hit a tree. He dropped his cane but didn't care as he released the zipper on his jeans. He grunted, feeling the relief from releasing his urine. Jason's long sigh matched the steady, strong trickle of pee falling to the forest ground.

Jeffrey laughed subtly. "I guess I should go, too."

Jason heard another stream pound the forest dirt. "You better not be looking at my dick."

"You better not grab mine," countered Jeffrey.

"Shit! I hope I'm not pissing on my cane!" Jason bellowed, His laugh pushed through his belly and his chest – making the stream jump and wiggle. Both boys, unable to stop, kept laughing for over a minute, maybe two. At that point, their chuckling diminished with their streams. Jason sighed heavily. "Best piss ever!"

"Good news," said Jeffrey. "Your cane is dry!" he said - handing it to Jason. "Here," he took Jason's arm and gently pulled it a bit to the left. "Step back a bit and sit. There's a fallen log right under you."

"Thanks. I needed a break. My back is sore from all the bouncing. How much further away is this place?"

"I think about another five miles." Jeffrey, sitting next to Jason, sounded tired as well. "I remember Mom and Dad taking us there about three years ago for some camping. I remember mostly how to get there. Dad and I kept saying, 'Jason's after us!'"

"Me?"

"No," said Jeffrey. "Jason Voorhees from the Friday the 13th movies."

"You really need to get a life," said Jason. "Any cell reception out here?"

Jeffrey quickly filled the pause. "Only one bar - but I got two texts from Mom. She's mega pissed at me."

Jason tried to pull his phone from his back pocket. "Oh, fuck!"

"What?"

"I lost another cell phone. Shit!" He added a grunt, slapping his own head. "Aunt Janie's going to kill me. Those are specially made for the blind and they're expensive."

"Let me see if I can find it." Jeffrey wandered behind Jason, first to the left, then to the right. It sounded as if he moved towards the minibike.

"More good news!" Jeffrey sounded joyful. "I found it!"

The comfort Jason felt superseded the relief his bladder just had. "You just saved my life, dude." He felt more reassurance feeling the phone in his hand.

Having the face memorized, his fingers activated it and heard the artificial intelligence voice give a report. "Three messages from Aunt Janie. Two messages from Robyn."

Jason uttered "Aunt Janie."

"Message one delivered at 4:00 p.m. 'Where are you?' Message two delivered at 4:20 p.m. 'Get back to your Aunt Jenny's house now.' Message three delivered at 4:45 p.m. 'You two shitheads better answer me!'"

"Oh, Jesus," whispered Jason. "She's going to kill the both of us, either way. Come on, now. Where's this place? We gotta find it fast and get back."

"I'm not 100 percent sure if it's due east, or northeast from here. I wish I could remember it better."

"We better figure it out, soon. dipshit." Jason sighed, now angry at Jeffrey. He scoffed, waiting for him to figure it out. "What about Gunner? Do you think he'll come out here if we texted him?" asked Jason.

"Probably not."

"How do you put up with that weenie dipshit?"

"Shut up, dude," snapped Jeffrey. "He's MY cousin. He's always been like a little brother to me. I'm sure you feel the same way about Justin – even though he's a jerk."

"Hey – I'm sure he could kick your ass." Jason quieted. "He means a lot to me. He was there for me so much when my brother and parents died. He helped me adjust to being blind." He sighed. "I felt like ending my life, but Justin kept me going." A smile broadened. "And he found me that blind surfing school. I never thought I'd be able to surf ever again. He may be an asshole, but he's also been the best person to be my brother. I owe him a lot."

Jeffrey sighed. "Yeah. Gunner's like a kid brother. He's naïve and …"

"Dumb."

"He's not dumb." Jeffrey's blunt words pushed Jason back. "He's just desperate for people to like him. Elise kept taking advantage of him and pulling pranks like when she tried to shoot an apple off his head with a bow and arrow."

"Holy shit! Are you serious?"

"Yep. Dad stopped her." He giggled. "She thinks she's Wednesday Addams – although I compare her more to Lizzy Borden. Anyway, Elise acts like Wednesday with her dead, monotone voice, twisted sense of humor, and expressionless eyes."

"Sounds creepy." Jason faltered. "Are you sure you want to find her? Maybe it's the demon that makes her do that."

Jeffrey sounded on the verge of tears. "I have to find her. She's my twin. We've always been close. Sure – she can be mega annoying, but I could always talk to her. You know what that's like. You should understand."

Jason barely nodded, thinking of Jimmy once again.

"What do you miss about your twin?"

Smiling, Jason nodded harder. "Surfing. We'd do it for a couple of hours then we'd talk about our best accomplishments. We competed with grades, sports, and girls. 'Course, he was always better with the girls. I wanted to kill him one time. We were at an ice cream shop, and these two girls were flirting with us. We walked over and

Jimmy blurts out, 'Ladies, my twin and I were debating. He says you're virgins, but I say no. So, we're wondering who's right. And if my brother's right, maybe we go to the park and change that?' They threw their drinks on our faces. All while he's talking, I was so embarrassed and wanted to hide in a corner and die. After they threw their drinks on us, I wanted to kill him." Although he remembered the utter humiliation, he managed to crack a smile thinking of his brother.

"How old were you?" asked Jeffrey.

"Thirteen. What was really embarrassing was that they went to the same school we did – and their parents called our parents. Mom and Dad were so pissed. All three of us wanted to kill Jimmy."

Jeffrey let out a thoughtful grunt. "Sis liked to take pictures of me in embarrassing situations: dancing in my boxers while lip syncing, while singing in the shower – and on occasion she'd snap a photo of me naked. She threatened to send it to her friends – but I had to remind her she has no friends because all the girls at school think she's mega weird."

"And your dad died?" asked Jason. He sensed Jeffrey nodding.

"Yeah. Drunk driver hit him when his rig broke down. He was setting out road flares to warn other drivers."

"My dad was in a wreck," Jason said. "The whole family was in the car. I was the only survivor." He turned towards Jeffrey and sighed. "You and I got a lot in common."

They sat quietly for a few minutes while cicadas sang. Despite knowing he was in trouble, the noises and smells of nature relaxed him. Sometimes, Jason found the cicadas annoying, but the cadence and rhythm resembled a gentle song that offered peace. Their song ceased abruptly – leaving a dead silence. An owl hooted. Then another one further away. The cicada noise returned, but with a softer sound. The noise of the tree branches blowing in the wind withered, fading like a soft echo in a cave. Jason stood for a second, but a wave of dizziness made him stumble to the right, falling to his knees.

"Dude," said Jeffrey, "are you okay?"

Jason grunted as his cousin's voice now faded in soft echoes. Hearing his own heartbeat, his blood rushing through his veins, sleep tried to take him in an instant.

He flinched as a dying scream reverberated. Covering his ears did not help – although the shrill noise dissipated along with every other sound. Jeffrey tugged at his shoulders, but Jason could not hear him. The horrid noise ceased and suddenly, Jason heard a whisper.

"Son," said the faint voice, *"you're close. And there ain't much time left."*

"Eli," Jason thought, *"... is that you again?"*

"Yes. I'm sorry, but sometimes I scream rememberin' the pain she did to me."

"Where do we go?"

Eli's voice echoed, then faded. *"It's not far. Keep heading a bit more northeast. Hurry, or the beast will mutilate that boy."*

Jason saw it emerge in his mind: a dark, deranged shadow, holding a hatchet drove it into his head – or rather Eli's head. He screamed, trying to reach for the handle and remove it. Unable to find it, losing his balance, he fell, staring in the face of a hideous beast. It towered above Jason, spreading dark wings, growing talons, and a hideous face. An odious stench of rotting meat, salt, and spoiled eggs made him gag. It hissed like a snake, only it burst into an annoying sound that shoved a hot spike into his ears. Jason screamed at the sight and sound.

Everything disappeared. Back in total darkness, Jason found himself on the ground with Jeffrey trying to rouse him.

"Dude? Are you okay? What's happening?"

Jason turned to his knees, inhaling deeply to calm his nerves. An old prayer Father Nelson taught him came to mind. He recited it. Jeffrey joined him. After crossing himself, Jason stood with the aid of his cane and cousin. "Jeffrey," he said, "I heard him again."

"Who?"

"Eli. He said we don't have much time to save Nathen."

"Where are we supposed to go?"

"This way. This way. This way."

Jason's head turned sharply towards the faint voice.

"Follow me. Follow me. Follow me."

"Dude! What's going on?"

Jason pointed towards the whispers he heard, only to lose it to the cicadas. "Northeast," he said while pointing ahead. "We gotta follow the voice."

"What voice? This is mega weird."

Jeffrey led Jason back to the minibike. Within seconds, the two had on their helmets and the minibike sped into action.

Chapter 28

Elise

Ceding to Victor's presence, I descended the steps. My volition had weakened and collapsed. Victor's cold, strong presence radiated in surges, spreading from my heart and mind into every bone, muscle, and limb. His spite slithered in my belly like a snake and his hate wrapped around me like a heavy winter coat. Oddly, it carried its own painful cold, blotting out any warmth or light that tried to escape from the sun.

At the bottom, about 15 feet deep, I turned ninety degrees marching under orders. Victor forced every step, pivot, and neck movement. I stared at Nathen and didn't stare at him. Victor, though, gazed at him as my mind visualized faint images of an empty cage. Would he send me back inside and lock me up?

I hummed the Addams Family TV theme as I stepped closer to Nathen. My feet, no longer my feet, found no strength or resistance to fight this strong and enduring power that dug into every inch of my body. I did not want it, but its force, overwhelming me with great energy, squashed what was left of my own free will. Having no control, my spirit panicked, almost flailing for some control back. Impotent, with no volition, I realized Victor had rendered me a spectator.

Five more steps and my feet – or rather Victor's feet – reached the bottom. Adjusting both lamps, their light intensified to a much higher level. A hideous, unholy chorus subtly creeped through my mind, filling my ears with a chilling sound that left me terrified. Just like Nathen, I was trapped without any hope of escape.

I dropped to my knees to put the tray down, then sat on the last step. There were more berries, along with a smoked fish and some water, and even my last Snickers bar. Nathen eyed me nervously, then licked his lips. His hands, shaking, reached for his food but immediately recoiled as if afraid of touching forbidden fruit. "Go ahead," I whispered. "Eat up."

"What's wrong with your voice?" he whispered. "You sound … different."

I could hear it. Victor's voice led and mine trailed, but with only a lag of a second or two. Victor's voice surged, becoming louder. "There are no stones, and if there were, you couldn't turn them into bread."

"What was that? Nathen asked. His eyelids narrowed and his head leaned left. "Elise?" His voice resounded in long, turbulent echoes. An ominous sound spread, thickening at one end of the spectrum, and thinning in another.

"Elise," Nathen asked, "are you okay?"

Dizzy, tired, I forced my eyes wider to remain awake and balanced. My mind and essence fell as if descending a sleek, metal slide. Victor's cold presence pushed me deeper into darkness, and into his cage he made for me. Naked, my hands rubbed my arms to generate some warmth. Confused, I searched for where the source of dim luminescence came from. My face squinted, trying to purge an awful flavor that sickened my tongue and stomach. Nauseated, my throat and chest heaved, but nothing regurgitated. "Victor!" I screamed. "I don't like this. Let me out!" Although I covered my mouth and noise, a horrid stench of horse shit mixed with rotten eggs and spoiled cheese choked me. Victor's hate spewed like a volcano - carrying an explosive sound only I could hear. Strangely, it almost knocked me off my feet. Feeling his disdain, spite, and cruelty, I knew this was going way too far.

Victor and I were one. Our identities mixed back and forth, although his will had a much stronger presence. Pushing my personality, and identity aside, he replaced it with an oppressive dread, and vile hatred. Not liking this, I pushed back – however it was like trying to push back heavy amounts of water with my hands. His presence drowned me.

"Victor, please! You're scaring me. I don't want to do this anymore. Don't hurt him. Don't make me hurt him."

"You're mine, now, Beautiful."

A giant wind lifted me as the cage disappeared. My … spirit whisked fast, feeling as if I shot up thousands of feet within a matter of seconds. Some light appeared, but it remained weak and dim. Only able to watch, I saw Nathen scarfing his food. Hearing him grunt with every bite, I tried to tell him to stop eating it, but Victor's scaly, clawed hand seized my throat, preventing me from talking.

Nathen's head wobbled as his eyes batted a few times. He moaned and grunted, as if trying to wake himself up. Grunting, he tried to stand but fell face down on the floor. Victor sneered and almost laughed as he tried to stand up.

"What'd … what'd you …" his voice echoed as if in a cave, "do to … me?" Nathen, weakened, teetering, tried to rise to his knees, but he dropped again and rolled on his back. He sighed, let out a long grunt, and passed out.

"Victor, we shouldn't do this. I don't like it! I think you should leave."

I tried to make my voice stronger, but it faltered as if choking on a drink. My soul and identity tried to cough out Victor's frighteningly cold essence, but it spilled into my lungs, filling every part of my spirit. Having no control, I panicked, as if flailing my arms against a strong ocean current.

Our minds intermingled, filled with doubt, anger, fear, and confusion. Who was this with me? Any memories of my family had vanished. I had a mother – but who was she? I had a dorky brother – but what was his name? Where am I? What's my name? Who was this with me?

"Who are you?"

"I am you."

"And who are we?"

"Victoria."

"Who are we?"

"Victoria."

Noticing a boy lying on the ground, I wondered who he was. Part of me felt like I knew him, yet I didn't know him. Still, I knew what I had to do and picked up his naked body.

Chapter 29

Jason and Jeffrey stood about 300 yards from the old structures. The cabin to the left had faced more decay over time: rotting wood, sagging walls, a partially missing roof. The barn seemed much intact with less deformities and better structure. The wood also seemed much thicker and stronger. They both rested at the bottom of a ravine where a large stream cut through between some rocks and near the trees. Looking over his shoulder, Jeffrey noticed the sun hovering just above the tall trees behind him. Soon, they'd lose a significant amount of light.

Jeffrey gasped looking at the grade in front of them. "This is pretty steep," Jeffrey said as he scanned every direction. "Probably 30 degrees or so - so don't move. I'll help you." Taking the inside of Jason's arm, Jeffrey took small steps to make sure neither of them fell down the sloped field.

"Wait," said Jeffrey as they reached the bottom. "Let me check something." Dropping to a knee, he felt the grass, noticing a slight impression in the soil. It resembled a hiker's shoe – although it seemed to be an adult's size. The toe section slipped forward – and just before it was a rock that looked as if a footstep displaced it. Looking forward, he noticed the pair of tracks heading towards the barn. "This is the place, and someone's been here." Hearing the stream, his head turned north, focusing on the trees that surrounded the small waterway.

Feeling slightly cooler, Jeffrey stared at the large barn

that loomed over them. A few rays of sunlight tried to bring it some life, but the trees above the grade provided a good block

Leading Jason by tugging at his inner arm, the two reached the bottom of the small glade.

Jason

"Wait, wait, wait," Jason whispered, "let me think." Taking a deep breath, he held it and focused on his heartbeat. Feeling the vessels compress in his limbs, chest, and his ears, his mind stretched. He heard the stream, the wind rustling through the leaves, a few small birds and … and the fast steps of some nearby rabbits. Aware, his mind reached out.

"Eli. Are you there?" Nothing. Focusing on his thoughts, Jason tried to find the scoutmaster again. *"Eli. We need your help. Is this the place?"*

Jason stopped thinking, desperately reaching out more with his ears as well as his mind. He kept anticipating an answer … but heavy silence remained.

"What's …"

Jason shushed Jeffrey. His mind focused again, spreading deeper and farther out. *"Eli … please? Help us."*

"He's here," the weak voice said. *"Hurry. That horrible thing has the girl and is going to …"*

Jason flinched as a loud wail exploded in his ears, shooting through his mind, and spreading through his body. His arms and legs shook as a fiery sensation spread through his entire being. Jason covered his ears, but the noise penetrated deeply, making him shake. A horrible, hopeless dread followed, leaving behind a despair that robbed all hope and faith. He wept as the sensation refused to budge, adding to his anxiety. A cold, inhuman, clawed hand slapped his left cheek, leaving behind a stinging blow. It burned, and Jason tasted blood where he bit his tongue.

"Jason!" yelled Jeffrey. "What's happening? Are you okay?" Jeffrey gasped after turning Jason's head. "Holy shit, dude! It looks like something … clawed you."

"Yeah," Jason managed to say between grunts, "I know. I can feel it and it burns and stings like a sonofabitch." Still shaking, he spit out a little blood. "It's here. It's got her – and it's going to hurt Nathen."

Jason stopped himself from holding his wounds, knowing the touch would add to the stinging and numbing pain on his cheek - spreading to his ear and scalp. His head thudded, keeping in time with his heartbeat. "It fucking hurts! We need help. Tell me we have cell reception down here."

"Shit," said Jeffrey. "We don't. We'll try to climb … no wait! I got one bar."

"Text Justin and Gunner. Tell them to get Father Matthew."

"He won't come! I know the sacrament. I can do it."

"Are you fucking crazy or just plain stupid?" Jason said amidst his swelling pain. He grunted a couple more times, unable to alleviate the throbbing and stinging pain. He heard the text send noise. "Tell me it went through."

"It looks like it. I also dropped a pin of our location." He inhaled deeply. "I'm going in." His voice trailed, moving away from Jason.

Jason rolled on his knees. "Jeffrey! Don't! You'll get the both of us killed!" Jason heard Jeffrey's strides crushing the twigs. "Jeffrey!" he whispered loudly, "don't go in there!"

Justin

Justin heard his phone vibrate. He glanced at the text:

"Get your asses back to your Aunt Jenny's house NOW!"

Worried, he widened his eyes and cleared his throat. "Our moms are getting really pissed."

Gunner's phone vibrated. "My mom's asking where we are, too. I better …"

"Don't answer it. Don't answer it."

Gunner sighed as his blue eyes showed confusion, fear, and desperation. "But she's … she's my …"

"Don't answer it, dipshit! Jesus – don't you have any balls? Or did your cousin psychically cut them off?" Justin took the phone as Gunner was about to use his thumb. "If we wanna save this kid's life … or his balls … we gotta be determined." Justin's head snapped. "Wait - did she want to cut off your balls AND your dick?"

"Does it fucking matter?"

Justin, clutching his own crotch, cringed heavily. "If you wanna pee, yes!"

A new text announced its presence on Justin and Gunner's phones. Both looked at the message, accompanied with a dropped pin. The message seemed to flash like a neon sign: "We found him. Get out here as fast as you can!"

"Great," said Justin. "You head out to the dropped pin on your minibike; I'll go get Father Matthew and we can trace it on my phone's pin."

Gunner, wide-eyed, shook, gasped, and stammered as he tried to talk. "No way. No way. I don't wanna go out there. I can't! She'll get me. She'll get me. You ride out there and I'll get Father Matthew and Sister Regina."

"I don't know how to drive a minibike." Shaking, Justin closed his eyes and took some deep breaths. "Gunner – I'm scared shitless, too – but we have to work together. My bicycle is here - so let me get Father

Matthew."

Gunner, almost crying now stood. Shaking his head, his chest heaving short breaths, he stammered. "I can't. I can't. Please don't."

Justin's voice exploded. "Go!

Gunner

His eyes scanned the dim yet not yet darkened eastern sky. Still, he'd need the headlight on as well as the helmet with side lights on it. Putting his phone on a mount, he activated the map app. Ready, he stood and put his foot on the starter … no he wasn't ready. He hesitated as fear tried to surge through his body again, carrying an ominous dread. His fingers and toes shook, and his jaw quivered. The cold terror latched tightly to his stomach, trying to keep him still. Closing his eyes, he sighed deeply. *"You can do this. You can do this. You can do this!"* His foot dropped on the starter, signaling the engine to come alive. It roared like a lion, probably making up for Gunner's cowardly heart. Taking some of its energy and strength, Gunner sped up and quickly got into high gear, breaking free of his reticence. One thought kept going through his head. *"I must be fucking crazy."*

Justin

Justin pedaled fast. Being a competitive bicyclist, he knew the proper cadence, how to use gears to get up hills, and swerve his bike from side to side. He was glad mom let him bring it with them to Newcastle. Just like his competitions, his energy gained, grew, and circled his heart. As a master, he used this force numerous times to maintain his drive and focus. He found it strange that when younger, he imagined his bike as a motorcycle with a viciously loud engine. If it existed, the noise would make him stronger, faster, and hurl him closer to being a man –

not just a boy with a vivid imagination.

Now, he only heard the cadence of his pedaling, the tires pounding on the pavement, the clicking of the gears, and the racing of his heart. For a second, he wished he was in his biking gear, with his clip shoes to hasten his speed. Doing this in his street clothes was a little encumbering – but he had no time to change.

Uphill towards Saint Patrick's Catholic Church, he flew through lights and shadows on the road. The horizon seemed to call the sun which heeded the command, leaving behind a brilliant orange light on the underside of the clouds.

Justin didn't bother to park the bike upright and tether it to something. He rushed to the parsonage. Hopefully, the priest was home. "Father Matthew!" he yelled while pounding on the door. "Father Matthew. We need your help."

Somehow, he remembered to ring the doorbell instead, but by then, the porch light ignited, and the door opened. "Who is this?"

Startled by the priest's irked voice and surprised to see him dressed in jeans and a Notre Dame T-shirt, Justin stepped back. He almost didn't recognize Sister Regina who wore sandals, khaki shorts and a King's College T-Shirt. "Father, Sister – it's me, Justin. We need your help. Jason and Jeffrey …"

"Calm down, please. Slow down and explain things to me."

His breaths, rapid and hurting, raged, not allowing him to find any of the peace the elder priest and nun possessed. Tears lifted in his eyes. Unable to speak, he felt like a little child, confused and frightened of the world. Sister Regina put one arm across his back and touched his shoulder.

"Shh. Shh. Justin," she whispered, "it's alright. It's alright." She walked him indoors to a living room full of light. "Just calm down, honey. We're here for you. Take some deep breaths, hold them, and let them out slowly. Just calm down." Her voice had a moderate pitch which was neither overly feminine, nor overly masculine. Guiding him to his couch, she lowered Justin to sit down and gently rubbed his back.

Taking in a few deep breaths, Justin's mind slowed from a whirlwind to a strong breeze, then to a peaceful, gentle wind. "Okay," he said repeatedly, "I'm sorry. But … Jason and Jeffrey, they found Elise and Nathen. I know where they are because they dropped a pin in their text."

Father Matthew's eyes flinched – as if overwhelmed by a bright light, or rather by regret and fear. He sighed deeply. "Justin, I don't have permission to perform an exorcism."

"Shit," Justin shouted as he stood, "we're not asking for an exorcism – just help. I mean, what good's a prayer if you don't back it up with some action?"

"Father," Sister Regina interrupted, "boys from your flock need you. I know you're scared, but we must do something."

"Dealing with demons is very difficult. It's not like performing a funeral, a marriage or baptism. I haven't fasted, I haven't prayed, I haven't taken the Eucharist, gone through liturgies – and I'm not qualified to do this on my own!"

Justin and Regina both jerked back at Father Matthew's anger.

"I don't have a Jesuit to guide me," his voice shook, " – and I've only assisted in three Exorcisms my entire life. I'm not ready!"

Justin exploded "Luke Skywalker wasn't ready when he faced Vader!"

Father Matthew scoffed. "I can't believe you just compared battling demonic forces with an exorcism to the fictional force of Star Wars." He shook his head. "Shit."

Justin, shocked by Father Matthew's profanity, started to talk – but Sister Regina interrupted. "Father, think of this: first of all, you were given permission to exorcise this demon 20 years ago. On that – nothing has changed. You still have that permission. Second, do you want Jeffrey and Jason and this other boy to face the same fate as Matteo and Luca? Please don't be blind to what you need to do."

Chapter 30

Nathen's eyes blurred. Flapping his eyelids, his vision cleared. He flinched but could not move. Feeling his heart race at full speed, he breathed heavily through his nostrils. A piece of cloth was in his mouth, and a bandanna had been wrapped around his lips. He tried pulling on some straps that immobilized him on some sort of board. His eyes clenched tight, sweat pulsated through his skin, and sobs made his chest heave. Trying to flail his arm and legs did no good. He was totally trapped and helpless.

His eyes pivoted left. The shadow had long arms, a huge head cloaked by darkness. It stepped into light, and he saw her! Elise. Her hand touched his shoulder – but it did not feel like a hand. Cold, scaley, and dry, it disgusted him. The horrid stench of salt and chlorine almost made him gag. Her eyes, snakelike, had a yellow, ominous glow. Her teeth appeared sharpened.

Nathen's mind rushed into a frenzy as she revealed her scalpels. The serrated one gleamed in a tiny bit of light, adding more panic to every inch of his body. The cleaner one did not appear any better. Then, he saw her syringe with a long needle. Cold terror froze his insides into tiny ice crystals that rolled up into a huge ball. He cried as the block of ice grew larger and larger in his center, spreading to every part of his body.

"I have two of these," she said, "just in case you wake up."

Her voice was bizarre. Aside from the sibilance, it

sounded as if something echoed just under her voice – like a moderate bass voice just underneath a soprano setting. Her hand now petted his head and caressed his face. He felt disgusted and petrified. Desperately, he pulled on some straps but found zero leverage. His heart raced to a panic, feeling as if it would rupture. Pure fear ran with his hot blood, causing him to sweat profusely. This was like something from the Holocaust! He grunted, squirmed, but aside from exhaustion, his muscles, joints, and limbs still suffered from straining during his almost successful escape.

"It'll be alright," she said. "Trust me. You'll wake up a different person."

The jab came first in his thigh. A burning sensation pushed through, finding its way into his vessels that contracted with every heartbeat, spreading the medicine around in his system. His mind sank deeper into an abyss, but not without a desperate cry for help from Mom and Dad. Realizing they would not come, or even hear his plea in the psychic realm, his hope sank deeper into his black sleep.

Jeffrey

Jeffrey eyed both syringes, hoping to get his hand on one of them and use it on Elise. They needed to get her back to St. Patrick's so Father Matthew could help. Or maybe Gunner and Justin would convince him to come. Jeffrey stealthily moved into her underground lair, trying not to make a sound. Dim lighting did not help as steps hid in shadows. He had trouble paying attention to both Elise and the stairs.

She turned around to face him. Her eyes flared with a yellowish glow, her skin blistered, dried, and cracked. Her wail terrified him, finding its way to his bone, muscle, and skin – even chilling him to his soul. A chaotic and cold panic paralyzed him in thought and action. Unable to remember the prayer of exorcism, his arms and legs froze when seeing her. He could only scream and fall back backwards.

A chain hovered above him and wrapped around his neck, constricting his throat. Frenzied, trying to find a breath, Jeffrey tried to loosen its links, but an invisible weight yanked him down several steps. He coughed heavily as he hit the ground. His throat was tightened under the strain of the chain, not only cutting off his air but also hurting his neck and skin. They loosened a bit, and he could breathe.

Catching sight of Jason, he yelled. "Jason! There's another syringe. It'll knock her out!"

Jason swung his cane back and forth, likely to keep Elise at bay.

Elise's deep cackle sounded amused as Jason tried to wallop her with his cane.

"Several more steps in front of you!" yelled Jeffrey.

Elise jumped, flipped upside-down, and planted her feet on the ceiling as Jason moved forward. She grabbed the end of his cane and yanked him down to the bottom. Coughing, he rolled closer to Jeffrey who ran up the steps, trying to seize the other syringe without jabbing his own hand and putting himself to sleep. Elise, still having Jason's cane, hit Jeffrey's nose. It swelled and spilt blood as he fell back to the ground again.

He frantically scanned for the syringe, having trouble finding it in such dim lighting. There it was! Before he could reach it, the chain became taut in mid-air, and one end wrapped around his wrists while the other end wrapped around Jason's wrists. The chains pulled them back across the ground and into a wall - knocking the air out of their lungs. Jason and Jeffrey coughed to retrieve their breaths. Jeffrey looked up to his right and saw Elise move back to her operating table. His eyes caught sight of the syringe on the ground just several feet in front of him. His mind scrambled, trying to find a way to free himself and jab Elise with it.

Gunner

Gunner brought his minibike to a halt next to Jeffrey's. He put his kickstand down and killed the motor. Keeping his headlight on, he saw the old cabin and barn amidst some trees. He glanced at his phone, seeing a text from Justin: "On our way!" Another text from Jeffrey was underneath. "We're going in."

Swiveling his headlight back and forth, he noticed a trail of crushed grass leading to the entrance. Keeping his helmet lights on, he hoped they would give enough illumination to help him find Jeffrey and Jason. He rushed, tripping twice on either uneven ground or large sticks. Regaining his balance, Gunner tried to calm down as he approached the barn entrance. He backpedaled, wondering if Elise waited inside to nab him, knock him out, and carry out her twisted scheme on him. Reality and fear met, causing his chest to heave rapidly. Sweat seeped through his skin like geysers – and he almost peed himself. His heart raced so fast, he worried it might rupture like a grenade. Taking one deep hard breath, he let it out slowly. He took another one, doing the same thing.

Something inside cajoled him to act. His cousins were inside, and they desperately needed help. Yet it was Elise - a girl who had threatened him so many times and almost succeeded in castrating him. Almost crying, he took one last breath and let it out slowly. *I can do this. I can do this,* he kept thinking to himself. Gunner pushed forward quietly.

His helmet's ambient light barely illuminated the barn. He saw a table full of journals, tools, and bottles of … something. Medicine? Potions? Not sure, Gunner noticed camping equipment near the table: a sleeping bag, survival gear, and a lantern. In front of him, he noticed a rope and pulley that hoisted a thick wooden door. Light tried to escape, but it was buried inside a cellar. He heard movement, shuffling, and a slight laugh.

Wait! What was that? As he moved closer to the opening, he noticed something on the floor. As he got closer, he noticed its size, and form: Those were legs, arms, a torso and … Gunner's shock erupted so fast his heart almost leapt from his chest. Seeing a decapitated man, a surge of terror froze his arms, legs, and joints. "Shit!" he whispered while scurrying quietly across the floor to the opening. His breaths shook through his nose and mouth while his hands and fingers tremored violently as adrenaline rushed through his blood. Strangely, the rush shocked him, causing racing winds to become thicker as they swirled within his mind. Finding no exit, his fear built, becoming thicker, stronger, and heavier, weighing him down and hindering his progress. *Come on. Come on. You can do this. You can do this. Jeffrey and Jason are counting on you.*

"Sis!"

That was Jeffrey's voice! Taking off his helmet, Gunner kept quiet as he scooted closer to the opening.

"I know you're in there," continued Jeffrey. "Fight it. Please! You don't wanna do this."

"It's taken her over and it's not going to stop." Jason's voice cracked with heavy fear. "Oh, shit! What if she castrates us next?"

Gunner, trying not to attract attention, barely poked his head through the opening. Elise was several steps down on a landing, next to a table with … *"Oh, my God"* thought Gunner. *"She's tied that missing kid to a table like she did with me!"* Retracting his head, Gunner felt all his terror return. Panic triggered tiny huffs through his lips and nose again. The dread thickened heavily, almost drowning him in terror. Icy pin pricks froze not only his hands, feet, and limbs, but also his mind. Sucking in a huge, quiet breath, he let it out silently, then poked his head down again.

Looking further down towards the bottom, he saw Jeffrey and Jason. A chain had wrapped around their wrists and had hoisted their hands above their heads. Making eye contact with Jeffrey, he suddenly felt a psychic connection. Jeffrey pointed to something on the ground. Gunner couldn't see it but knew it was something he needed to get. Something else caught Gunner's attention. It lay on the landing about ten stairs down: Jason's cane. A weapon … if only he could get to it.

Metal clinked together, sounding as if Elise sharpened her blades. She was going to castrate whoever she had on that table. When she's done with that kid, Gunner knew he'd be next. His terror returned, causing his internal organs to shake. Now stuck in a perpetual state of indecision, he didn't know what to do. Instinct told him to turn and run as fast as he could, however, a tiny spark of loyalty and duty remained. Taking a few deep breaths, panic gave way to thought, and urgency pushed horror aside, goading Gunner to barely poke his head in again. Seeing Jeffrey move his lips, Gunner read them easily.

"HURRY."

Although unsure, frightened, Gunner nodded. He worried Elise could hear his erratic heartbeat and the blood rushing through his arteries and veins. He doubted it for a second but remembered she had a demon, and he did not know how well they could hear. He lifted his foot quietly, then placed it gently on the next stair. His right foot joined his left foot. His heart tightened. Taut, it refused to relax. Gunner took a quiet breath and went down another step.

His eyes shifted back and forth between Jason's cane and Elise. She looked taller, more muscular – and her head was deformed. From behind, he noticed her arms were certainly longer as if they had grown. Her ears, now deformed, spread wider. Her laugh changed, becoming lower in pitch, and sounding more sinister. Her legs grew, and deformed knees stretched awkwardly.

Third step, fourth step, stop, look at the cane, glance at Elise. Fifth step, sixth step, stop, look at the cane, glance at Elise. A frozen heart and silent breath cooperated, however, Gunner worried tiniest sound would have Elise looking back. Seventh step, eighth step, stop, look at the cane, then Elise. The next board barely moaned as he fully planted his weight on it.

Elise turned. Her large and enraged demonic eyes widened as her wicked smile stretched from ear to ear - revealing her sharp, jagged, teeth. The rancid smell from her breath sickened him - almost causing him to vomit. Paralyzing shock spread through his mind, blocking any sane thoughts or actions.

"Gunner!" Her low, scratchy voice sounded happy. "It's so good to see you!"

He jumped down two steps as she hurled herself at him. Falling to his knees and then to his stomach, she missed. Grabbing the cane, Gunner stood fast and swung it at her.

She dodged his blow, jumping up and flipping upside-down, and planting her feet on the ceiling boards. She grabbed the cane, and her uncanny strength jerked Gunner to his right. He partially landed on the table, rolled off the boy, dropped to the lower five steps and fell to the bottom with Jeffrey and Jason.

Elise must have lost her concentration as the chain fell limp. Freed, Jason and Jeffrey rushed in a frenzied panic. "Get the syringe," yelled Jeffrey.

Gunner, although sore, had to get up and defend himself. He looked for the syringe Jeffrey mentioned. Catching a glimpse, he reached for it, but Jason kicked Gunner's hand while scrambling away. Ignoring the pain and lurching forward, Gunner tried to seize it again. Panicked, his fingers missed, pushing it closer to Jason. "Jason!" yelled Gunner. "The syringe! It's in front of you!"

Elise had a scalpel in her hand. She swung at her brother but missed. Another swing jabbed Jeffrey in the arm. He pushed her away after another stab sliced his shoulder. Jeffrey's screams hurt Gunner's ears. Seeing her arm rear back to deliver a massive blow, Gunner tried to push her away, missed, and landed on top of Jeffrey.

The blade sank and sliced deep into Gunner's torso. The agonizing pain spread through his chest, causing him to flinch. She yanked it out, pulling flesh and blood with it, splattering on Jeffrey's face as well as her own. Jabbing it a second time sent a huge wave of pain deeper and wider in Gunner's chest. Again, he spasmed and screamed as more blood sprayed on their faces, drenched their clothes - and stained the nearby walls. Gunner coughed up some blood. Frantic, he could not think - even more so when she pulled it out again - causing his body to jerk again and flay more blood. Gunner tried to beg her to stop, but his voice stammered as a menacing terror swirled violently in his mind. His arms flailed to stop her, but in a panic, he couldn't stop her continual stabs into his pectoral, stomach, and shoulder muscles. Frenzied, horrified, he choked on his blood, phlegm, and other bodily fluids. The pain from multiple stabs swelled to such levels he could not comprehend - adding to a heavy dread that pushed on him like heavy weights. Every cough and breath added to the swelling pain.

"I hate you!" Elise kept yelling at Gunner. "I hate you! I hate you!"

Gunner had given up trying to block her blows with his arms - mostly because they stopped working. Feeling his own blood retreat to his heart, he lost sensation in his hands and feet. Terrified, Gunner tried to talk, but the pain and shock overwhelmed him. His muffled screams and coughs ejected more blood through his mouth. Tasting it, his frenzy wanted to cover his wounds with his hands and scoop the blood back into his body, but he forgot his limbs did not work anymore. The blood that provided life kept oozing, with no end in sight, covering his hands, clothes, and chest - and splattered across his and Jeffrey's faces. Even Elise was unrecognizable.

"I hate you." Elise let loose a stab with every syllable while repeating her hatred for Gunner. Elise froze, then fell out cold. Jason pulled the syringe out of her back and tossed it aside.

Gunner's kidneys spasmed and he peed himself. His breaths raged, along with violent coughs that had him vomiting both the contents of his stomach as well as more blood from his veins. His favorite shirt was ruined - but that thought faded as waves of pain circled his head, chest, stomach, and back. He tried to inhale, but the excruciating pain dug deeper with every breath. A chilling silence signaled his definite fate.

"Gunner, Gunner … please don't die." Jeffrey's voice strained as his tears tried and failed to clean the blood off his face. "You'll be okay," he said while holding Gunner's head up. "I promise you'll be okay. Just don't die. Don't die - please!"

Gunner wanted to reach up and grab Jeffrey's arm or hug him, but his arms and legs no longer worked as his life seeped from his arteries, veins, organs, and mind. His vision blurred at the periphery, and he felt cold. Resigned, defeated, he cried. Struggling for breath, he mustered up just enough strength. "Dude … I'm not … going … to make it." A stabbing pain exploded through his chest, spreading like an inferno – making it harder to breathe and speak. "Shit," he bellowed between grunts, "this … really … hurts."

Just arriving, Sister Regina and Justin appeared in Gunner's misting vision. Images faded on the far edges, succumbing to a blackness that crept closer. Gunner felt their warm touch for a brief second, but their hands were too weak and impotent to provide any life or help.

"Gunner," Justin whispered, "… stay with us. You're going to be alright. We're gonna getcha help. Please, hang on."

Gunner's emotions retreated, leaving behind no anger or fear. "Can't," Gunner struggled to speak as it hurt to say every word. "Can't last." He even struggled to grunt and cough - and he couldn't even reach up and touch Sister Regina. She held his other hand, although he was unsure if he could feel it. She prayed in Latin while his life drifted further down, as if sinking into a dark, freezing ocean.

Feeling further away, he cried. "I'm … so … scared. I don't … wanna die." He whimpered as pain flared like a fire finding oxygen.

What was going to happen? Noises and voices faded, and images bent and ebbed as darkness spread across his eyes from the outside in. Blackness eddied like water down a drain. Unable to feel anything, Gunner sensed his soul desperately clinging to something in his body … maybe his stomach or heart? He knew his spirit couldn't hold on much longer, but it did not scream or beg for more life. It waited for the right moment to abandon its Earthly vessel before jumping into its afterlife. While he was scared, his soul wasn't – as if ready to embrace what was coming. Still, he panicked, wondering what would happen when his spirit deserted his body. Will he see Jesus, or will everything go dark? Right now, memories flashed in fast motion. After a grunt, and a cough, he felt his heartbeat weaken.

Jeffrey still cradled Gunner's head, bawling incessantly. "Gunner, please don't die. What am I gonna do without you?"

"You … you … got other cousins." Knowing he had little time, Gunner mustered a bit of strength for a whisper. "Jeffrey … I'm going … to miss you … so much. Tell Mom I love her." The last image of Jeffrey froze in his mind as his vision dissolved into blackness. His heart thumped one more time, as his last breath exited his body. His soul let go and drifted away…

Chapter 31

Father Matthew crossed himself, then Gunner. "I commend you, my dear brother, to Almighty God, and entrust you to your Creator. May you return to him who formed you from the dust of the earth. May Holy Mother Mary, the angels, and all the saints come to meet you as you go forth from this life. May Christ who was crucified for you bring you freedom and peace."

The solemn silence hypnotized the group of mourners. Jeffrey felt part of himself die in his belly. He could not describe the hurt – although it felt similar to when Dad died. Strangely, he didn't cry but just felt a cold and empty numbness spread, cooling the adrenaline that rushed hot through his blood a few moments ago.

"Boys," said Sister Regina, "we need to get this other boy to the hospital."

"And we need to get Elise to the Church," said Father Matthew.

"What about Gunner's body," mumbled Jeffrey. "We can't just leave him."

"There's not enough room in the van," said Sister Regina.

"There will be if I ride my bike back."

Justin put his arm around Jeffrey. "Are you okay to ride?"

Barely nodding, Jeffrey mumbled. "Yeah."

"Somebody get the chain," said Jason, "and find the lock. We're gonna need it to restrain his sister if she wakes up."

Justin found it, as well as the padlock with the key in it. Jeffrey, still shocked, barely went through the motions as they wrapped one end of the chain around her ankles, and the other end around her wrists. They put the locks through the chain links around her limbs.

Father Matthew and Jason, although strong, could only help so much until they got to the stairs. Justin and Jeffrey took Nathen up first. Jeffrey almost heaved from the boy's odor. He looked emaciated, covered in dirt and soot. Bruises and scrapes were all over his body, and blood stained his long hair and scalp. Once they had him in the van, Jeffrey returned to the basement to help. He hesitated helping Elise, so he let Justin and Sister Regina pull her up. Jason helped Jeffrey take Gunner, but they had to stop at the stairs and wait for Justin for the final haul.

"I vote to leave the headless dude behind," said Justin as they passed by the body.

The doors to the van slammed shut once Jason, Justin, Sister Regina and Father Matthew got Nathen, Elise, and Gunner's body into the van. "I call 'shotgun'" quipped Justin. "I swear being in the back will mega freak me out!"

Jeffrey ran to the other side of the barn, up the slope, put on his helmet, and kick started the engine. It awakened and its eye lit up the area in front of him. He zipped around the barn and followed the van. On natural terrain, they had to take it slow at first, but once it found the road, both vehicles sped up.

It seemed something drained from Jeffrey's body and spirit as he followed the van. No thoughts ran through his mind as they traversed the lonely, dark roads. They were unfamiliar, spooky, winding, and confusing – just like his life had been lately. Mom's about to go to rehab, and he'll be living with Aunt Beth and … No – he won't be living with Gunner. A couple of tears obscured his vision. He slowed, reached up behind his face shield and slid the tears away with his finger. Would Aunt Beth still take Jeffrey? Would she be angry at him, Elise, and Mom? Would that be the end of their relationship?

Maybe Gunner will return to life in the van, and they'll be reunited at the hospital, hugging each other, hanging out and watching horror movies together again. Maybe Father Matthew could be like Jesus and touch Gunner to bring him back to life again. Or perhaps a random miracle would resurrect him. He knew all the thoughts were wishful thinking that were snapped away from reality's hard crushing presence.

Riding subconsciously, it seemed his minibike did the thinking as to how fast to go, when to lean to the side, speed up, and slow down. The present moment, ever changing, seemed frozen as he pursued the van. Every mile was a minute – and every minute seemed longer. He gripped the handlebars tighter, to keep his hands from shaking and keep him grounded in reality instead of lost thought.

"Sorry, but I was lost in thought since it's unfamiliar territory for me."

Usually, Jeffrey smiled at Gunner's verbal mannerisms – which he referred to as Gunner-isms. More of them rushed through his head.

"I was having a great day until my alarm went off."

"Now for that nap I've been daydreaming about."

"Don't play dumb with me - I'm better at it than you!"

The Gunner-isms faded as the night lit up when approaching the hospital. It flashed like a beacon of hope but faded as Jeffrey looked at it. What? It took 30 minutes to get there. It seemed like only five or ten minutes.

A security guard tried to dissuade them from parking in ambulance pickup and drop off, but he conceded seeing Gunner's mangled and bloodied body as well as Nathen's condition. "This is the missing boy," said Justin. "We found him. He needs help."

Jason and Justin went inside while Sister Regina closed the van door, got back in and raced to the church as Jeffrey followed. Once there, she and Jeffrey took Elise inside. Thankfully, the security guard didn't see her. Inside the Church, the chains were removed and Jeffrey and Sister Regina used ropes to secure her ankles to the chair legs and her wrists to the arm rest handles. They finished by tying her torso to the back of the seat.

Jeffrey noticed the minor cuts on his forearms and shoulders, and he also sensed bruises on his back, legs, and chest. A bruise on his forehead throbbed. He finally noticed his shirt was drenched in blood, as well as the dried blood on his arms, hands, and face. He twitched, knowing it was Gunner's.

Glancing at Elise for the first time, he felt a revulsion in his heart. It hated her with such intensity – he wanted to do the same to her. Why would she befriend a demon? It was her fault. She brought death to Gunner, pain to Mom, Aunt Beth, himself … and she showed no remorse.

Even Father Matthew's and Sister Regina's touch did not provide any comfort, healing, nor did they soften the hate that festered in his stomach. Instead of being cold, it radiated a searing heat that erupted more and more, as if getting ready for a volcanic explosion. It didn't show, but he sensed its veracity and magnitude.

"Okay, Jeffrey," said Father Matthew, "you're going to assist me. Don't talk to it, don't listen to it. Focus on the prayers in this book. Think of it: you'll be the first altar boy to assist with an exorcism."

He nodded lightly. Jeffrey wanted to talk, but the sadness dragged him down, trying to drown his faith and his love for Elise. Licking his lips, he tasted a bit of Gunner's blood. His paralyzed mind had no thoughts or emotions - not even enough to muster a single tear. At that second, he felt closer to his cousin than his sister. She teased Gunner, taunted him, and put him in jeopardy so many times. Elise hated him for some reason, and he had turned a blind eye to it.

"Jeffrey," said Father Matthew, "are you alright?"

He barely nodded as he spoke. "Yes, sir." Barely audible, he spoke a bit louder, although his words hesitated like lies trapped by a dam of rocks. "I'm okay."

The priest began by crossing himself, praying, and then going into the first prayer. He nudged Jeffrey and looked at him. "Please, start the prayers."

"In Latin or English?"

"Latin," whispered the father. "For some reason, it's much more effective."

Jeffrey said a prayer … and didn't say a prayer. He found no heart, no faith, nor any love of God with it. Maybe the prayers would loosen his hate and fear, but they could not dissolve the emotions clinging to his spirit at this moment. Sister Regina recited her prayers, but they had life, meaning, and power. Should Jeffrey tell Father Matthew? Faith shaken, stirred, and faltering, Jeffrey felt like a failure to the one person who he loved like Dad. Almost crying, he tried to speak his prayers with more conviction.

Victoria

Elise found identity – or at least a little bit of it. For

the first time, she wanted Victor gone. His uncanny strength, and evil, was far more powerful than she imagined. It slithered into her body, even pushing into her legs, arms, and head. It seemed as if her spirit and body were both tethered to Victor. She wanted to tell Father Matthew, Jeffrey, and Regina to run, but Victor clamped her throat.

Victor's mind merged with hers, although both fought for dominance. Their voices mixed, although the deeper voice came first as hers lagged behind by a millisecond. Victor pulled all the strings, as if being a puppeteer who manipulated her. She wanted to speak, act on her own, be her own person, but Victor dominated. As their personalities mixed, Elise lost her agency and identity, even forgetting her name.

No. She remembered it now. Her name was Victoria.

The Latin words from the priest thundered, almost rupturing her eardrums. She heard a few angels flying close, wailing as if sad she was captured. Victoria hated the pity. A cold spite surged like a small twister as the chair lifted off the ground. An angel took a swipe at her leg, leaving a deep gash. Yes, Victoria recognized them all. Once brothers, they now remained stupid, foolish sycophants, rushing to bow their heads in respect for the Almighty instead of casting the disdain he truly deserved.

The chair returned to the floor gently. "Is that all you got, Matthew? Last time you didn't have the strength, what makes you think you got it now? I blinded you twenty years ago – but tonight, I'm going to kill you, rape that bitch, and twist that little sack of shit next to you into a million pieces. You just want to bone him, anyway – like so many of your cohorts. Pathetic, sick ..."

"Unclean spirit," Matthew spoke gibberish, but the

demon fully understood. "Identify thyself in the name of the Father, the Son, and the Holy Spirit." The thundering booms returned, wreaking havoc on its ears. Even if it could cover Elise's ears, it would not help alleviate the discomfort of sacred words from a holy man.

He looked at the boy who showed no emotion. "Jeffrey – Gunner's in here with me. I can't wait to get my hands on him and butt fuck him for all eternity." Seeing the boy's sadness, the demon laughed again.

"Unclean spirit!" Father Matthew this time released his holy water and splattered Elise with it – causing painful, blistering burns to her skin. "Identify yourself."

After writhing in pain, the demon glanced at the priest, worried about the angels behind him. It thought up a lie – which was easy for it to do. Its essence was nothing but lies to both humanity as well as itself. "Call us … Victoria. And we'll kill her and take her soul with ease if any angels try to drag me out."

Father Matthew and Sister Regina prayed fervently, although it could tell doubt and fear riddled Jeffrey's mind. "One of you doesn't have the faith to do this," it said. "It's a mind full of doubt, hope, fear and dread." Its voice got deeper and rougher as the chair lifted a second time.

Instantly, its mouth released a string of blasphemies, knocking the humans down on the floor. The wind blew church hymnals, the crucifix swayed, the candles blew out, and the holy water swayed in their bowls. A couple of smaller tables flew, knocking Father Matthew and Jeffrey down while communion plates smashed into Sister Regina's head.

The chair fell hard, splintering into several pieces. Elise, now Victoria, stood, separating herself from the broken pieces of the chair. Yes, she felt bruises and some cuts, but she also felt the surging power reign over her. She loved it – even savoring it. Or did she hate it?

"Victor," she thought, *"am I Victoria, or is that you?"*

"We're both Victoria now, Beautiful."

Still frightened, she accepted her new identity and let her best friend continue. "I am Victoria."

Humming the theme to the Addams Family TV show, Victoria ventured into the kitchen, found some food, and put it in a sack. On her way out, she rifled through Regina's purse, taking her wallet and the van keys. Victoria took Jeffrey and Father Matthew's wallets but only kept the cash. She walked out to the van, stepped in, pushed the ignition button, and put on her seatbelt. She knew how to drive as Dad let her drive the family van on their land, and even Mom encouraged her. Still humming the old TV theme, she drove away.

Chapter 32

Jeffrey pulled off his helmet and killed the power of his minibike. Immediately the rumbling noise was replaced with Aunt Beth's shrieking. Her wails cut through the cold numbness inside his chest. It felt like a hot knife that plowed through and left behind an agonizing pain that pulsed with every heartbeat. Her cries threatened to drain Jeffrey's empty chest even more - but nothing was left. An awful dread slowly sank through his spine.

Licking his lips, he tasted the dried blood of his cousin. The taste reminded him of Gunner's horrific death. His face squinted, somehow hoping to blot the memory out of his mind. Feeling a tear stream, he wondered if it might belong to Gunner as well. Could enough crying wash off all that blood?

Whimpering, he feared stepping inside the house to face Mom and Aunt Beth. Jeffrey opened the door, and the lights hurt his eyes, revealing the reality of Gunner never sleeping over to watch movies, or joining him for a minibike race. It also unveiled his guilt that grew like plants finding nourishing rays of sunlight. Afraid of Mom, and more so Aunt Beth, he prepared for their wrath.

"Jeffrey!" yelled Mom, "thank God your back!" Crying, she wrapped her arms around him, causing him to flinch as waves of pain spread from his sore joints and aching muscles. "Sweetie!" she said, crying on his shoulder and holding him tightly. Mom clutched him by the elbows and shook him violently. "Where the hell have you been?" Her loud voice, filled with agony, despair, and anger, sliced into his ears, sending a chill through his whole body. It shattered his numbness as it gave way to the shuddering pain of reality that slithered down, making him so sick, he felt like puking. Mom's yell punched him so hard he almost fell backwards. "Why didn't you come home when I texted you? What were you thinking? Your cousin is dead!"

His eyes, already clamped, cried painful tears that lurched hard. "Don't you think I know that?" Never yelling that loud, Mom, took a couple steps back. "All this blood on me is his! And I had to watch my best friend die. And it's … all … my … fault." He hoped they could understand him. "It's all my fault. It's all my fault! I'm so sorry, Mom. Aunt Beth, please don't hate me. I'm so sorry. We just wanted to help. It's all my fault. It's all my fault!" Even repeating it several times did not purge away his heavy guilt. His crying caused him to quake. Even his breaths came in short, uneven spurts.

Mom's familiar arms wrapped around him as he sobbed uncontrollably for the longest time. He recognized Aunt Beth's hands that held him tightly as she sobbed with him. He savored their tight hugs, holding onto them with all his strength. Their touches offered empathy and healing - although his wounds ran so deep, they seemed anemic.

Right now, Jeffrey sorely missed dad's hugs, which were more like strong grips that hoisted him away from danger, and protection from the traumas of an ambivalent world. Dad's strong, masculine touch passed on resilience, strength, and determination. They once provided added strength - almost like a blood transfusion or a jolt of caffeine to help him wake up and face new challenges.

Those feelings resurfaced as another set of hands

clutched his open shoulder, and then his back. "It's our fault, too," said Jason.

"We're all in on this together," Justin muttered softly. "We're so sorry."

The horrendous, ugly feelings ebbed, losing some power - although a stubborn remnant lingered. While feeling small relief from the pain, Jeffrey knew he was far from being cured. The embrace lasted long – but not long enough. He wanted to stay within that bond he just formed with two cousins he barely knew. He sobbed for minutes, but they never let go until Jeffrey caught his breath. He remained in that connection, crying so much that his tears tried to wash the stains of Gunner's blood from his skin and shirt.

***

In the shower, Jeffrey scrubbed hard to rid himself of Gunner's blood. Maybe that would remove the memory of Elise stabbing him with her scalpel over and over. He also hoped the shower might wash his mind of hearing Gunner's final words to him. Strangely, he also wanted to keep that moment perfectly etched in his thoughts … and his soul. The hardest recollection was watching Gunner's spirit depart his body. No matter how hard Jeffrey tried, he could not get those images out of mind. Their last conversation played in his head repeatedly, recalling every detail of the trauma. His tears mixed with the shower water until it turned lukewarm, and then cold.

After leaving his shower, he felt no cleaner. The guilt stained him into a much deeper part of his essence. His mind returned to memories of Gunner's voice, his laugh, his silliness, and his sincere heart. His cousin was gone, and they couldn't forge any more memories together.

After drying and getting into some shorts, Aunt Janie

tended Jeffrey's wounds, providing healing ointments and bandages on one elbow, another on the opposite wrist, and on his ankle. Mom went to Aunt Beth's house to get some of her things, because they felt it best if she didn't sleep alone for a few nights.

Sitting on his bed, Jeffrey knew he'd never have Gunner over to sleep on the floor. They couldn't talk, make jokes, watch movies, ride their minibikes, or call each other "dude." Freddy jumped up, nuzzling his nose on Jeffrey's hands, sniffing and licking them. Jeffrey almost smiled when his dog hopped up on his hind legs and licked Jeffrey's cheek. Freddy whimpered, as if mourning the loss of Gunner as well.

Hearing the door push open, his head turned to see Samson stride in. The German Shepherd, out of his service vest, hopped on the bed, tilted his head, then nuzzled Jeffrey with his snout and sniffed Jeffrey's cheek. He laughed for a second as the licking tickled him and made him feel better for a brief second. He cried again, although both Freddy and Samson whimpered while licking Jeffrey's face – as if trying to lap up his tears. They were the perfect mourners and counselors, willing to be present and just listen. Jeffrey's hands ran through their fur, seeking solace and peace.

Still, so exhausted from sobbing, he wondered if he could ever have a life where he didn't feel like crying every day.

A quick rap on the door alerted him to Jason and Justin. Their somber and sad eyes kept them quiet for a minute. "We wanted you to know," said Jason, "that when the police and the chaplain brought us home, we told your Aunt Beth what happened. We told her the shithead died bravely to save you and someone else."

"Quit calling him names," Jeffrey whispered.

"For us," said Justin, "'shithead' is a compliment."

Jeffrey, still riddled with the surrounding guilt, barely looked at them. He noticed the gauze on the side of Jason's face where the demon slapped him. Remembering how they found Elise and her victim, Jeffrey asked a question that kept running in his mind. "Jason – I was wondering …" He hesitated, staving tears. "Can you hear him?"

After a long silence of either a minute or an hour, Jason shook his head. "No." Another quiet moment passed. "But I'm listening – and I'll let you know if I hear him."

"Guys," he said softly, "…would you mind sleeping in here tonight? I could really use the company."

Chapter 33

Nathen treaded water in a calm ocean. Looking left, looking right, he sought any ships that might see him. The water, lukewarm, felt comforting to his aching muscles and joints. Strangely, the water receded, falling deeper into the ocean valleys below. Although it drained, the water never spiraled fast like an eddy. Reaching the dry ocean floor, he turned on his side, then batted his eyelids open.

The soft mattress and sheets surrounded him with warmth. Wondering where he was, he looked for clues. The first was some sort of hose that had air coming through two openings that fit into his nose. A needle, inserted into his arm connected to an I.V line with medicine was the next clue – indicating he was in a hospital. Sunshine beat through a window – reminding him of the daylight he missed for … how many days? Two, three … or four? He relished the light as well as the blankets and sheets that provided the warmth and security he craved.

Nathen remembered a psychic scream for Mom and Dad just before he was rendered unconscious. He flinched, remembering the sadistic psychological torture, being trapped, his helplessness, and facing unwanted surgery. Terrified, he gasped and reached down to his crotch. His mind sighed with his lungs as he felt some morning wood. Grateful his testicles and penis were still attached, he nearly cried tears of joy. *Thank you, God. Thank you, thank you, thank you!*

Sitting up in the hospital bed, he gasped at the sight of

his parents. Speechless for a split second, his voice got caught in his throat. So happy to see them, he spoke louder. "Mom. Dad."

Mom's ears first heard him, and they seemed to command her eyes open. Immediately, tears swooped down her cheeks. Dad quickly followed, being the first to stand and rush to Nathen. Both of them hugged him, then covered his head and cheeks with kisses. For a change, he didn't mind it, desperately craving it over the last … how long was it? "I missed you so much," he said. "I thought I wasn't ever going to see you again."

"We're so glad to see you, too," Dad choked back. "We're glad to have you back."

"Everything'll be alright now, honey. I promise you," Mom said between her kisses.

"I don't know, because I'm going to need a shit load of serious counseling."

A brief laugh allowed them to relax.

"How'd I get here?"

"Some boys … and a nun found you and brought you here."

Scared, his eyes frantically searched the room. "Where's that girl? Did they catch her? Please tell me they found her."

"Son," said Dad, "there wasn't any girl we know of. We haven't heard what they told the police - but I know the police want to visit with you."

A gentle knock interrupted their reunion.

Nathen noticed the boy standing in the doorway. A little shorter than him, his dark hair, parted just left of center, framed his eyes and nose perfectly. He wore a Friday the 13th T-shirt with some jeans. He had a few bruises on his arms, one on his forehead, and a wrap on one of his elbows.

"Hi," said the stranger.

Nathen, Mom, Dad, all responded politely with "hello."

"My name's Jeffrey."

"Are you one of the boys that found our son?" asked Mom.

He nodded. "Along with my cousins and Sister Regina, a nun at my church."

Mom hugged the strange boy who seemed distant, cold, and possibly hurt. Nathen sensed he lived with a great pain that wrapped around him like a thick heavy chain, linked to weights that tried to keep him captive. He looked tired, as if walking with those encumbrances for miles in the desert with no water or food.

"We can't thank you enough," said Mom.

"How'd you find him?" asked Dad.

Jeffrey faltered, as if afraid. "Well … the person who kidnapped you … was my … sister."

Nathen's voice became louder. "Your sister? But she wanted to …"

"Castrate you – I know."

Nathen still shuddered at the thought, remembering his ghastly fear. It clutched him like the chain Elise wrapped around his neck in the dungeon. His stomach whirled in a circle, then bounced up and down and side to side. It settled, then sank a bit as an unforgotten terror still remained attached to his psyche.

"My sister has …" he balked, as if embarrassed. "She has … serious mental problems."

"Where is she?" asked Nathen.

"We don't know. She disappeared after we found you."

The entire room froze like an ice statue.

Jeffrey moved closer to Nathen. "I'm sure the police will find her … or someone else will. You're okay now."

Sensing a huge pain with Jeffrey, Nathen worried. "Are you okay?"

Jeffrey shook his head. "My sister killed my cousin. He was … trying to save me and you."

Nathen sighed as a sad, disheartening chill fell down his spine. Unable to face Jeffrey, his eyes fell to the floor. "I'm sorry."

Jeffrey stepped closer and handed Nathen a photo of a boy. "I … just wanted to give you … this."

Nathen took the photo from him, then looked to see a boy. His piercing blue eyes contrasted his blonde hair. His thin lips stretched far, barely revealing his teeth. "Is this your cousin?"

Jeffrey nodded, then clenched his face as if to prevent himself from crying. "His name was Gunner."

"You need to tell us all about him," said Mom.

Nathen, sad, let out a long breath and nodded. The memory of his terror faded as he connected with Jeffrey's complete loss – which was for Nathen's sake. Should he feel guilty? Sad? Grateful? His feelings meandered through his blood vessels and mixed in his heart - with none of them becoming dominant. He tried to think of something to say, barely opening his mouth. "I'm really sorry about that," whispered Nathen. "It must be hard."

"He was my best friend – and I hope you'll think of him as your best friend, too." Jeffrey took a few steps back. "Well – I gotta go and talk with the police about what happened. Hope you get better."

Nathen took the picture and stared at Gunner's image. Unable to hear his voice, or shake his hand, his mind went deep into thought – feeling Jeffrrey's emotional pain. He glanced at Mom and Dad who stared at the floor, appearing just as guilt-ridden and sad.

He saved me, Nathen thought. *His cousin died saving me. How can I thank the kid in the picture and honor his memory. How can I talk to him? How can I show him my gratitude?*

"Jeffrey?" Hesitant, afraid of saying the wrong thing, Nathen blurted the first thought that entered his mind as Jeffrey turned around. "Could you please write your number on the back of this photo – because I want to visit with you and learn all about him."

"Maybe you could come over for a visit and tell us all about him?" Mom suggested.

"I'd like that," said Jeffrey. He smiled and a brief flash of light dashed across his eyes. He nodded, then extended his hand as Nathen returned the shake, locking his thumb with Jeffrey's. The tight, strong grip felt as if it held him, preventing a long, disastrous fall. Jeffrey's free hand patted Nathen's shoulder. Nathen returned the motion despite an IV connected to his inner elbow. "I can't thank you enough," he said between a whisper and a whimper. "I thought she was going to mutilate me."

Jeffrey wrote his number on the back of the photo and left.

Chapter 34

Father Matthew, with his hands on Jeffrey's shoulder, sighed heavily and rubbed the boy's back. Matthew remained solemn like everyone else. Jenny stood to his right, and he felt her onus emotions lacked tears yet still felt defeated. At the end of her rope, she kept sighing as if desperate for help.

"I guess this is it," she said.

Always able to hear a faux smile, Matthew stepped closer to her, hugged her, and kissed her on the forehead. "Father, guard this woman, guide her steps so she may find healing in your Son's miraculous touch. In the name of the Father, the Son, and the Holy Spirit." Stepping back, Matthew's hand found Jeffrey's shoulders again.

"Mom," said Jeffrey, "we'll visit you. You can do this – I know. I really need you."

"I need you, too, sweetie."

Matthew, this time, heard a sincere smile full of a mixture of faith, fear, and doubt,

Janie stood next to her husband, Dan, who arrived yesterday evening. She moved towards Jenny. "Sis – you can do this. You were always the rock in our family."

Justin and Jason echoed her confidence. "Aunt Jenny, you're gonna do it." Their words turned towards Jeffrey. "Give us a call, dude. If you ever need to talk, we'll listen. You're mega-awesome."

"You shitheads take care of yourself," said Jeffrey.

Father Matthew knew Beth felt devastated, clinging to

the memory of her son. Her hurt, the strongest at this moment, radiated a deep melancholy – empty of hope and comfort, and full of dejection, anger, and doubt. Was the anger at Jenny? Or at Jeffrey? Perhaps God? Matthew knew it was aimed at all of them, with no clear direction or focus, she was lost without guidance. The confusion likely had her spinning in all directions, not knowing which way to go.

"Beth," said Jenny, "I'm so sorry."

Beth's voice stammered softly, as if having no idea what to say, nor having the courage to speak the words flying angrily in her mind and heart. "Jen," she said quietly, "…I'll take care of Jeffrey just as I promised you."

Janie hugged Father Matthew. "Thank you so much for all your help."

"Thank you," he nodded.

"May God be with you and direct you safe passage back to Albany," added Sister Regina.

The doors on Janie and Dan's SUV closed. The engine started. Facing the general direction, Father Matthew waved at the family with a grim, yet sincere smile. He silently prayed for their journey.

His thoughts turned to Beth and her incomprehensible pain of losing her son. As a trained Psychiatrist, he knew of the agony of losing a child and the potential for severe depression. Taking a step forward, he mustered his faith and love and reached out to her. He heard her sigh, detecting she looked down at the sidewalk instead of at him. "Beth, please call the Sister and me if you need to talk. We can get you the proper counseling, help, and support you need …"

Rushing forward, she hugged him and pulled him so close, he felt her agony all the more. He felt all her questions, confusion, hurt, and anger pulse through every heartbeat. "You've always been a good priest and an even better friend …" she paused. "But I'm not sure what I believe anymore – or even if I believe. All I know is … if God is real … why did he let my boy die? Of all the things to take from me." The last part ebbed into silence.

Father Matthew immediately wanted to defend the existence, power, and justice of God – but knew best to keep quiet. Nothing he could say or do at this second could ease her spirit full of hurt. Sensing her mountainous doubt, he let her vent. "Let god know how you feel," he whispered. "He can take it."

She kissed him on the cheek.

Father Matthew nodded, hoping she might find God's healing. Hell, he wondered about his own anger at the Lord for letting such a sweet young boy die. He, too, would never hear Gunner laugh, tell a joke, ask a bizarre question, post confession, or offer the priest a hug. His grim smile displayed his mourning without tears. Maybe it was hearing how disappointed or angry people felt towards God and listening to their hurt. It was not that he didn't care for them, but rather he built a strong wall to keep from wallowing in misery. Many priests, preachers and Rabbis could easily fall into a depression - as well as practicing psychologists and psychiatrists.

He turned towards Jeffrey. "My son, I must speak with you about something important. Is there a bench where we can sit?"

Jeffrey

Somber, nervous, and reflective, Jeffrey led Father Matthew to a nearby bench. It was a bit wet from a summer evening sprinkle that moistened the pavement, grass, leaves, and part of the bench. He tried to dry it with his hand, then coaxed Father Matthew to sit. The priest rubbed Jeffrey's shoulder more.

"What is it?"

Father Matthew let loose another grim smile – although its sincerity remained strong as ever. Although his eyes saw no light, something else shined from the inside – allowing his face to emit its own illumination. It revealed empathy, faith, peace, and love. He sensed great sadness in Father Matthew.

"Jeffrey," he said, "I've been keeping something from you – waiting for the right time to tell you. Since no time seems like the right time, especially now, I realized I owed you the truth."

Jeffrey cringed, wondering what Father Matthew was talking about.

"A little more than a week ago, I heard from Father Paul from the Vatican. He found six other exorcism cases going back to the early 16th Century. These were people delivered from possession who remembered everything – just like you. The most recent one happened in 1943 in Austria.

"In every case, the person who remembered everything – within several years – was possessed by several other spirits. None of them survived the exorcism."

Jeffrey whimpered as his head fell against Matthew's shoulder. His voice cracked, likely representing his soul under all the pressure. Dad was gone, just like Mom and Gunner. Aunt Beth was so despondent. He felt so alone against all the pain and coming anguish. Worried, scared, his wails bellowed like a catastrophic earthquake. His sobs continued for several minutes as the sorrow refused to budge. Again, he longed for a day when he did not feel like crying.

Finally, the emotions retreated. Father Matthew gave him a handkerchief to dry his eyes and then blow his nose. Afterwards, he took a huge breath, then let it out slowly. He needed just a few more sighs before he could talk. "Please don't let me go back to that. Please don't. I don't wanna go through that again. Please help me. I'll do anything."

Father Matthew continued to rub Jeffrey's shoulder tightly and pulled him as close as he could. It felt as if he and Sister Regina were the only strong support he had. Longing for companionship with someone like Gunner, Justin, or Jason, he muttered. "I feel so alone. I don't know what I'm going to do." Jeffrey realized he said it to nobody in particular - except maybe to God.

"I promise you that Sister Regina, and Father Paul are going to study and prepare for this battle. We're onto it so we can be ready. And we will support you in every way we can. And when your mom gets out of rehab, you'll have her full support, too." Father Matthew sighed. "I just wish you could've stayed with your Aunt Janie and get the support of your newfound cousins. You do need a friend,"

"I have an idea," he said softly.

***

Stepping off his minibike, Jeffrey put down the kickstand and slowly walked up to the door. The house, situated on the edge of a small town and the woods, was surrounded by trees along with an orange glow of a setting sun, as well as songs from cicadas. Rich, thick grass cooled the sticky heat of late July. He usually wore shorts out on nights like this, but preferred jeans when riding his minibike. It was a long ride, and he was glad Aunt Beth said 'yes.' However, he didn't want to stay too long so he could spend time with her and comfort her sadness.

He noticed a really nice inground pool as his feet lightly treaded across a deck leading up to the backside of a house. Although smaller, it was much nicer than his own home as it was fresh brick at the base with thick, bright wood that had a cabin-like presence, yet having plenty of windows. The deck also had nice patio furniture, including a huge round table with several chairs. Going up to the glass doors, he knocked on them, noticing the family in the living room. The adults stood smiling as they pulled the sliding glass door to his right. Once open, he felt the cool blast of refreshing air conditioning.

"Jeffrey!" said Nathen's mom.

"Hello, Mrs. Rhoades," he said while smiling.

"Please," she said, "call me 'Elaine.'"

Her tall, lean husband extended his hand. "And you can call me 'Steve.'"

"Thank you, Mr. Rhoades … I mean Steve."

They ushered him inside and closed the glass door. They all sat on a plush couch that was matched with nice end tables, coffee table, and a fancy area rug on a wood floor. "We're glad you could come over."

Jeffrey nodded then glanced around at the other kids. A boy, probably 12, was mesmerized by a game on his pad.

"That's our middle child, Ethan," said Steve.

Immediately a young girl, likely nine or ten, came up to him with a sneaky smile. "I'm Alicia," she said proudly. "I'm going to be a gymnast."

"That's our baby," said Elaine.

"This is one of the boys who saved your brother," said Steve.

Hearing footsteps coming down the stairs, Jeffrey looked over his shoulder.

"Jeffrey," said Nathen, "I'm glad you could come over."

He stood and moved closer to Nathen for a handshake – but the kid yanked him close for a hug. It reminded Jeffrey of Gunner's grip. Although a year younger, Nathen stood a couple of inches taller than Jeffrey. His wide smile and light blue eyes radiated much more energy as opposed to a couple of days ago. The hair was long, falling to his shoulders.

"Sorry I couldn't make it to your scoutmaster's funeral."

Nathen sighed. "It's okay."

Jeffrey wondered if he should tell Nathen that Jason heard Eli's spirit and helped them find Nathen. No. Nathen and his parents would think Jeffrey was crazy.

"What about your cousin, Gunner? When's his funeral?"

Jeffrey took his turn to release a sad sigh. "Probably next Tuesday or Wednesday."

"Just let me know when, and I'll be there," Nathen said quietly.

A Jack Russell Terrier rushed downstairs and circled Jeffrey's legs, sniffing his shoes and the lower part of his jeans. It barked several times, begging him to kneel and pet him. The dog's curiosity brought a smile to Jeffrey's face.

"That's our dog, Woody," said Nathen who also knelt to pet the dog.

"Cool," said Jeffrey. "Next time I'll bring my dog, Freddy."

"How'd you get here?" asked Elaine.

"I rode my minibike over. It's outside."

Nathen's eyes widened. "You have a minibike? Can you take me for a ride?"

Jeffrey, smiling for the first time in a few days, nodded. "Sure."

Nathen looked at his mom. "Can I, please?"

"I'll give him my helmet," Jeffrey said.

"I don't know," said Steve.

"It's okay," said Jeffrey. "My mom always said there's absolutely nothing in my head."

Nathen's parents laughed, although it sounded seriously silly to Jeffrey.

"Okay," said Elaine. "But be back within ten minutes. It's getting a bit dark. Then we can sit around the table and visit."

Jeffrey started outside but halted and looked at Elaine and Steve. "By any chance, do you have a Pepsi to drink?"

"Sure," said Elaine.

Elaine moved closer to the boys, hesitated, then latched to Jeffrey. "Thank you so much for saving our boy," she said, her voice cracking. "Thank you." She said it with more confidence and strength. "I can't wait to visit with you some more – so don't take too long on your ride."

Steve put his arm around his wife, pulling her tightly. He then leaned over a bit to look Jeffrey in the eye. "I can't thank you enough, either. Because of you, we got our son back."

Somber, Jeffrey nodded and grinned. "We'll be back quick because … I can't wait to tell you all about Gunner."

Chapter 35

Brandon walked along the dark two-lane highway with Max. The Rottweiler kept pace, but he had to keep his thoughts focused to keep the dog in line. A few times, he thought of ditching Max to get to his destination faster.

The small droplets of rain multiplied, becoming bigger, and dropping faster. A few coyotes howled, triggering Max to bark – along with some other dogs in the wooded area. A brief flash lit the sky, followed by a bit of thunder. The storm crawled closer, as if trying to smother and capture him. For a moment, he thought of finding a place to keep himself dry, but Brandon continued.

Bright headlines outlined him, much like the eyes of God that searched for him meticulously. Of course, they weren't God's eyes because the Almighty obviously didn't care about him for many reasons. The auto's eyes, though, did find him, he moved aside, but they already identified their prey. A short honk summoned him.

As the rain changed from a sprinkle to a light drizzle, he opened the door, realizing he was hungry. Hopefully, this was another one of many assholes who was too naïve or stupid to do anything about him. However, to his surprise, he found a young girl driving the van. Probably 15 or 16, she seemed close to his own age – although many people underestimated it.

"Hop on in," she said.

"Thanks. I appreciate it." His thoughts immediately turned to sex, followed by some good food. The girl wore oversized glasses and had ashen skin, much like his. Before the cabin light shut off, he noticed how her dark hair matched the black Wednesday Addams T-shirt. "I'm Brandon."

"I'm Victoria," said the girl.

She continued the drive as the rain pounded heavier on the pickup trucks' roof, and the pavement below. Hail followed, pounding the pavement and the vehicle harder.

Brandon put on his seatbelt, although he really didn't need it. He had to fit in. Although hungry, he kept it to himself, wanting to wait until the thunderstorm to pass before he got to gorge. Maybe he could get some of this chick before he ate. *"It's gonna get dangerous tonight,"* he thought.

"Is that your breath I smell?" she asked.

"Yep. It's not going to get any better. Sorry."

His mind focused on her heartbeat. Hearing her blood pump through her veins intrigued him, goading his appetite, until … the dread descended on him, coupled with an uncertain shaking just beneath his skin. The temperature dropped heavily – but it wasn't from the air conditioning. Looking at her, he noticed her sinister, glowing eyes. A flash of lightning contorted her image into something else that had long, hideous ears, cracked skin, and taloned claws that turned her into a frightening beast. It cast a sulfurous stench that pushed him away. Her heartbeat surged into a foreign rhythm no mortal soul could ever have. Even the blood sounded different.

The lightning cracked the sky again, proving his assumption true. It was the apex king, one of the few things stronger than his kind. Knowing this was not his meal, he gulped hard. For a change, he wasn't the most dangerous thing.

One Month Later

Usually, Jason's sleep ebbed, fading into nothingness as he gradually woke up. This time, it scurried away as if trying to warn him. His eyes bolted open, instantly taking him to alert status. What time was it? Sitting up, his fingers ran across his Braille clock. What? Only 4:15 in the morning. "Shit."

His head dropped to the pillow. Savoring the warm, yet not too warm sheets, he rolled over to his side, frustrated that something disturbed his slumber. Feeling a tad chilly, he pulled his sheets and blanket higher to his neck and sought the comfort of sleeping.

He yelped as an icy cold finger scraped his neck. His body exploded with shaking tremors as he felt the room turn colder. Part of him wanted to yell, but all his mind did was beg God to make it go away. He followed with a prayer and he crossed himself.

"Over here."

His head turned left.

"Over here."

His neck snapped in the other direction, trying to isolate the whisper.

"How do you make a supernatural 'Do not disturb' sign?" he wondered aloud.

Samson, awake, growled for a split second, then whimpered. The dog huffed then moved towards the door, then over towards Jason's closet. Jason wished Samson could talk and explain what it heard, smelled, and possibly saw.

"Jason ..."

Barely hearing his name, Jason tried to stretch his ears. At least that's what he called it. He found this ability a double-edged sword. Sure, Eli was helpful to help find

Nathen, but now ghosts were disturbing his sleep. "Come back during normal business hours," Jason whispered.

"Jason ..." The voice seemed to dance from one side of the room to the other. "Jason ..." This time it echoed and circled around, drifting further away and then returning closer.

"Gunner ..." he thought. *"Is that you?"* Jason waited for a minute, then was startled when Samson jumped on the bed and licked his ear.

"I'm not Gunner."

Who could it be? The voice was childlike – not like a teenager, but rather a pre-adolescent boy. It could be a deception. He knew demonic things were deceivers, often pretending to be something else. He reached for his crucifix as well as his rosary beads. Jason kept his guard up, although the slight drop in temperature indicated a ghost rather than something overtly evil. Also, there was no rank stench accompanying the voice.

"Who are you?" he thought again. He hoped it could hear him and would respond this time. He waited for a minute ... or had it been two?

"I'm your Uncle Bobby."

Jason, confused, tried to sort his thoughts and memories. His mind could not think or find such a person. "I don't have," he thought aloud, "an Uncle Bobby."

The silence accompanied an eerie stillness in the air. *"I've been dead a long time."*

"How long?"

Jason wondered why such a gap existed when conversing with spirits.

"I'm not sure. Time works differently where I am now."

Becoming skeptical, Jason felt defensive, clutched the

Rosary Beads and his crucifix tightly. His mind recited one of the many prayers, then threw out an angry thought. *"You're lying. I never had an Uncle Bobby."* Holding his chest, he prayed fervently.

"Jason - I would have been your Uncle Bobby, but I died in the car wreck with my sister - your Aunt Janie."

Shocked, Jason dropped the crucifix. The noise of it clanging on the floor startled him.

"It's hard to talk." The voice faded in and out like a radio on the edge of receiving a broadcast. *"Something's ... coming ... for ...."* The voice, weak, dissipated into nothing. It tried to return ... barely reaching the threshold of being heard. It died again, leaving Jason waiting in silence.

Only hearing Samson's breath, Jason's jaw quivered. Time passed - although he was unsure how long it lasted. "Uncle Bobby?" he thought as his mind and ears reached for any tangible sound. "Uncle Bobby, what are you trying to tell me?" His mind and ears tried to focus, hoping to continue the communication and solve the cryptic message.

A frigid swathe of air wafted up through his body while a vile stench of excrement mixed with rotting meat wrapped around him. His whole body twitched as he covered his ears - unable to stop an ear-splitting scream that bellowed through his mind ...

About the Author

Stephen W. Scott was born in Tulsa, OK. He attended the University of Oklahoma and graduated with a degree in Journalism – Professional Writing. He has worked for a few newspapers, then moved to Wilmore, KY in 1991 to attend Asbury Theological Seminary where he received his Master of Divinity in 1995. After returning to Oklahoma, he served as a pastor and chaplain in the United Methodist Conference. He has been working in education since 2001 and resides in Tulsa, OK. He enjoys bicycling, weightlifting, photography, reading, playing guitar and writing.

Other Books by Stephen W. Scott

The Blind Faith Series:
Do You Hear What I Hear?
The Demon Inside Me
My Best Friend is a Demon

Other Books:
Wonderful & Terrifying Nightmares
Abandoned

Visit him at
www.swscott-author.com